Wildman

Wildman

J. C. Geiger

HYPERION

LOS ANGELES • NEW YORK

First Edition, June 2017
10 9 8 7 6 5 4 3 2 1

Library of Congress Cataloging-in-Publication Data
Names: Geiger, J. C. (Jeffrey Clayton), 1979– author.
Title: Wildman / J. C. Geiger.
Description: Los Angeles ; New York : Disney-Hyperion, 2017. •
Summary: Lance Hendricks, eighteen, is an over-achiever headed to
the last big party before graduation when his car breaks down in a
remote Washington town, leading to life-changing experiences.
Identifiers: LCCN 2016029359 • ISBN 9781484749579
(hardback) • ISBN 148474957X (hardcover)
Subjects: • CYAC: Self-actualization (Psychology)—Fiction. Conduct
of life—Fiction. Interpersonal relations—Fiction. • BISAC: JUVENILE
FICTION / Social Issues / Adolescence. JUVENILE FICTION / Social Issues /
Dating & Sex. JUVENILE FICTION / Social Issues / New Experience.
Classification: LCC PZ7.1.G448 Wil 2017 • DDC [Fic]—dc23
LC record available at https://lccn.loc.gov/2016029359

Printed in the United States of America
This book is set in 10¼-pt ITC Slimbach Std, Spectrum MT Pro,
Strayhorn MT Pro, Grotesque MT Std/Monotype
Designed by Maria Elias

Reinforced binding

Visit www.hyperionteens.com

SUSTAINABLE FORESTRY INITIATIVE Certified Sourcing
www.sfiprogram.org
SFI-00993

THIS LABEL APPLIES TO TEXT STOCK

For you

A riddle, a clue, a gift

Tell me, what is it you plan to do with your one wild and precious life?

—Mary Oliver, "The Summer Day"

1

The song skipped.

A crackling beat, a brief tremor in the steering wheel—and Lance Hendricks noticed the gap in the music. He knew every last note of *Classical Trumpet Ballads*, which had been jammed in the cassette player of his '93 Buick since the unfortunate day his mother gave him the tape. Now it was his only option. No radio this far from the city. He thumbed the useless eject button, then stared at the speedometer. The needle was suddenly frozen, pointing straight up and down, like a compass finding north.

"Hey," Lance said, tapping the dash.

The needle hovered like a slender middle finger, then went slipping off to the right: 65, 75, 85, gone. A blank face of numbers. Like he was going no speed at all. Sitka spruce and Madrones blurred past. Douglas fir, and the flash of a small sign:

ENTERING WILDERNESS AREA

Evergreens and sky vaulted into a new layer of atmosphere, and the car's dome light flickered. A wet grumbling in the engine.

Lance turned up the trumpet solo, trying to ignore the sound. He hummed along, forcing himself to smile. The gas pedal went squishy, and the Buick jolted so hard it made his teeth click.

"Hey!" Lance said, pointing at the steering wheel. "No. Not happening."

Not tonight. Not with six hours left to drive.

When the song skipped again, Lance's mind skipped with it, launching his thoughts over 370 miles of rivers and roads to Bend, Oregon. It was 3:35 P.M. Right now his friends would be at Jonathan's house, preparing for the party of a lifetime. Piping vodka into a hollow watermelon. Regulating the hot tub. Fastening Post-it notes to the rooms of vacationing family members. *Lance + Miriam,* one note would say. It would be their first overnight in a bedroom together.

He considered the factors that had finally qualified him to share a plus sign with Miriam Seavers on a Post-it note equation. Seven years of dedicated trumpet practice. Four years with a 4.0 GPA. The $16,500 scholarship to OSU both she and his mother agreed he should take. All this multiplied by two years together, X hours spent on the phone, Y hours on the sofa in Miriam's basement. Their rare make-out sessions, like flinching marathons. Under suffocating blankets, the threat of parents' footsteps, whiplash jerks of the head—

The Buick shuddered. Power steering went gummy.

Miriam!

Attractive and intelligent. Deep somehow. She swore but went to church on Sundays. Her favorite food groups were vegetables and candy. Gentle with animals and children, yet vicious with inanimate objects. Like the way she banged shut the paper drawer of the school's copy machine. A lean little pivot, then *KA-SHINK!* with her hip. If Lance was being honest, it was primarily The Hip Bump *KA-SHINK!* that had sparked his imaginings of the wild, sexual beast lurking just beneath Miriam's church-girl façade. She was an erotic volcano, just barely holding herself back.

Holding back for going on two years now.

Because there were so many nights, waiting through a three- or four-hour date wanting only to kiss her. Then leaving her front porch or basement, unkissed, to walk calmly around the corner then race blindly into the night. To try running off the fire in his blood, down one block, then another, only to go home, collapse onto his bed, hold his pillow over his face, and scream.

But tonight in the bedroom, floodgates would open. Lives would be changed.

The stereo skipped again and Lance hit the power button. Life Radio was no longer playing trumpet, nor *Songs to Lose Your Virginity To.* The only station coming in was NEWS RADIO: PANIC EDITION: *You are in a twenty-five-year-old Buick,* said the DJ in Lance's head. *You are 370 miles from everyone you know and your car has 145,238 miles on it. You will not make it to Bend. You will break down and be barbecued on the side of the road by Uneducated Forest People.*

On either side of him, a parade of roadside evergreens, stiff and straight as soldiers. The occasional odd shape, flickering through the pines.

Meth labs! Bigfoot!

Lance rolled down his window, tasting the wind. He breathed deeply, summoning his mantras, centering himself:

You are valedictorian.

You are the first-chair trumpet player.

You have a full-ride scholarship.

Miriam Seavers is in love with you.

The mantras helped. He was The Lance Hendricks Machine. He solved problems with the application of math and clear goal setting. Around the next curve, a blue sign rotated into view.

EXIT 126: BARING, WASHINGTON.

No rectangular logos. No fast food. Stark white symbols of a tent and a gas pump.

Ghost camping. Ghost gas.

Jonathan would've been whistling "Dueling Banjos."

Lance reached over and touched the black hard case of his Wild Thing trumpet, strapped in beside him like a tiny passenger. Miriam had watched as he buckled in the horn the morning he left for Seattle. Probably a mistake, letting her see that.

I feel like you and the Wild Thing are running away together.

He patted the case.

"Don't worry," he told his trumpet. "We got this."

Lance kept one hand on his trumpet case as he steered the Buick toward the exit ramp. A long, gradual climb. The car slowed, sputtered, and died just shy of a stop sign. Lance unfastened his seatbelt and squinted up at irregular blobs of daylight in the metal. Bullet holes.

This stop sign had been murdered.

Lance put his foot on the brake, shifted to park, and took what his mother would've called *a deep, cleansing breath*. But the Buick wasn't good for deep breathing. Sunbaked upholstery. Stale fries and cigarettes. His father, lingering at the molecular level.

Lance opened the door and climbed out. The air had the familiar nip of wilderness. Tree bark, baking in the sun. The mix of scents and adrenaline conjured his father with uncanny clarity. Over the years, he and his dad had lain on pavement beneath broken-down vehicles in remarkable locations throughout the Northwest. They'd unscrewed hex nuts and replaced fuses in three national wilderness areas, and Lance remembered most of their seven-step engine diagnostics ritual: The Seven Stages of Grief.

Leaning on the Buick, he removed his right shoe.

Lance popped the hood and went to work on the battery terminals first. He whacked them hard with the sole, knocking off corrosion crystals, rotating them around their posts. He pounded the starter next. Then the alternator.

That's it? he'd asked his dad. *You just bang on stuff?*

It's an art form, kid. You'll never be stranded, so long as you got your shoes.

But when Lance climbed back in and turned the key, the engine gagged, then died. Lance pounded the steering wheel. He cursed and climbed outside, then lay on his back. Cold, pebbled pavement. The breeze cut through his sock. Inching beneath the car, Lance tapped the exhaust line with his fingers. *Hot!* He jerked back, scraping his knuckle. Bleeding. He cursed again and whacked the gas tank with the rubber heel of his shoe.

Never, he'd once told his father, *in the history of time and mechanical troubleshooting, has it ever worked to bang on a car's gas tank.*

But when Lance got back in, the car started.

Dome light blazing, Lance whooped. He punched the sagging fabric ceiling.

"Yes!" he hooted. "Here we go!"

He pressed on the gas and the Buick rolled forward. He would make it, half an hour late with a great story. He could feel Miriam's arms pulling him close. Taste the creamy perfection of Jonathan's famous White Russian. The engine popped. Convulsed. The brass treble clef hanging from his rearview mirror rattled, pecking glass. *Ticktickticktick.* Lance's hands strangled the wheel. He could only steer away from the highway and down the hill to whatever was there.

At the bottom of the slope, a stand of pines and a small white building.

Lance shifted to neutral and the steering locked up. The dash, a checkerboard of red and orange emergencies. Gravity threw its weight behind the bumper and Lance had to stand, one foot pumping a squishy brake, his whole body draped over the wheel, grunting as he angled the Buick into a jackknife parking job across all three marked spaces in the parking lot.

According to the marquee, he was now at JOE'S PLACE.

LAST GAS FOR 30
MEAT OAF 5.99
BROASTED CHKN 6.5

MARLIGHT PK 7.88
KEYSONE! 6 PK 12 PK
CLD BEER
CLD SUNDAY

In these parts, CLD meant "closed" and "cold."

Cobwebs stuffed the building's eaves like cotton candy, and the nearby gas pumps were museum pieces—boxy, with faded red fishbowl tops. The smell of gasoline, like it was being ladled from open barrels. Clearly, he could not leave his trumpet unattended.

Carrying his case, Lance left his car and opened the door to the service station.

A bell clanged overhead. It made an awful sound, like hitting a tuba with a tack hammer. The man behind the counter glared. A black man. Bearded and frosted up top, like he'd come in from a snowstorm and had never run a hand through his hair. Joe, apparently.

"That your car?" Joe said.

"Yeah."

"Why do you need three spaces?"

"Sorry. It's dead or something."

"Or something," he said. "Dead's dead." Joe looked down at a pile of paper tickets on the counter. He turned one over. Tore off little strips.

"Do you know if there's a mechanic in town?" Lance's voice was shaking.

"Ain't nothing in town," Joe said. "You'll be needing a tow."

"Tow," he said, tasting the word's weight. Three letters full of lost time. Lance needed a different answer. His *break-glass-in-case-of-emergency* solution. The dreaded red lever: A Phone Call to Mom. His phone's battery would never last. Not the way she talked. He returned to his car, got his charger, and walked back inside.

The bell clanged.

"Damn it," Joe said to no one in particular.

"Could I plug in my charger?" Lance asked, holding it up. "Is that okay?"

"Plug in by the nachos." He pointed to a dusty back corner of the store. A giant nacho cheese pump half blocked a single dust-clotted outlet. Hair-curling heat radiated from the box, and Lance held his phone up to keep the cord from melting into cheddar. The odor was a mix of hot plastic and cumin. It smelled good, which meant he was starving.

"Hey hon," his mother said. "Almost home?"

"The car's dead."

Saying the words made it real.

"Dead? Oh my God, Lance. Where are you?"

"Exit 126, I think. In the Wenatchee Wilderness."

"Wilderness? Lance. Are you kidding me? Is this really happening?"

Lance licked his finger and touched the top of the cheese box. Spit sizzled, hopping around on the surface.

"This is really happening," Lance said.

"Are you safe? Where are you?"

"A service station," Lance said. "Joe's Place."

"Joe's Place. Why don't you get back in the car. Lock the doors."

"Mom. It's the middle of the day. I'm not going to be murdered."

"So what do you want me to do?"

"I need your help, Mom. That's why I called."

His voice went half an octave higher. It had done that since he was a toddler. She had to make this right. This was The Party. The solitary glimmer of hope in a year of windowless study sessions. An evening planned with the care of a shuttle launch. Orbits, accounted for. Equipment, secured. Excuses, made and believed. A miraculous alignment of circumstances.

His mother must fix this.

"I've got to get to Jonathan's tonight," Lance said, bouncing his right leg. He had the crawlies in his calves and it wasn't even dark yet.

"I swear, Lance. This little trip of yours." She tsked. Sighed. The sound of gears turning. "Get back in the car. Promise me you'll get back in the car immediately."

"I promise."

"Right now, Lance."

"I will."

They hung up. Lance looked out the window at his Buick and didn't move. He took out his phone and composed and deleted three separate texts to Jonathan and one to Miriam. He couldn't send the messages:

breakdown, stranded, stuck

Those words could not apply to him. His mom would make this right.

When his phone rang, she opened with her classic line:

"Okay, Lance. I've got this figured out."

Her words soothed. Lance's shoulders lowered. Breathing resumed.

"I called you a cab. A train leaves from Bellevue in two hours. Take the six forty-five to Eugene, and I'll have Dave pick you up. You'll be at the party by eleven, midnight at the latest."

"I won't get back until midnight?" Lance asked, a full octave higher now. He did a frantic half pirouette by the nacho machine and knocked his wrist into metal. A hot pinch. Burning hair. He shrieked and dropped his phone. *Crack.* He picked it up: tiny lines, spiderwebbing through his screen. Frozen ripples in a pond. He wiped the phone. Licked his finger. Wiped again, grunting. Cracks. Cracks! Permanent!

He made a high eeping noise.

"Lance? Lance! What is wrong with you!"

"You made me drop my phone."

"Lance."

"My phone's broken."

"We're still talking, Lance."

"I'm going to miss the party. I can feel it."

"Calm down. Just stay in the car. You are in the car, right?"

When they hung up, he gripped the phone and felt its edges. Reassuring angles of glass and steel. What if his phone had died? For the first time, he felt incredibly distant from Bend.

He stood very still.

A familiar sensation, beginning with a spontaneous tingle up the back of his neck. Then a swelling in his chest, and he reached for a napkin. Fished a pen from his pocket. He drew on the soft paper surface, pressing too hard, leaving small gouges, until he had created a blank five-line musical stave. He began to blacken the lines with heads and stems, the first pair of notes in a new composition.

He was humming, scratching out a time signature, still trying to pin the magic to a napkin when the door to Joe's Place blasted open. That bell. The sound was all wrong, knocking him out of the song. A cool breeze swept through the shop. When Lance looked up at the strange man who had come for him, the rest of his notes blew away.

2

The man at the door was so bone-thin wiry you could almost hear him jangle in his denim overalls. Blue eyes, wild and burning. Emblazoned on a stained white oval, his first name, last initial: WILLIAM S.

"Guessin' it's you whose momma called. C'mon out."

Momma.

Outside, clouds had darkened the sky. William stepped in close to Lance, stale cigarettes on his breath. Not his father's brand. More like tobacco and sawdust soaked in whisky, and the guy's teeth had a motor-oil sheen, as if he drank the stuff by the glassful. He stared at Lance. One angle, then another, cocking his head like a curious dog.

"You a car guy?" William asked.

"Excuse me?"

"You know a little about cars?"

"A little," Lance said.

"Knew it! Knew it the second I looked at ya." William laughed a full, raucous laugh that ricocheted under the eaves. It was a sound too big for his body—a flute of a man who blew like a saxophone. This man in dirty overalls now stood between him and a night with Miriam. William S, asking questions:

What kinda noise did it make?

Did you give it gas?

What happened with the lights? They flicker a little?

It had started to rain. Water dribbled through the gaps in the rafters and they had to keep shuffling around, standing at awkward angles. Together with the dead Buick, they were an isosceles triangle. Acute. Equilateral.

"You think the car's fixable?" William asked.

"Me?"

"Yeah. What do you think?"

He didn't know, but William had called him a Car Guy.

"Oh yeah," Lance said. "I think it's fixable. Definitely."

"Good. Yeah, me too," William said. "Well. I got a garage. Don't advertise or nothing, but I'd be happy to take a look."

"Tonight?"

"I can sure try." William forked over a business card, glossy as an oil painting. And beautiful. It depicted a suspension bridge over a blue ribbon of water. Clusters of trees, clear sky. The back of the card read: GOODVIEW TOWING, WILLIAM SCHOLZ.

Lance checked the name against William's overalls, then stuck the card in his pocket.

"Wait," Lance said. "Where were you planning to tow the car?"

"Lady told me to take it to The Boneyard."

"Boneyard?"

"Junkyard," William said.

Tires crackled on blacktop, and a green taxi bounced into the parking lot. The creak of brakes. A door popped open and a large man *unfolded*, stretching skyward, stacking legs, trunk, shoulders, and beard. He wore a rust-colored duster. Rain droplets stained his coat a darker brown.

"You Lance?" the taxi driver said.

"Yeah," he said.

"Meter's running."

Lance's phone vibrated. A text from Miriam.

Hey you. What time are you heading over?

"I have to make a quick call," Lance said. He stepped under the eaves. Cracked phone and a wet screen. His finger was shaking and would not land on the call button. He tried twice. Three times. And finally:

"Hi there!" his mother said. "Back on the road?"

"What are you doing with the car, Mom?"

"Are you in the taxi, Lance?"

"What's happening to the Buick?"

Silence.

"A junkyard, Mom? You're taking the Buick to a junkyard?"

"Did you think I was having it towed to Bend?" she asked. "The tow would cost more than the *car*."

A little twist of disdain on the word *car*, like the Buick didn't deserve to be called one. William and the driver were facing each other. Rain pattered on their shoulders—*taparatataratatap*—like distant drums.

"Maybe you can go back up to Washington," his mother said. "Get it later."

"How's that going to happen?"

Water dribbled down through a hole in the roof, tapping his shoulder.

"If I leave the car, I'll never see it again," Lance said.

"That's a little dramatic."

"It's true."

His voice was going reedy.

"They'll pay you something for the parts." She sighed. "You can keep the money."

So that was it. Her angle. His car for a cab ride. His car for a night with Miriam.

"What else are you going to do, Lance?" his mother said. "You're not going to spend the night in *Washington*."

Her words twisted in his stomach. That clammy feeling, like when she'd told him he wouldn't drive to Seattle. His friends had chimed in: *You're too busy. You won't go by yourself. You're afraid of the city.*

Yet, he'd gone. He hadn't been afraid.

Streets teeming with people: so many voices, accents, cultures. His eyes too wide and too small at the same time, straining to peel back the skin of the place and get down to where the notes were humming. He could sense music, quivering along the edges of skyscrapers, cutting long, clean lines against the sky. Solos hiding on street corners. Symphonies in the sewer.

"I'm staying with the car," he said. Was that him talking?

"You're staying."

Worse, hearing her repeat it. With one swift sentence he'd painted himself into a corner, his mother had applied the second coat, and Miriam and the party were on the other side of the room.

"Really, Lance?" His mother laughed. "You're staying. Miriam is going to love that."

He could already hear their conversation. His mother's ripe chuckle. Miriam, giggling. *And then he told me he was staying. No, really? He did. He really did. Oh, Lance.*

But they'd only laugh if he came home.

"Lance?"

"I'm not leaving Dad's car."

Lance launched the D-word. A rocket, dragging a vapor trail through the sky. It pinged off a satellite and rushed over mountains, roads, and streams to land with the precision of a sniper's bullet in his mother's ear.

His mom was quiet. Dead, maybe.

"So that's what this is about," she said. "Has your father been in touch with you?"

"Seriously, Mom? No."

"You want to keep the car? Go ahead and stay. I hope you enjoy your night in the wild."

"I'm at a gas station, Mom. Not the Serengeti."

His mother hung up. A low ringing, between Lance's ears. Once, freshman year, his friend Darren had kicked him square in the balls. There had been a swimmy, head-buzzing moment just before his body processed the injury and brought him down in a heap of gut-clenching agony. That's how he felt now—floating through frozen time, about to feel the pain. He walked quickly to William.

"William," he said. "Can you tow me to your garage?"

"Yeah? Sure thing, bud. I'll hitch her up."

"It would be great if you could fix it tonight."

"I'll do my best," William said.

The taxi giant stepped into their conversation. "So, you ready?"

William walked to the truck, leaving them alone.

"Hi," Lance said. "So I guess I don't need a ride anymore."

"What?"

"I don't need a ride. I'm going with William."

"You got a ride," the man said. "You just ain't paid for it yet."

"I don't understand."

"I had to drive out here. I've been waiting ten minutes. That costs something." The man had severe gray eyes. Out of place in his wide, bushy face.

"How much?"

"Fifty," the man said.

"Fifty dollars for ten minutes? That's insane," Lance said. He looked around, and there was no one to appeal to. William was hitching up the Buick. "You expect me to eat the gas on this ride?" the man said. He pursed big red lips.

"I'm not paying you fifty dollars."

"And I ain't leaving until I get paid." The man hitched up his jeans.

Lance looked down. He was still wearing the clothes from his audition. Khakis. Polished shoes. Still, he'd rip the man's eyes out. Clutch his keys into a spiny fist and pummel his face. He would take out his wallet. Hands trembling, he would take out his wallet and hand this man fifty dollars.

The driver took Lance's money with a thick, grease-stained hand, rubbing each bill between his fingers. Careful as a bank teller. Then the taxi driver got in his car and rolled away with Lance's fifty dollars. Lance checked his wallet. Yes, the bills were gone. He felt sick, like the money had been carved out of his belly.

He picked up his trumpet case and walked to William's truck. Inside, the murmur of talk radio. He grabbed the door handle, and something exploded against the window. A pompon of orange and white fur, claws skittering on glass. Lance shrieked. A barking cocker spaniel, and William yanked it back by the collar.

"Daisy, goddamn it!" William shouted. "C'mon, kid. Get in."

William clutched Daisy to his thigh, and Lance climbed into the cab of the truck. The cocker spaniel snarled. The truck rattled to life, and Joe's Place shrank in the rearview mirror. They turned onto Highway 2, dragging the Buick behind them. Towering conifers swallowed them. Day had already tipped into evening, and darkness hardened in the gaps between trees.

"So. Where you headed?" William asked.

"I'm trying to make it back to Bend."

"I mean, where you headed now, bud?"

He was headed to the party, of course. William would fix his car tonight and he would make it. He'd be with Miriam in a matter of hours. What else could possibly happen?

"Trainsong?" William said. "Don't know why I'm asking. It's the only place."

"I'm sorry. I thought you were going to fix the car tonight," Lance said, warble in his voice.

"I can try," William said, flipping on the windshield wipers. Drizzle, coming and going. "We better head to the Trainsong. Nice little motel."

Motel. The word had never entered Lance's travel vocabulary. There had been chain hotels with his mother and campsites with his father. Motels were squat, neon-lit habitats one went rushing past on the way to better places. Would there be amenities? A pool and hot tub? Miriam was probably in the hot tub now. In a swimsuit. That blue one, for sure. The one that gapped in a mind-altering way when she leaned forward, and he could just lean over and—

"Easy there," William said.

Lance's right leg was jackrabbiting up and down. William and Daisy, eyeing him.

"Sorry," Lance said.

"Ha! Felt that shaking. Thought my truck was about to break down."

"Restless legs syndrome," Lance said. He held his leg still. Felt the crawling. Calves, pulling and tightening.

"What's that?"

"It's a condition. Makes me bounce my legs sometimes."

"Heard of that," William said. "Not just while you're sleeping?"

"It can happen anytime."

"Kinda young to have a syndrome, aren't you?"

"Yeah, I guess so." Lance smiled. Tightness in his cheeks. He hadn't smiled in a few hours.

"You in school?"

"Yeah. High school," Lance said, looking out the window. So much darkness. Hundreds of miles of rivers and roads between him and Bend. "I graduate next Friday."

"Play trumpet? Your mom said you were up here for an audition."

"That's right," Lance said, tightening his grip on the case.

"How'd it go?"

"Pretty good. The Seattle School of Music has some amazing musicians."

The three panelists had been friendly when he'd walked in, laughing about campus parking, offering water. But you could smell the experience on these guys: a thousand smoky club nights and street-corner gigs. Seasoned in hundreds of orchestra pits. They had chops. And when they watched him blow, their eyes hit him like the unnerving peal of a triple C sequence he hadn't yet learned to play.

"I did my best," Lance said.

"So you could be making music up in Seattle."

"Probably not," Lance said. "I've got a scholarship to Oregon State."

"Corvallis, right? Beavers."

"They've got a satellite campus in Bend. I got a full ride."

"For music?" William asked, eyes glimmering.

"Business," Lance said.

William turned back to the road. He looked uncomfortable, like something was itching him under his overalls.

"And I've got a job this summer. At Bank of the Cascades. I can live at home and save up money."

The truck swallowed white stripes on asphalt, sucking them under its carriage. William gnawed the inside of his cheek.

"And my girlfriend is going to OSU too, which is perfect."

"Well," William said. "You got me convinced. Now, what kind of sputtering do you reckon it was, just before the car died? Was it a clicking, or more of a dinging? Did it kick in all of a sudden, or come on slow?"

As William talked, the road got darker, more remote. Like they weren't traveling across the wilderness so much as tunneling into it. Moments later, a white blaze of light struck the sky. A giant, luminous flotation device—like the kind you'd throw a person who was drowning. It was the size of a car, mounted on a building. White with red lettering: THE FLOAT.

"The Float?" Lance said.

"Ha!" William's smooth, baritone laugh. "Spent plenty of time there. Might not be driving this truck if it weren't for all them nights at The Float."

"What is it?"

"The Float *is* it. For twenty miles in any direction. Roadhouse. Only place to get a meal. Or a drink. You'll get to know it real quick."

"Roadhouse," Lance said slowly, tasting the word's rural mystique.

Just before The Float, William turned in and parked between a pair of motel buildings. Long two-story structures, divided by a parking lot.

"Here's the Trainsong. This is where you'll be staying."

"Until you fix the car, right?"

William cranked up the hand brake. "I'd go ahead and get yourself a room."

The rain had returned, a thickening drizzle. Lance collected his things from the Buick. Orange duffel bag, suitcase, backpack. He stacked them neatly around his trumpet case. His pile of things looked small and wet.

"Gimmie a call in a few hours," William said. He slapped Lance's back, his hand like a soft sack of bones.

William hopped in his truck and fired the engine. Then the Buick was being dragged away, taillights smearing red trails through the rain. In Lance's stomach, the hole the cabdriver had carved ripped wider.

Loss. Something was gone.

"William!" Lance shouted. He ran. "William! Stop! Wait!"

The truck rolled forward. Lance's foot shot out over loose gravel and he stumbled, scooped up a rock and flung it at William's truck. A deep clang, like a church bell. He'd nailed the side, just under William's window. Taillights flared. William climbed out into the rain. Backlit in red. Frizzy hair, cocked head. With a chain saw, he would've been a one-man horror movie.

"Boy. What in the hell?"

"Sorry," Lance said. "I left something in the glove box. It's really important."

"So you throw a rock? That's what you do?" They stared at each other through the drizzle.

"Well, go on," William said, shaking his head.

Lance tore into the glove box: insurance, registration, and starlight mints. It was still there. Thank god. The worn envelope with his name. LANCE. He kissed the envelope and put it in his back pocket. William climbed back into his truck. The Buick lurched out of the parking lot and shrank down the length of highway, taillights turning to mist.

Gone.

Lance gathered up his things and walked toward the front office. The sign in the window said WELCOME TRAINSONG, and looked like it had been drawn by someone in elementary school. Inside, the lobby was small. A shoe-box diorama of a real hotel. Straight ahead, a wooden counter with a brass bell and a nameplate:

CHERI FRONT DESK

He assumed Cheri Front Desk was the woman in the tiny squeeze of a workspace between the counter and the back wall. She was staring at a dinosaur of a computer monitor, tan and boxy. Cheri and the monitor were of the same era. Her skin was orange and looked overpixelated, as if her face had missed an essential software upgrade everyone else in the world had gotten around 1990. Long fingernails pecked at the keyboard.

"Excuse me," Lance said. "Excuse me."

Cheri's fingers, swift and violent, crushed down on the home row.

Lance rang the bell.

Cheri stopped, then craned her neck at a crazy angle, like her head had a swivel option most humans did not. Her eyes blazed blue and she looked in every way like a mythological creature who would ask him riddles and eat him.

"Was that you, got towed off by William?" Cheri asked.

"Just now?" Lance asked. "Yeah."

"Where's he taking your car?"

"Back to his garage."

"Lordy."

"What?"

"Oh, nothing," she said. "You looking for a room tonight?"

"Yeah."

"One night or extended stay?"

"One night. Definitely. He might even have the car fixed tonight."

"William?" She laughed. "Hoo-ee. You sure you don't want extended stay?"

"What do you mean?" Lance asked.

"Oh, nothing. Here's your paperwork. Go on and sign."

The forms covered things like make and model and maximum occupancy and insurance and evacuation routes, pet policies, maximum seasonal charges. When Lance turned the sheet over, Cheri snapped the paper out of his hand and poked her finger at the X.

"You don't have to read the whole thing. Just sign."

"Sorry," he said. "I've never done this before."

"Wowee. If I had a nickel for every time I heard that. Look at you, blushing."

Cheri slapped down a metal key attached to a cartoon train with its smokestack snapped off. Brittle plastic.

"Room two twenty," Cheri said. "Welcome home." Lance loaded his things onto his shoulders and walked around the side of the building. The steps leading up to the second floor were painted blue. The same blue as the building and the banister and the doors and the *hinges*, suggesting the entire Trainsong Motel had been painted all at once by an air tanker dropping a single load of high-gloss periwinkle.

On the balcony, Lance had to step around a pair of muddy black boots. The mud was hard, like the boots had fused to the floor last winter. In the room just before his, someone was watching a game show turned up to action-movie-volume levels. Laughter and applause rattled the windows.

LET'S SEE WHAT'S BEHIND DOOR NUMBER TWO!

Lance opened his door to the warm odor of a nursing home. He took a final gulp of fresh air, then plunged in, groping for a light switch. It was smaller than hotels he'd stayed in with his mom, but not cramped. A queen bed, covered with a floral spread that might've been quilted in Cheri Front Desk's basement. A window, facing the parking lot. To his left, a small desk wedged in the corner. Two wall hangings. One: a puffy, homemade tapestry of a keeling sailboat on wooden dowels. Garage sale material, the fifty-cent pile.

Wall hanging number two was something special.

Right above the bed, an enormous framed photograph of twin tabby cats. The picture could've been cute, but the tabbies looked like they wanted to maul the photographer. Giant, angry cats. Staring straight at him.

"Nice, Cheri," Lance said. "Charming."

He set his horn by the desk, then took the envelope out of his pocket and searched for a place to stash it. In the nightstand drawer, a Bible and a slender phone book. He opened the yellow pages to AUTO REPAIR.

One advertisement on the page. **ROBERT'S AUTO REPAIR: A _REAL_ MECHANIC**. That was all it said. Lance traced his finger down the listings. Between **GOODBAR GARAGE** and **GREAT AMERICAN AUTO PARTS** was exactly nothing. **GOODVIEW TOWING** wasn't even listed. He took out William's card with all its depth and shading and perfectly inked letters. Somehow not in the yellow pages.

Lance grabbed the phone on the nightstand.

No dial tone.

He pressed down little white nubs. Dusty.

"Seriously?" he said.

He sat. In silence, the motel room settled around him like an itchy blanket. He stood. Paced. He ran his finger along the top of a lampshade and came away with a curling spiral of dust. He flicked it onto the carpet, then followed a charcoal-colored stain into the bathroom and jerked the shower curtain aside.

Antennae!

Roaches in the drain. Obscene feelers splayed out on white porcelain. His breath caught in his chest. Nothing moved. Dead roaches. Or hair. Dark strands trailing down to places unknown. Hairy drain. *Well that's it.* He heard the words, spoken with his mother's voice.

Down in reception, Cheri Front Desk continued to stab her keyboard.

"Breakdown Kid," she said without looking up. "What's happening?"

"I need a new room."

"Why?"

"The phone doesn't work. And there's hair in my drain." He planted his palms on the counter. "A bunch of hair."

"Maybe it's your hair."

"What?"

Clacking keys.

"It's not my hair," Lance said. "The hair is black."

"Do you like it?" she asked, facing him with her moon of a face.

"The hair? No, I don't like it."

"So why's it still there?"

"Because it was there when I checked in. The room wasn't cleaned."

Cheri stood. "That room was cleaned."

"Maybe it was *cleaned*. But it's not *clean*."

"What do you want me to do?" she said. "Housekeeping is gone."

"I want a new room."

"That's the only room left."

"So what am I supposed to do?"

"You could leave," she said. "I'd refund your money. Or, I'll tell you what. Since there's no one else here, I'll hire you for the night. The drain should take you about ten seconds to clean." Cheri pulled a quarter from her pocket. "Here's a quarter. That's a pretty good hourly rate."

She turned the coin in the light, grinning with her wide mouth.

Lance's phone buzzed in his pocket. Miriam was calling him.

"I thought your phone was broken," Cheri said.

"The room's phone is broken."

"Ooo," she said, pointing to the cracks. "Your phone *is* broken."

He pressed his phone to his cheek.

"I'll be back," Lance said.

"If I had a nickel for every time a guy—"

Lance slammed the door behind him.

"Hey," he said.

"Hey you," Miriam said. "What's going on? Are you really missing the party?"

How did she know? His mouth had no saliva. It could not produce words. His feet were thumping up the steps. Muddy boots in the hallway.

"Lance? You there?"

He stepped back into his motel room. The reality of his situation came into focus incrementally, like tiny letters during a routine vision check. He could hear the metal-and-glass slide of the Phoroptor, lenses dropping in front of his eyes.

schlink, schlink, schlink

Clarity, increasing.

"Party," he said.

"The party. Tonight. Lance?"

schlink, schlink

"Yeah," Lance said. But the party did not exist in this room.

Not to be attended, nor to be missed. The Trainsong Motel could not occupy space on the timeline of his actual life. There could be no choice between Miriam and the Trainsong, because this was a parallel reality. A time-out.

"This can't be happening," Miriam said.

Lance agreed. But, somehow, time was still moving in Bend. He could hear the party warming up through the phone. Faint music. Scattered laughter.

"I'll make it," he said. "You have no idea how bad I want to be there."

"You have to come," Miriam said. "You'll make it. We just need to—"

A voice in the background: *Is that Lance?* Miriam was handing him over.

"Lancelot! What in the hell have you gotten yourself into?"

Jonathan, already dialed up to ten.

"Hey, man. I'm stuck. The car is dead."

"What? This is The Party, Lance. Do you understand? The. Party. You have the penthouse suite. I changed my parents' sheets for this. Which was gross, Lance. Super gross."

In the background, Miriam said something he couldn't make out.

"Jonathan, I have no car."

"Rent one."

"I'm in the middle of nowhere."

"Steal one."

"Dude."

"Lance. Over the course of a life, what's more important? Doing what's strictly legal, or experiencing the culminating moment of, literally, your entire life? I'm sure your dad taught you how to hot-wire a car."

His dad had talked about it, but there had never been a hands-on demonstration.

"You're serious," Lance said. "You want me to steal a car."

"Damn right I'm serious," Jonathan said. "Lance. You've had zero fun this year. Old Man Disco Davis has partied harder than you. You're about to turn into a shitty little bank-telling turtle for the rest of the summer. Listen, Lancelot. You're better than this. You have to pull out something amazing right now. Defy expectations, okay? I'll hold my toast until you arrive."

A distant *oooooo*, like somebody spilled a drink. Miriam's voice, orbiting closer.

"Lance. Lance?"

"Hey."

"Sorry. Jonathan Davis is in rare form. Two White Russians and he's already into the disco."

"It's not even seven," Lance said.

"Your mom said she could get you home. Can't you leave the car?"

"Did my mom call you?"

"Yeah. So?"

"It's weird when she calls you," Lance said. "I feel like I'm in an arranged marriage."

"I'm glad *someone* called me."

"Miriam."

"Lance."

"Did my mom tell you her plan? She wants to junk out the Buick." The end of his sentence came out a croak. On Miriam's end, stunned silence. He pictured her, locked in a soundless scream, shock and disbelief. Until she said:

"We'll be at OSU next year. You won't really need the car."

"What?"

A thud of bone-jolting bass—choppy, syncopated guitar from Mr. Davis's underground disco collection. The party, getting better by the minute.

Miriam! C'moooooon. Let's get funked!

A male voice, closing in. Some idiot who couldn't tell funk from disco.

Yeah! Shake that thang!

Who was that jackass? Darren? Had Darren heard Lance wasn't coming? Darren had been waiting two years to take Lance's place in the Miriam equation. He was probably eyeing the bedroom Post-it with a Sharpie.

"Miriam, can you go outside? I can't hear anything."

"Hang on."

"Miriam, who is that talking to you?"

She was laughing, then nothing.

"Miriam. Hey, can you go back outside? I can't hear you." But there was no music. No Miriam. Lance's phone vibrated against his cheek. He stopped breathing. His stomach hit a speed bump, hung in the air, and refused to come back down. He pressed the power button. Again. Then again.

Dead.

"No," he said.

Panic came in quick, hot waves. Because there was no phone charger plugged into an outlet in his room. No phone charger in his suitcase or backpack or trumpet case or the orange duffel bag, which he had not opened, which he would not open. He clawed through everything else. Unzipped and rezipped and heaved out and scattered and paced the room until panic dulled to fact.

His charger was at Joe's Place.

"Nachos," Lance said.

He picked up the landline. Still dead.

Somehow, his life had taken the wrong exit. He'd flipped over the guardrail and was going down. There was no taxi. No train. His car was broken and would remain broken. His virginity, intact. It would spend the night with him. Him and his virginity, curled up alone in bed in a shitty motel room with pissed-off cats and a drain full of hair that was not his.

Nothing in this room to throw. Nothing he could afford to break. A sickening feeling in his chest, and he needed to get it out.

Hands shaking, he unsnapped his case. He took out his trumpet, palms damp on cool brass. Then he yanked open the window and aimed the bell of his horn at the opposite building. With one breath, he reached inside, yanked out the hot feelings twisting in his guts, and blatted a wild, true sound out into the night. A growling wail, slapping the building across the parking lot, bowling over its roof, crashing somewhere off in the trees.

The air trembled with the noise, and Lance let the horn drop to his side.

Breathing.

There was a distant pop of glass and metal, like breaking a

window with a home-run baseball. He stiffened. A warbling sound hovered in the distance, close to an F-sharp. Growing louder. The sound attached itself to a lone yellow light. A will-o'-the-wisp, bobbing behind the trees. The sound was a car horn. With the chug of a broken engine, a ruined white SUV bounced into the parking lot, hood metal skinned down to bone. One headlight dangled from its socket.

The car stopped and the horn blared.

The driver's-side door popped open and a girl climbed out and her yellow sundress was covered with blood and she was screaming.

3

Somehow, he had white bath towels in his hands.

He was in a dream, outside, moving in slow motion, and the girl in the bloody yellow dress was screaming and jerking at the passenger's-side door. She'd been driving, and a man was trapped inside.

Get out, Stone! Get out, goddamn you!

A small crowd had gathered, but they were standing in the wrong places to be performing a rescue. Just watching. Stone had short hair and a leather jacket, one leg hung up on the shifter. He jolted to life, trying to move. His head rolled fast and loose, like his neck was made of straw. The girl was frantic. A yellow streak bolting from door to door, jerking at the handles.

Get out! Get out of the car!

"Don't move!" Lance pulled open the driver's-side door. The girl was suddenly in his face. Cheeks flecked with blood. *Who the fuck are you?* Alcohol, a hot wave from her mouth. She knocked Lance aside, groping for Stone.

"Stop!" Lance said.

He grabbed a fistful of her dress, yanked her backward.

"Don't move him," Lance said. "He could die."

Shock in her eyes. People did not tell this girl *stop*.

"Don't touch me!"

"Someone call 9-1-1," Lance shouted. "Call the police!"

"No one's calling the police!" She kicked off one shoe, screamed at the pavement. She should've been beautiful, which made her ugliness worse. Bloodshot eyes, face pinched with disgust. She'd been driving.

Lance knew from his first-aid course to secure the victim's head. Never move the victim. And Stone's head was lolling like something in his neck had split. His right arm jerked up, as if trying to swat a fly. Lance ducked into the car and *shhhh* and *it's okay* and *relax* and packed white towels around Stone's neck, bracing his skull. His eyes fluttered, white slits. Blood trickled from his mouth. Blood, in the cup holder, like spilled soda. Blood on Lance's fingers. Warm. And a noise in his right ear. Shaking his eardrum. The girl.

"Out of my car! Get the fuck out!"

"Stand back!" Lance planted one foot on the pavement.

She charged.

It was instinct, putting his hands out. It didn't feel like a push, and it didn't feel hard, but then this girl was sucking air like her lungs couldn't find it, and she was stumbling backward, hands paddling. She rocked back on her heels, tipping like a chopped tree. She fell on pavement. Her head made a soft sound when it hit.

"He just pushed Breanna!" someone shouted.

"Yo! Back the fuck up!" someone else shouted.

Shadowy faces, men's voices. The crowd constricted. The voices, coming for him, then the front-office door burst open and someone was coming faster. Cheri Front Desk, a wrecking ball snapping loose from its chain—crashing into the crowd, scattering the men and their voices, grabbing hold of this whole ugly thing.

Get back! Stand up! Back to your room! Rocco—I will call the police! Shut up, Meebs! Get up, Breanna! On your feet!

Breanna, the one he'd pushed. She wrestled off her other shoe and flung it into the parking lot, then turned and ran barefoot toward the field, feet slapping pavement. Lance climbed back into the SUV.

"Stone—is that your name?"

"No," he said. "James. My name is James."

"What's your last name? Can you tell me what day it is? James? James?"

Sirens approached, grew shrill. Emergency lights transformed the car into a fun house and James was red and white and barely moving. Lance grabbed James's hand because it felt like he should, and someone's palm clapped on his back. Lance turned toward a strong set of eyes, looking into his.

"Thank you, son," the officer said.

Lance got out of the car. Police swept in, people who belonged here. Lance's hands clenched to fists and James's blood pulled at the short hairs on his knuckles. An unsettling flutter in his chest, like the beginning of a shiver. He stood, frozen. He ached for goosebumps, a shudder, a sneeze. Some kind of release.

"Come here, kiddo."

Cheri had him by the arm and through a door, beneath a naked yellow bulb. A waist-high sink. An oval of pink soap. The water was scalding, steam blanketing the mirror. Lance scrubbed red hands until they were raw and pink shavings had replaced the blood beneath his nails.

Back outside, the stretcher stood at a crooked angle. The straps were tangled as if it had just been pulled out of storage. Police stood in small clusters, pointing in different directions. These men were not neat and trim like the Bend police. They had beards and bellies, like someone had yanked them off their barstools and stuffed them into sky-blue patrolmen shirts. A pair of them walked into the field, flashlights bobbing in the dark.

Had he saved someone's life? Committed assault?

They would have questions.

But he could not make a report. He could not have his name in an official file, anchored to this place. This was his chance to walk into the shadows with freshly scrubbed hands and no one would ever know. He calculated the best route back to his room, and was moving as quickly as he could when he saw her.

She was watching him.

A girl in the darkness. In possession of perfect stillness. Her stillness made him stop, and because he stopped, it came. The feeling he'd been aching for. Toes in ice water. Feathers up his calves. A hair-prickling, teeth-rattling rush of a shiver so good it made his eyes sting. He took a deep breath and looked at her.

"I saw you," she said. "You're the guy with the trumpet."

He nodded and tried to see her, but her attention was like a spotlight. Hard to look at straight on. She was maybe his age, or a little older. Possibly beautiful. They were on the wide concrete slab of the motel parking lot, but it felt like a small room. Like he should say something important, or ask her to dance. The silence was getting heavy, their instant on the verge of thickening into a moment.

Behind him, voices and emergency lights. He had to move. Now or never. So he didn't talk. He turned away and stepped to the side, and once he was moving inertia carried him around the corner, away from this still girl, and up the stairs.

Back inside his motel room, police lights flared through the blinds and did strange things to the wall hangings. The cloth sailboat turned orange, the water, crimson. The cats' eyes were flashing marbles. Lance picked up his phone and cradled it. His hands were no longer bloody. His phone was cracked and dead.

He took a shower. The first blast of hot water sent the dark hairs scurrying down the drain, almost before he noticed them. Time passed with a dull, white roar, and when his lungs were heavy with steam he shut off the water. He reached out, pawing bare wooden shelves.

There were no towels.

His feet slipped on linoleum. Back by his suitcase, Lance balled up a white T-shirt and rubbed it over his body until he was dry.

He was damp and dressed in a clean shirt and jeans. Socks and shoes. Shaking hungry.

Out here, The Float is it.

The emergency lights were gone, and he hadn't eaten in twelve hours. He walked out of his room, down the stairs, and out toward the giant glowing flotation device, feeling wobbly and light, like a moth dancing toward a flame.

4

The shortest distance from the motel to The Float was through an overgrown field. Too hungry to think, Lance bushwhacked through the scrub and was scratched and nettled and soaked from the thighs down when he finally stepped onto pavement. He circled around to the front of the building, where a laminated sheet of paper was nailed to a windowless wooden door.

THE FLOAT

7AM–CLOSE

DOGS, CATS, AND (SOME) PEOPLE WELCOME

WARM BEER! TERRIBLE FOOD!

The rumble of voices and a standard 2/4 rock beat pulsed inside. Lance opened the door and was greeted by a towering wooden statue of a female pirate, standing where a host should be. She wore a savage expression, one leg cocked up on a rock. She could've been solemn—even noble—but someone had done her up with a pink bandana, a wench's skirt, and a skull-and-crossbones bikini. She still had a sword. Long and broad and sharp. It looked real. Like you could wiggle it right out of her wooden hand.

"Hey! I can't see you. Dude! Step away from the pirate!"

Lance stepped to the right. Fifty feet ahead and behind the bar was a college-aged guy with a mop of dark hair and noticeable gap between his two front teeth. He held himself like a bear; hunched forward, slump-shouldered.

"Oh, I know you," he said. "You're the guy who knocked Breanna on her ass. Nice work, friend. Come on in!"

The Float was cavernous; much bigger than it looked from outside. Wooden and dark. Lance skirted the pirate and scanned the mismatched tables. People stared back. Everyone at the road-house looked like they played on the same team. Their uniforms involved flannel and denim of a certain character. They probably had their own roadhouse customs and sacrificial rites involving wooden pirates and angry tabby cats and—

Shoelaces.

A black shoelace, dangling in front of his nose.

Lance looked up. The shoelace was attached to a black sneaker, hanging by its twisted lace around exposed wood. Shoes were everywhere. Tangled around rafters the way they sometimes draped from lonely telephone wires, but *hundreds*. White Keds, battered work boots, fluorescent sneakers, polished wing tips, thick-soled skater shoes, all types and sizes, strung up and swinging above his head.

The Shoe Gallows.

"Have a seat," the bartender said.

Lance found a stool.

"Are you still serving food?" Lance asked.

"Yeah," the bartender said. "But we lost our fry cook."

"Oh."

"Yup. You had his blood all over your hands about an hour ago."

"The guy from the car?" Lance asked, checking his hands. "James?"

"Stone," the bartender said. "His name's Stone. *James.* Y'all hear that?" Down the bar, a few people laughed. *James, James,* they repeated, like a word they'd never heard before. "My name's Mason."

"I'm Lance."

Mason's paw swallowed Lance's hand, pumping it firmly. Before he let go, he said: "Want to make a bet, Lance?"

"A bet?"

Mason tossed a glossy menu on the bar, then leaned on his elbows. "I'll bet you ten bucks I can tell you where you got your shoes." He slapped a ten-dollar bill on the table. Mason's eyes, a hazel confusion of blue and green and brown. No real color at all.

"That's okay," Lance said. "I'm good."

"Think about it," Mason said, then turned away.

Lance glanced at his shoes, which he'd gotten in Bend at Gronski Family Shoe Shoppe. Mason couldn't possibly know that. On the menu, a long column of burgers. His jaw ached. He was salivating. Close to actually drooling.

"Decide yet?"

"Yeah," Lance said. "I'll have the Black and Blue Burger—"

"About the bet," Mason said, tapping his ten-dollar bill. "Really. I can tell you where you got your shoes."

Mason's stare was a wall between him and his cheeseburger.

"Okay, sure," Lance said. "I'll take the bet."

"Let's see that ten."

The fold in his wallet was loose, still holding the gap where his fifty dollars had been. Now, another ten. He'd just been to an ATM in Seattle and was nearly out of cash. Mason took the bill, holding the money as if he already owned it.

"All right, gambler!" Mason said, lighting up. He wasn't talking to Lance anymore. He was talking to the whole bar. "I can't tell you where you *bought* your shoes. Target? Payless? How the hell would I know? But I can tell you where you *got* your shoes. You *got* your shoes on your feet, and you *got* your feet in my bar. The Float, mile marker one twenty-five in Baring, Washington. And that's exactly where your ten dollars is going to stay!"

He pulled Lance's ten-dollar bill taut so it made a popping sound.

"Woo!" shouted a guy at the end of the bar. He had floppy blond hair and a flannel shirt. A surfer, abandoned at birth and raised by rednecks.

"What's your name again?" Mason asked.

"Lance."

He took a marker from his pocket. Tongue twiddling out from the corner of his mouth, he etched giant bold letters onto the front of the bill. LANCE, it said. The *N* perfectly centered, slashing diagonals over Hamilton's face. He walked down the bar to a wall-size

American flag, strung up like window blinds. When Mason pulled a cord, the red and white stripes accordioned together, going up.

Behind the flag, a fortune of ten-dollar bills.

Bills four or five deep, hung with pushpins and tagged with blocky letters. ANDREW, MELANIE, STEVEN, RICHARD, DANA, BRADLEY. Mason stuck Lance's up near the center. Hundreds of tens. Thousands of dollars.

"Wall of Shame!" said the floppy-haired guy. He clapped, dragging along some limp applause from others. Lance's fingers clawed into the menu, bending it.

"May I take your order, sir?" Mason asked, grinning.

"I'll have the Black and Blue Burger with fries. Hey, do you have a phone charger I could use?"

"Nope," Mason said without a beat. "But you can ask around."

Lance turned to his right. Down the bar, the floppy-haired guy and someone else were staring at him. They gave him the chin-up. Lance gave it back a little too hard. Like giving himself an uppercut.

He smiled. They did not smile back.

Lance reached for his pocket, but had no phone to look at. No TV in the bar. Only liquor bottles. Dusty shelves. Bins of paper tickets labeled PULL TABS.

He was sitting in an actual bar.

He wondered what Miriam was doing. He had not stolen a car. He had not defied expectations, nor done anything amazing. Turbulence in his chest. The swell and flutter he'd felt at Joe's Place, and every day in Seattle. He grabbed a napkin from a metal dispenser, a pen from his pocket. Music was coming. He scratched out a rough stave, holding the napkin taut to keep it from tearing. Then notes. Right there in the bar. Eyes stinging. Pulling this thing down from the sky.

The server set down his plate with a CLINK.

The burger. A thing of beauty. Piled high with thick peppered bacon. Chunks of blue cheese. A nest of beer-battered fries. He dropped his pen and grabbed hold of the bun.

"Tasty burger?" asked Floppy Hair, suddenly beside him.

Lance stared, blinking him into focus.

"Hey," another voice said. "Drop the burger. He asked you something."

The guy beside Floppy Hair was carved from mahogany, wide eyes, goatee the size of a toothbrush head. Lance set down his burger and took a long, rattling breath.

"I'm Rocco," the mahogany man said. "This is Meebs." Rocco slapped Meebs on the back, flopping hair into his eyes. Odors of smoke clung to them in atmospheric layers, wafting up from their clothing: cigarettes, campfire, beef jerky.

"I'm Lance."

"We already saw your name, Ace," Rocco said. "On the wall."

"You pushed our friend," Meebs said. He was giddy. Happy to say it. Like he'd been keeping it a secret all week.

"What?"

"Breanna," Rocco said. "The girl from the accident. You pushed her. You proud about that? You look proud about it."

"I didn't mean to."

"To push her, or look proud?"

"Push her."

"Wow. How do you accidentally push someone, Meebs?"

"I don't know. Weird," Meebs said.

"Like that," Rocco said, shoving Lance's shoulder.

Lance teetered on the edge of his stool for a second, then slipped off and was standing.

"Was that an accident?" Rocco asked. He was not tall, but his muscle groups were scientifically identifiable beneath his T-shirt. Meebs had knobby joints and stretchy limbs and could probably tangle himself around an opponent like a spring-loaded spider monkey.

And Lance's burger was right there. Steaming fries.

"More interested in this?" Rocco asked. He grabbed Lance's plate and lifted his meal to eye level. With a twist of his wrist, he dumped Lance's dinner on the floor. Fries on hardwood. The burger, mostly in its bun. Lance stared down and could not move.

"You could still eat that," Rocco said. "This place is pretty clean."

"Go ahead," Meebs said. "We won't bother you anymore."

They turned to leave.

Trembling, Lance lowered himself toward the floor. Rocco turned and stomped down. His boot heel cleaved through bread and meat. A gray smear. And suddenly Lance was up. His stool clattered on the ground. Welded to his palm was a butter knife. Lance held its rounded tip inches from Rocco's nose.

"What are you going to do, wild man?" Rocco asked.

"I'm going to stab you in the face," Lance hissed.

"It's a butter knife," Meebs observed.

"Go on, dickhead. Just try and break the skin."

"Hey! What the hell is going on!" Mason's voice boomed.

No one moved. A song on the jukebox was the only sound. Electronic, with high vocals. *Yeah, yeah, yeah,* it said. *Yeah, yeah, yeah, yeah.*

"Obviously, I'm being assaulted," Rocco said.

"Jesus, kid. You're a maniac," Mason said.

"He won't stop until we're all dead," Meebs whispered.

"This guy stepped on my cheeseburger!" Lance said. His final word reverberated, an octave too high. Cheeseburger. A word that tended to resist seriousness. Like a butter knife.

Mason flopped his meaty arms onto the counter. "Siddown. Both of you."

"No way! Rocco's gonna hand him his ass!" Meebs prattled, shaking like a nervous dog. "He's gonna—" Mason grabbed a stack of cocktail napkins and flung them in Meebs's face. A white explosion, fluttering all around him.

"Move your ass, Meebs," Mason said.

Meebs shuffled down the bar, sat.

"Gentlemen," Mason said. "Can you sit?"

"I prefer to stand," Rocco said.

"Me too," Lance said, right leg jackrabbiting on the ground.

"What happened?" Mason asked.

"He pushed Breanna," Rocco said.

"Punched her!" Meebs called out.

"So what?" Mason said. "Breanna's an idiot. She cost me my fry cook. And then she runs *here*. Is she trying to shut me down? Answer me, Rocco."

"How do I know?"

"You're her keeper, right?" Mason said. "That's why you're here pushing strangers and throwing my food around. Right?"

"You don't push girls," Rocco said.

"Oh. Now Breanna's a girl," Mason said. "She's a wildebeest. She tried to lock herself in my walk-in. That was some werewolf-movie bullshit, back there. *Lock me in! I don't know what I'll do! They'll take me to jail! Please! Heeeelp meeeee!* She had fangs and shit. I do not lie." Rocco laughed.

"Here's what's going to happen. Lance, right? Lance is going to put down his cutlery before he gives someone an abrasion."

Lance set the knife down.

"Good. I'm gonna comp you another burger. You can have Stone's shift meal. And Rocco's gonna clean up his food mess."

"Bullshit," Rocco hissed.

"Easy, killer," Mason said. "I'll pour us a shot. We'll drink to Stone. Guy barely has a pulse to begin with. It's a miracle they brought him back."

Mason ran his finger along several bottles, stopping at one called Teacher's. He sloshed whisky into three shot glasses. It smelled like disinfectant and burning leaves.

"I'm just gonna need some proof you're twenty-one," Mason said to Lance.

Lance patted his pockets, as if searching for something that existed.

"Dude. Kidding," Mason said. "Loosen up."

"Yo! Can I get in on that shot?" Meebs called from down the bar.

"No, Meebs," Mason said. "Go eat your grilled cheese, you vegetarian fucker."

Rocco, Mason, and Lance touched their glasses together. "To a fresh start," Mason said. The liquid went down with a burning gulp and left ashes on his tongue. It tasted like something he might enjoy someday. Like when he was fifty.

"First Scotch?" Mason asked, refilling his own glass.

"It's good," Lance whispered. It had also chewed away part of his throat.

Mason laughed.

"Yeah. Well, thanks for saving Stone's ass," Rocco said. "Enjoy that burger." He grabbed Lance's upper arm and squeezed. Lance was glad they hadn't fought.

Ten minutes later, the universe narrowed to the miracle of a cheeseburger and fries on his plate. Everything was hot and delicious. The meal hit him like a calming wave. Good food, stilling his hands, quieting his brain, bite after bite until he was drifting through the soft haze of a food coma. A new state of existence.

After red meat and whisky, the night had a whole different flavor. The loose, freewheeling feeling of a true adventure. *You saved someone's life. You drank Scotch in public. You pulled a knife in a bar fight. In a roadhouse bar fight.*

What a list! He smiled, playing it over. But he could already hear his friends back home: *Lancelot did what?* The stories seemed too wild to belong to him. He grabbed hold of his memories, replaying the facts, kneading them into his brain.

This happened, he told himself on the way to the bathroom. *This is happening.*

Condom machines bookended the urinals. Lance took the one farthest from the door and stared straight ahead at a crack in the wall someone had decorated with blue pen to look like a vagina. He thought of Miriam and it disturbed him, having this thought. Someone banged through the door behind him.

Rocco.

Lance froze and Rocco sidled up beside him. He looked Lance straight in the eye, smiled, then blasted the porcelain with a confident stream. Lance couldn't go. He felt it retreating, crawling up toward his stomach. He went back to his mantras, seeking courage. Sometimes this helped.

You are valedictorian.

You are the first-chair trumpet player.

You have a full-ride scholarship.

Miriam Seavers is in love with you.

Nothing. Lance pretended to shake off, then zipped, flushed, and walked to the sink. Rocco was still there.

"Hey," Rocco said. "You didn't go."

"What?"

"You didn't pee."

Lance stared at him. He'd never see this guy again.

"Yeah. I didn't pee. So what?"

"No shame in it," Rocco said. "Good instinct. That's what keeps animals from getting eaten. I won't tell anyone. Male code." He put a finger to his lips, then left without washing his hands.

Lance stood in the bathroom for a minute. He still couldn't go. Back in the bar, Meebs and Rocco were standing beside the giant wooden pirate along with someone else. The girl from the parking lot. Dark hair, jeans, a T-shirt. Watching.

That girl.

He wanted to spin and run back to the bathroom, but they'd already seen him. The three of them somehow together, like everyone at The Float was a cast member in the same small movie.

"Dakota says you're staying at the Trainsong," Rocco said.

Dakota.

"So? Are you?" Rocco said.

"What?" Lance said.

"Staying at the Trainsong?"

"Yeah. Looks like it."

"C'mon," Meebs said. Lance understood he was supposed to leave with them. Outside, the air had cooled and had a wormy after-the-rain smell. The group huddled by the rear bumper of a green station wagon.

"This piece of shit," Rocco said, kicking the tire.

"This piece of shit will leave you in the parking lot." Meebs turned to Lance. "Hey. What do you drive?"

"A Buick. It's in the shop though."

"With a mechanic out here? Good luck," Rocco said. "You might have to walk home. Don't lose your shoes."

"Lose my shoes?"

"Inside," Rocco said, pointing to The Float. "The prize wheel is rigged."

"It's not. That couple in the Chevy Malibu won a thousand—"

"Meebs, motherfucker."

"Guys," Dakota said. "We have company."

"You all live here?" Lance asked.

"We do," Dakota said. She tucked her chin while she talked, hiding behind a dark curtain of hair. "We used to be just like you, Lance. On the way to better places. But our cars broke down. On a night just...like...this." Her voice had a soft, steady quality, like a hypnotist counting down from ten.

"Yep," Rocco said. "It's true."

"My car still drives," Meebs said, patting the wagon's rear window. "This sweet baby."

"Your parents' sweet baby," Dakota said.

"It's half mine," Meebs said.

"You're half full of shit," Dakota said.

"So what brought you out here?" Rocco asked Lance.

"I had an audition in Seattle."

"You an actor?" Rocco asked.

"Musician," Dakota said.

"Cool," Meebs said, bouncing from foot to foot, flipping back his hair. "So are you in a band?"

Lance froze. The word *band* had been loaded. Meebs didn't mean marching band, or honor band, or any other school-based embarrassment. He meant a *real* band. With gigs and fans and between-song banter. Just last week, Jonathan and Miriam had said they couldn't imagine Lance in a real rock band. Jonathan had done an impression of Frontman Lance Hendricks:

C'mon, Mick, we can't fade the song out! That's not rock and roll! Can we try this with a different time signature, mate?

Now that Meebs was asking The Band Question, Lance felt a door opening. Like he could reach into a closet of new identities, try on what he wanted, and keep what fit. And Meebs was staring, because Lance still hadn't answered the question.

"No," Lance said. "I mean, not now. I'm busy getting ready to graduate."

"College?" Dakota asked.

Lance hesitated. "High school." A collective *oooooooh*.

"Just a pup," Rocco said.

"Told you," Meebs said to Dakota.

"Well, congrats," Rocco said.

"On what?"

"Graduating," Rocco said.

"You made it, dude!" Meebs said, slapping his back.

"They gonna let you walk?" Rocco asked.

"You mean walk, like leave?"

"I mean, are you allowed to walk in the graduation ceremony?"

"Yeah," Lance said. "Oh yeah. Why wouldn't I be?"

"I've only known you two hours and you pulled a knife on me."

"Did a shot of whisky," Meebs added.

"Knocked down a girl," Rocco said. "Fled the scene of an accident."

"Did *my* shot of whisky," Meebs went on.

"I didn't really flee the scene."

"Did he flee the scene, Dakota?" Rocco asked.

"Oh, he fled all right," Dakota said, meeting his eyes.

"No," Lance said. "I'd say I slowly backed away from the scene."

"Let the record show he slowly backed away from the scene, Your Honor," Meebs said.

They howled. Meebs drummed the hood of his car. The way they were talking made him smile. He was suddenly *expulsion material*. And this was an actual scene in his life.

"Did the cops go after Breanna?" Dakota asked.

"No. She and Stone got a story they're cooking up," Rocco said. "Breanna just totaled the Mustang, what, two weeks ago?"

"Mustang Sally!" Meebs sang.

"She totaled another car?" Lance said.

"You know you'd better slow that Mustang down!"

"Have you talked to the police yet?" Rocco asked.

"No," Lance said.

"Lance is a loose cannon," Dakota said. "He doesn't work with police." She winked at him. A wink, sending chills up his arms. So *that* was how a wink was supposed to work. He looked at the ground. Too much.

"Talk to Breanna before the police," Rocco said.

"Why?" Lance asked.

"She and Stone have got a plan."

Meebs began singing "Folsom Prison Blues," doing a decent Johnny Cash: *"I hear the train a comin', it's rollin' round the bend...."*

"Can we go, dude?" Rocco said. "I'm already tired of you, and we still have to ride home together."

"I said *biiiiiitch*," Meebs said, taking out his keys. So he was driving. Lance wondered how many car accidents these friends got into.

Rocco turned to Dakota: "You safe alone with the wild man? Can we trust him?"

"It's Dakota," Meebs said. "She'll ice him down."

"Don't worry," Dakota said. "He still has to use a hall pass."

Lance's cheeks burned. Meebs and Rocco hooted as they walked away.

A moment later, headlights flared, washing over them. He and Dakota were onstage. The brights flickered on and off and Meebs stuck his floppy-haired head out the window:

"Hey kids! Don't get frisk-y!"

Lance looked up just in time to see Dakota try to ignore them while he tried to ignore them and tried to ignore her trying to ignore him trying to ignore them.

"C'mon," she said, walking toward the field.

Dakota had a walk to her. Faster than she looked, like she stole an extra bit of ground with every step. She led him to the parking lot's edge, where pulverized concrete gave way to Spanish broom. His eyes adjusted, and a narrow path materialized in the blue-green shadows.

He wanted her to turn around and look at him, and it was also the last thing he wanted.

She kept moving. Blackberries, goldenrod. Strange grasses: sharp tips and feathery plumes, others bowed over with thick, stoppered ends. Nettles pecked from the path's edge. Lance was turning his legs, watching for jagged leaves, when he saw them: Splashes of white scattered in the undergrowth. Small flowers he hadn't noticed before, fanning out petals like cupped, ivory hands.

He stopped with one inches from his right toe.

The center of the flower's bloom was imprinted with a delicate shape—a spindly star, faint as a shadow. Was it really a star? He widened his legs to avoid crushing the petals as he bent down. Yes, a violet star, reflecting back the light like a cat's eye. And the bloom gave off a sweet scent, close to lavender. Like the most expensive bar of soap.

And the sudden sensation of being watched.

Dakota. She had stopped and turned around just in time to see him—the high schooler, the kid in need of a hall pass, the wild one, the stranger—hunkered down over a little white flower. And obviously sniffing it.

He could hear Darren and Jonathan reacting.

Dude, Lancelot. Did you just stop to smell the roses? What the hell are you doing?

But only Dakota had seen him, and she was quiet. Maybe smiling. Then she turned and he struggled to his feet and they were walking again, back to the Trainsong parking lot. Just them and evening-gray cars. Dark windows.

It felt like something was supposed to happen. Like he should say something.

"Thanks for walking me back," he said.

"Thanks for saving Stone's life," she said. She tilted up her chin and her hair slipped back like curtains. White lights from the parking lot struck her eyes—somewhere between green and gray. Blazing when they looked at him dead-on. Long hair was a good idea. Without it, she'd spend all day frying people's retinas.

"You leave tomorrow?" she said.

"Yeah," he said. "I hope."

"Well. Enjoy the trainsong."

She smiled then, like she'd just decided against saying more.

"I'll do my best."

The air tightened between them. What else could he say?

"Goodnight," she said.

"Goodnight."

Good. Done.

He turned away, finally able to breathe again. Nothing weird had happened. Everything was okay, aside from a sudden concern for his trumpet. He'd left it unattended in his room, which was unwise in a place like this. *Who knows who has keys to these rooms?* He was also out of towels. Luckily, Cheri was still lurking down in reception. She must be plugged in somewhere behind that desk.

"Breakdown Kid," she said, barely looking up.

"Hey. Can I get a couple towels?"

"What happened to the ones in your room?"

"I brought them down to the accident."

She leapt to her feet. "Wait. Did you get blood on my towels?"

"Yeah, I—"

"Those weren't emergency towels! Those were bath towels. That's why they're in the *bath*room, not the *emergency* room."

"What was I supposed to do? I was trying to save—"

"Kidding," Cheri said, slapping the counter. "A joke, Breakdown. Ever hear of a joke?" She gave him a fresh stack of towels.

"Thanks," he said.

"Wait a sec," she said. When he turned, something bright flashed through the air and he caught it. A quarter.

"For the clean-up job," she said. "Welcome to the team."

Lance managed to fall asleep. His eyes shot open when his trumpet started playing itself.

It was a horrible blat of a sound he'd made before the accident. His horn was doing it again, loud enough to shake the room. Lance wrapped his arms around his head. He had to stop it.

He kicked off tangled bedsheets and crashed to the floor, smashing his mouth. The taste of iron on his lips, and he was scuttling across the carpet to his horn. He threw himself down and wrapped his arms around the case, trying to muffle it. The case trembled along with the room. Drinking glasses went *tick-tick-tick* on a porcelain sink, the cats' frame tapping at the wall, and a strangely familiar *calack, calack, calack* that did not belong to his trumpet.

He loosened his grip.

It was a train. A train that sounded like it ran through the center of the motel. Another whistle. It would never stop.

Enjoy the trainsong.

Trainsong Motel. Another one of Cheri's jokes.

"Damn it," Lance said.

He climbed into bed, and even when it had long been quiet, he could not sleep.

He tried his usual technique—a fantasy he'd played dozens of times. Him and Miriam in a bedroom. He was removing her clothes, slowly. Somewhere in the middle of the scenario, his mind drifted and landed on Dakota. His legs went still, shocked at his behavior.

He absently wondered what Dakota looked like naked, and it was stunningly easy to imagine. His mind was suddenly full of painters, sculptors, cinematographers. Like they'd been awake all night, just waiting for a project. Naked Dakota was standing in his brain, wondering what he wanted to do. But he couldn't do that to Miriam.

He opened his eyes and heard something in the walls.

The things made a tooth-and-nail scratching sound. Slow and steady, like they'd be burrowing all night. He imagined mouths and whiskers and dark little claws. The sounds could almost be distant footsteps if he shut his eyes and pictured them that way. Shoes tapping up wooden steps, pacing along the balcony to his room.

He remembered the way she'd walked through that field. He could picture her perfectly.

He woke himself hours later, bolting upright in bed. "Hello?"

There was no response. He looked around the strange room and had no idea where he was, or how he had gotten there.

5

Cheri Front Desk stood outside the office, murdering shrubbery with a high-powered hose. The water was strong enough to strip paint. She grinned up at Lance, shredding bushes like confetti.

"What's happening, Breakdown?" she asked.

It was confusing, what was happening. The day had come on bold and bright, and he was somehow standing in a motel parking lot, holding his trumpet case. Time had passed. The moon had gone down and taken away the party of his life. And the sun had risen on what, exactly?

Cheri Front Desk and denuded boxwood.

"I need to get to Joe's Place."

"Sure," she said. "Just down Highway 2. About a ten-minute drive."

"But I don't have a car."

"Ohhhhh, right." She stopped spraying. "Want me to find you a ride? Ladies around here would line up around the block for a tall drink of water like you." She giggled. "But I won't be held responsible for what happens."

Lance took a step back. *Tall drink of water.* He wasn't sure what that meant, but he didn't want Cheri filling the glass. He had to be careful. He'd met others with Cheri's bizarre, life-bending powers. Neighbors. Proprietors of general stores. Innocent-looking people who could grab hold of your morning with one unsolicited comment and swing your day completely off course. Lance moved away slowly, before Cheri's powers could take hold.

"Wait, wait," she said, scanning the parking lot. "There's a taker! Lookee there!"

Too late! Too late!

He was caught in a Cheri Front Desk tractor beam. She was sending him across the parking lot in the direction of someone familiar.

Dakota.

The girl he'd last visualized naked in the privacy of his motel room, now existing in broad daylight. She was sitting in a green plastic chair, tan legs stretched out in front of her and crossed neatly at the ankles. He felt like he should apologize for taking her clothes off. Or give her flowers. Something. Then Dakota was looking at him and he was taking one step in her direction, more steps, until he was standing right in front of her.

"Go on!" Cheri said. "Ask her for a ride. Hey, Dakota!"

"Hey," Lance said, his voice coming out low and stupid.

"Hey," Dakota said, squinting into the sun. "You're still here. Is your car fixed?"

"I don't know. My phone's dead. I left my charger at Joe's Place. It's about—"

"I know where it is." She smiled. "You need a ride?"

Her question tingled under his skin and projected a word onto the backs of his eyelids. DANGEROUS. Like black letters on a white screen. This word, coming from nowhere. Cheri Front Desk would not be held responsible.

He nodded.

"Good," Dakota said, pulling out keys. "I was just out here thinking up a good reason to leave."

"Glad I could help."

"You're perfect."

They climbed inside her sky-blue Ford Focus. A green tassel hung from her rearview mirror, tangled up with a bacon air freshener that thankfully didn't smell like bacon. It smelled like a freshly peeled orange, or Dakota did. A warm smell, coming from her neck. She had a little blue vein there, tracing up around her jaw. They seemed to be sitting really close in this car. Maybe the Ford Focus had a weird thing about smashing their passengers too close together. Or maybe Dakota sat this close to everyone.

They drove for a few minutes. It was quiet.

"I don't usually give rides to strangers," she said.

"Well, thanks."

"Had a bad experience with a hitchhiker," Dakota said. "Hell of a story."

"Really?"

She pursed her lips, then didn't go on.

"So what's your story, Wildman?" Dakota said.

"Which story?"

"Your best story. You're going to be gone forever in five minutes, right?"

"Well, I was supposed to go to an amazing party last night."

"That's your best story? You were supposed to go to a party?"

He laughed, surprising himself. "Yeah. I think that might be it."

She smiled. A nice smile. A little crooked. Not showing a lot of teeth, but lips. The kind of lips Darren and Jonathan would've commented on crudely and specifically. The kind of lips Lance had never noticed until now.

"Want to get coffee?" those lips asked.

"Yeah," he heard himself say. "I do."

A fluttering anxiety rose up in his chest, like a warm breeze scattering leaves, spinning up behind his lungs. This was a choice he could not easily explain later. A few miles down the road, they pulled into a parking lot.

"Whiggley's!" Dakota announced. She sounded like a little kid.

Whiggley's was the real deal. An actual DINER. Every spot in Bend had just been a cheap knockoff of this: homemade pies spinning in a glass case, a steel tank of a cash register, booths with padded red seats, and hollow, glass-topped tables stuffed with '50s knickknacks and memorabilia. Their waitress was actually named Maude. She was one of three bustling white-haired ladies in aprons and striped shirts. They could've been identical triplet Maudes, possibly fathered by the diner itself.

Maude #1 flopped a few giant menus on the table and filled

their mugs to the brim with hot coffee. Steam unraveled, perfect in the sunlight. Folding and uncurling, stretching slender fingers toward the ceiling. Lance warmed his hands on the ceramic cup.

"Lance," Dakota said, leaning forward. "I need to ask you something."

"What?"

She beckoned him forward. They leaned toward each other.

"What's with the case?" she whispered, cupping her hands.

"Which case?"

"The one you carry around like a suitcase full of money."

"Oh," he said, touching it with his foot. "That's just my trumpet."

"I figured. Is it handcuffed to your wrist?"

"Maybe. I'm not allowed to say."

"Can I see it?"

"Right here?"

"Yes," she said. "Let's get crazy."

He pulled out the case and set it on the glass-topped table. He unsnapped the buckles, and there was his trumpet. Sunlight broke over its hammered brass like an egg yolk, and Lance saw himself smile in the bell of his beautiful horn.

"Wow," she said. "It *is* like a suitcase full of money."

"Not cheap," Lance said. "Two summers as a bank teller, right there."

She reached out to touch the horn. Instinctively, his hand jerked up to stop her.

"Wow," she said. But she touched the horn anyway, running her index finger along the trademark etching of a windblown tree.

"Wild Thing, eh?" she said, tracing the letters.

"Yeah," he said. "That's what it's called. That's the brand." He quickly snapped the case shut and put it under the table. It felt better there. Safe.

"So, musician. Knife-fighter. *Bank teller.* Are you a good student?"

"Pretty good."

She sat back and shook her head. "You're interesting, Lance."

His heart was pounding because suddenly he, Lance Hendricks, was interesting. And did that mean she was *interested in him*? It did, at least literally. And, also—wait, was this a date? This was just coffee. Which was fine. Everyone drank coffee together. Friends. Relatives. They could be related, if someone asked.

"Tell me a story," she said.

"What kind of story?"

"Any story," she said. "I don't know anything about you."

This girl never checked her phone. She did not look away.

He lifted his menu to face level, but did not look at the column of Piled-High Country Skillets nor the Barn-Buster Breakfasts. He needed to hide. Safe from her eyes, he rifled through his stories like a deck of old baseball cards. *What had he ever done?* Behind his menu, under the bright lights of Whiggley's Diner, he was forced to give his stories a good, hard look.

There was the night he and Darren threw folding chairs in the deep end of Bend Public Pool. Shopping-cart races at Walmart. His craziest, spur-of-the-moment trip when he skipped trumpet practice and drove exactly forty-five miles before turning around at a gas station with a blended coffee drink.

His mantras came rushing back, trying to save him.

You are valedictorian.

You are the first-chair trumpet player.

You have a full-ride scholarship.

Miriam Seavers is in love with you.

But he did not have stories. Just achievements.

And all the coffee cups were rattling in their saucers. Silverware, shivering against the glass-topped case. That damn train. It must be coming back.

"You okay?" she said.

"Yeah, why?"

He looked outside, bracing himself for the earsplitting whistle.

"Your left leg is a seven-point earthquake."

Lance planted his feet and the table stopped shaking. He attempted to resume normal breathing.

"Are you nervous?" she asked.

"No, it's just a condition."

"Like PTSD?"

"Restless legs syndrome."

"Is that a twitchy spasm thing? Like Tourette's?"

"No. It's not like that."

"You don't swear uncontrollably?"

"I don't."

"I can't believe that's a syndrome. I'm going to look it up." He thought she might pull out her phone and give him a break. But she just hit him with another question.

"Do you get nervous when you play music?"

"Not usually. I was a little nervous at my audition. The guys there—you could just feel how much they'd played." Improvising for that panel had felt like improvising for Dakota: He could play his whole heart out, and it might not be enough.

"So you're going to school for music then?" she asked.

"No," he said. "I mean, I'm going to keep playing music, but I'm going to school for business."

Her eyes shot open and Lance looked over his shoulder, because maybe someone behind him had just picked up a giant bloody hatchet. But there was no ax murder. That look was just for him, studying business.

"Business," she said.

"What?"

"Why would you study business?"

Lance's stomach prickled. But he knew the answer to this question. He had the script.

"There are a lot of places you can go with a business degree," he said. "Most competitive employment sectors are looking for business graduates, so I want to give myself the academic freedom to find something I love."

"Wow. You love music, right?"

"Yeah. But I need to make good money."

"Why," she asked. "For what?"

That solid stare. Was she serious?

"You need to know *why* I want to make good money?"

"Yeah. What do you want to do with all your good money?"

Lance had a specific vision of himself with money. Wearing expensive sunglasses, he walked out of an important meeting and into a parking lot. He opened the door to a new white convertible, threw himself into the front seat, and jammed a key in the ignition, music blaring as he peeled off to kick ass at his next important meeting. He'd never considered the purpose of these meetings. Only being rushed and valuable. He smiled, picturing it.

"So?" Dakota asked.

Lance shrugged and said: "I want to be able to do what I want."

"What do you want?"

According to his five-second mental film clip, he wanted to be between meetings.

"I want to travel," Lance said, remembering Seattle. "Play music."

"So why not just travel and play music?"

"Oh, right." Lance laughed. She wasn't smiling. He frowned. "Because you can't just do that. I need to make money first. I mean, do you know the average business graduate can make over sixty thousand dollars a year? That's really good money. After a couple years, I'll be able to do whatever I want."

"Sure," she said. "But by then you'll want different things. Maybe you'll want a nicer car. And a nicer house. You could be married with babies and knickknacks and window treatments."

"What's wrong with that?"

"With window treatments?"

"With the whole thing."

"Nothing. If that's what you really want," Dakota said.

"It's not what I want right now."

"Exactly! Right now, you really love something. That's rare. You carry your horn around like a newborn baby. Right now you stop and smell flowers."

His cheeks burned, full of blood.

"Cute," she said.

"Great," he said, touching his cheeks.

"That's rare, Lance. That's precious. I like Lance Right Now. I don't know about Business Lance. We might not get along."

"And obviously this is all about you," he said.

"Well, sure." Dakota smiled.

"Do you always start fights with strangers?"

"Only when I like them."

"Did you pull boys' hair in grade school?"

She stared back at him, considering this.

"No. I didn't mess around with hair-pulling. I just knocked them over. Flat on their backs. Usually when they weren't looking." She laughed. "I can't believe I'm telling you this."

"It's great," he said. "I'm sure they loved it."

"Maybe. I liked more boys back then. It's harder now. There are fewer people I want to knock down."

"Should I be careful?" Lance asked.

"No. You're safe. You're a high school student with a promising future in business."

She was now taking a tone with him. And his own tone was creeping up the back of his throat like the first tickle of a cough. How did this girl spend her time, anyway? Did she still live with her parents? Hang out with the drunks from last night?

"I just believe long-term happiness is about delayed gratification," Lance said. This was the voice he used when he raised his hand in class. The voice he would use in front of a gymnasium full of people when he gave his speech this Friday.

"Oh yay," she said. "Let's talk about delayed gratification."

"Have you ever heard of the Stanford Marshmallow Experiment?"

"Nope."

"It's a really famous experiment," he said. She did not react. "Here's how it worked. They would take a five-year-old kid and put him in a room with a marshmallow. So here's the marshmallow."

Lance tossed a white sugar packet in the center of the table.

"The researcher gave the kid two choices. Either eat the marshmallow now or wait five minutes and get *two* marshmallows."

Dakota grabbed the packet and tore it open. Dumped it in her coffee.

"Well," Lance said. "Now you won't get two."

"I only wanted one."

"Fine. But you know what they learned? The researchers followed these kids for twenty years, and they could trace all their successes back to the marshmallow decision. One marshmallow now or two marshmallows later? It tied into how much money they made, where they lived, and whether or not they'd been in prison. Kids who could wait for the second marshmallow made more money, lived in better neighborhoods, and were generally happier. Kids who ate the first marshmallow ended up getting arrested or dropping out of high school."

"Sounds like the first marshmallow was laced with something."

"No," Lance said. "They just proved it. Success is about delayed gratification."

Dakota was looking at him evenly. Chin out.

"So who won?" she asked.

"Won what?"

"The marshmallow contest."

"I don't think anyone *won*."

"That's what success is about, right? Winning."

"Well. I guess whoever ended up with the most marshmallows."

"Right," Dakota said. "That makes sense. That's very mathematical."

"What's that supposed to mean?"

"I just want to make sure I got this right. A five-year-old who wants to eat a marshmallow is eventually going to prison. The winner is the kid who would rather hoard his bullshit marshmallows in a lab with creepy grad students."

"In all fairness, we can't know they were creepy."

"Yes, Lance. We can know that. And you know what I think? A five-year-old who won't eat a marshmallow is a freak. And that's who's running our country right now. A gang of freakish children, all grown up, who never learned what the fuck a marshmallow was for. They just learned how to count them. Probably at business school."

"Oh, good. Because I'm taking Statistics and the Marshmallow Economy next semester."

"Good for you," she said. "Start pricing window treatments."

Dakota grabbed a second sugar packet. Tore it open.

"You said you only wanted one," Lance said.

She stared right back. Poured in the sugar.

Just then, Maude came by: "Any food?"

"No," they both said.

Maude left and Lance tried to keep his leg still. He'd probably just lost his ride to Joe's Place. People were eating all around them. Obnoxious sounds. Laughter and slurping and lip smacking. A woman at the next table, chomping ice cubes. Like chewing glass.

"You're fighting your leg," she said. "It wants to move."

A bar of sunlight slanted across Dakota's face, brightening her eyes. Fixed on him. Moss-colored in this light, with sunflower halos. No one ever looked at him this long. And this girl didn't blink.

Dangerous.

"C'mon," she said. "There's somewhere we need to go."

"Where?"

"Aux Sable Cemetery."

Not helping.

6

Back in the Focus, Dakota was listening to folk rock with predictable harmonies, but at least the songs didn't fade out. They ended on a specific note, the way songs should end. The band was singing about ghosts. Maybe she was playing this on purpose, to scare him.

The car tunneled through low-hanging trees, and the road turned from pavement to gravel to dirt. A green bird spun and plunged toward the windshield. Lance jerked back, and the bird slipped past them, spinning in the updraft of the car. Not a bird, a leaf. The trees all around them were distorted, like fun-house mirrors.

"Bigleaf maples," Dakota said. "Aren't they cool?"

"Whoa," Lance said. That was it. "Those leaves are enormous."

"Bigger than car tires," Dakota said "You should see them in autumn. Golden kites, all over the road. It's amazing." Dakota drove too fast, but it felt good and a little out of control, like a raft spinning down the rapids.

Aux Sable was impressive. It took them five minutes to drive its fenced perimeter—a big graveyard for such a small town, like the whole population had died and been buried there a hundred times. They parked near the front gate.

The air here felt cooler than it had near Whiggley's. Maple leaves rustled like the hiss of drum brushes, and the sky was putting on a good show. A silver crease tore through a mass of cotton-topped, lead-bellied clouds, spilling chutes of light. Golden puddles lay in the hills. They looked good enough to swim in.

Good job, Sky Team, his father would've said. *Remember this, Lance. It's the most important thing you'll see all day.*

But the sky was hard to remember, exactly as it was. Could you pin it down with notes? Capture it with a song?

Dakota was looking at him. She'd just said something.

"What?" he asked.

"I like how you look at things."

Goosebumps sleeved his arms and he walked quickly, unsure of what to say. She stopped at the front gate.

"Remember your cemetery etiquette," she said, pausing at the threshold. "Thank the dead for allowing you to visit. When you leave, remember to say: *I truly appreciated our time together. I must ask that you please don't follow me home.* Then spin three times."

He laughed. "And that works?"

"It has so far."

Inside, the cemetery was incredible. A silent city of monuments and obelisks. One fifteen-foot marble statue of a woman spreading her arms. Two men riding tall black horses. A gravel path snaked up through the grass, taking them close to what resembled small stone homes in a medieval village. Glass doors and walls. Knobs and keyholes. Some had chairs inside. One had a stack of magazines and a coffeemaker.

"Lots of rich people buried here," Dakota said. "Their relatives come to visit and just sit inside the mausoleums, like they're getting used to the idea."

"The idea of what?"

"Being dead."

Dakota had done a headstone rubbing project, and knew things about the cemetery. Names and dates. Information you have to research and remember: family histories, the reason some markers faced the sun and others faced the shade. As they walked farther, she grew quiet. She was ahead of him, and he remembered something his father said:

If it's five miles into the woods, it's five miles out.

Every step, taking him further from Bend. Complicating Lance + Miriam with two new variables: time and footsteps. How long had they been walking. Ten minutes? Twenty? They should probably turn around.

"Dakota," he said. "Dakota." But he had that breathless feeling, when the words wouldn't come, and Dakota was too far ahead, already climbing the cemetery's tallest hill.

When Lance reached the top, he paused to catch his breath. Dakota stood waiting for him. The breeze was cool, and all four sides of the surrounding iron fence were visible from where they stood. Carved into the distance, a straight line of stone and steel. Railroad tracks.

"Can't escape the train," she said.

"Enjoy the trainsong," he said. "Thanks for that little tip."

"Ha!" Dakota said, punching his arm.

"I almost died. It literally knocked me out of my bed."

"Happens," Dakota said. "My dreams have all made room for the whistle. I have a banshee dream, a giant teakettle dream. There are more."

"Does it come every night?"

"Two twenty-six A.M.," she said. "You could set your watch by it."

"Don't people complain?"

"People complained when they tried to stop it."

"What!"

"Oh yeah," she said. "Five years ago, a neighborhood association tried to get a noise ban and people came crawling out of the freaking woodwork. I mean, a hundred people. The Float turned into the King County Fair. Grandmas and grandpas and broke-down lumberjacks all trucked in from the woods to save their precious train whistle. Folks got straight-up weepy, Lance. I do not lie."

"Why?"

"They grew up with that whistle. It was in all their best memories and two A.M. teakettle dreams. It's like a part of them."

"That is the single dumbest thing I've ever heard," Lance said.

"Kind of makes me love people," Dakota said. "Kind of makes me hate them."

She was looking off to the right, toward the cemetery's bad neighborhood. The grass was bunched and twisted. Stubby headstones poked up from the ground like molars. In the center of a loose ring of stones stood a giant willow tree. Spaghetti branches dangled to the ground.

"Outlying graves. Most old cemeteries have them, for the dead who don't belong," Dakota said. "Atheists. Suicides. Murderers."

"I should probably go back," Lance said.

She smiled. "Are you scared, Lance? You're totally scared."

"I'm not."

"Then come on. That's Unger's Willow. It's a rite of passage. It's why I brought you."

They kept walking and the ground sloped down toward the willow. Tablets and wedge stones turned blank, their letters wiped clean. Bindweed caught the tips of his shoes, making him stumble. They were near the willow when the sound came, a piercing *squee, squee, squee.*

Lance froze. Craned his neck slowly. To his right, a small clawed thing on a headstone. On its hind legs, chest puffing.

"What the hell is that?" he whispered.

"A chickaree," she said.

"Are they native to Washington?"

"A squirrel, dude. It's a squirrel." The rodent dropped on all fours and looked more like a squirrel. It scampered down the backside of the headstone, then followed them all the way to the edge of the willow's green curtains, chittering and scampering, claws clicking over headstones. Dakota pressed her right hand through the willow's limp branches. Her fingers disappeared inside.

"It's haunted in there," she said.

"Dakota."

"It is," she said. "Our best ghost story is in here. Come on."

She parted the branches. Vanished.

Greenery tickled the back of his neck as he followed her inside. The whisper of small, rattling leaves. The space beneath the willow was cool and dim, an emerald dome supported by its beam of a trunk. The bark, malformed. Like someone had turned the wood to taffy and twisted hard to the left.

"The guy who built the railroad died here," she said. Dakota's eyes stole snatches of color from wherever she was looking. In the filtered half-light, they looked green and unnatural. "Here we remember Lawrence Unger."

The air was too still. No breeze. Only the squirrel, still scampering overhead. Rustling branches in sudden, uneven bursts.

"Is that true?" Lance asked.

"Yes. Lawrence Unger was rich and lived alone in the East Hills. Had some guy bring him groceries every morning. The guy showed up one day and Lawrence wasn't home. It took them a week to find his body." She stepped forward, tapped her foot beside the trunk. "They found it here."

Lance took a step back. "How did he die?"

"Hunting knife," she said, dragging her fist across her neck. "Slit his own throat."

"Oh god." Lance touched his bare neck.

"He carved a note into this tree," she said, fingers brushing over wounded bark. Dim slashes, still visible. "A question."

"What did it say?" His voice barely came out.

"Can you see me now."

"Can you see me now?" Lance said. "What's that mean?"

"We can't ask him."

"What do you think it means?"

Her lips came together. She pressed her palm to the bark.

"I don't think anyone knew Lawrence Unger," she said. "He was like a ghost, all by himself in a big, lonely house."

"And now he is a ghost," Lance said. More rattle-scampering. He looked up, but couldn't find the squirrel.

"Yeah," she said. "It's a problem, wanting to be seen. That's got to be why ghosts haunt. You spend all day with living, breathing people, but no one notices you. Maybe if you're a ghost you try to whisper first. Or sit on the edge of someone's bed. But after a while, you'd have to scream. Throw things around. I think you'd be willing to scare the living shit out of someone just so they'd finally see you."

The space beneath the willow constricted. It felt like they were standing in one of those small stone buildings. Stippled sunlight fell on Dakota's cheeks.

"You have to put one hand here." She pressed her hand to the trunk's wood. He placed his hand beside hers, but their skin did not touch. The bark was warm and taut as the belly of a garter snake. Beneath it, Lawrence Unger's words. Carved letters, surfacing.

"With your other hand, reach up into the tree," she said. She raised her right arm, tangled it in long, slender branches. "Then you close your eyes and say three words."

She closed her eyes.

"I see you."

Her mouth formed the words carefully, sculpting them. Her jaw clenched—a panicked moment, like she was about to be bitten. She jerked her hand back and exhaled, eyes open.

"What happened?" Lance asked.

"Nothing," she said. "I escaped the curse."

"What curse?"

She looked up.

"You really have to see Lawrence Unger in your mind. If you don't see him, he'll keep you here. Trap you. You'll never leave this place." Lance pictured Lawrence Unger at Dakota's feet. Blood pumped from his throat. Sightless eyes.

They were underwater. Lance couldn't breathe.

You can never leave.

Danger he could feel in the back of his throat. If he spoke the words or touched Dakota's skin here, under this tree, there would be a green flash and he'd bolt up in bed at the Trainsong Motel, forty years old. Working for Cheri Front Desk. Still waiting for his Buick.

He faked a laugh.

"I should really go."

"Right now?" she said. "But you haven't done it."

"You did it," he said. "It was good to see. I've really got to go."

He clawed his way out from the willow. Breathing hard, he kicked through the weeds, walking back toward the entrance and Dakota's car. If her car was still there. If the willow didn't snap shut like an umbrella and jerk down into the dirt and drag her and him and the rest of Baring with it. In the ground, like they were never there at all.

At the top of the hill he looked back toward the willow and could not find Dakota among the headstones. A faraway wail. In the distance, a patchwork line of boxcars pushed themselves through the trees. A single yellow car. A parade of browns and grays. The train kept going. Ten more cars. Twenty. The train could run forever, and there would never be another yellow car. He wanted to see one more. It felt like good luck.

"C'mon," he said. How could there be just one?

Then Dakota was coming up the hill. He'd been holding his breath and when he inhaled he smelled Darren, which meant Dakota smelled like pot. Her eyes were glassy and bloodshot and he couldn't smell any citrus. None of the smells he liked. Lance shook his head.

"What?" she said.

"Nothing."

"No, what?"

The train was gone. No more cars.

"Do you ever get used to the train whistle?" he asked.

"No," she said. "You never get used to it."

They walked down the hill and Lance made a deal in his head. If he saw that squirrel again—the one from before—the Buick would be fixed and he'd make it home okay. Halfway down the hill, he changed the deal so it could be any squirrel. Not necessarily that one. But the cemetery was silent all the way down through the gate and across the parking lot.

Dakota stopped at the gate and spun three full circles.

By the time they both got into her car, they hadn't spoken in a long time.

"Lawrence Unger," Dakota said, staring straight ahead.

"What about him?"

"That guy had a lot of marshmallows."

7

At Joe's Place, everything felt safe again. Through the shop's front window, a tableau of modern conveniences: Soda fountain. Terraced racks of candy. Motor oil and blue jugs of washer fluid. From beside Dakota's Focus, the highway was visible. A hum of white noise. So many cars, driving wherever they wanted.

Dakota popped her trunk, and her car exhaled the odor of melted Popsicles and hot plastic. Five black garbage bags, stuffed full. She hauled them out with a clatter so loud it tickled his eardrums.

"All cans?" Lance said. "Wow."

"The worst," Dakota said. "It's Moody's Soda season. Grape flavor. My mom and my sister suck the stuff down like mosquitos." She made a desperate sucking sound, wide-eyed and frantic. "Sickening." She twisted her wrist into black plastic and lifted.

"I'm sorry I didn't do the thing with the tree," he said.

She stopped. "You're sorry? Why are you sorry?"

"Because it was really cool of you to bring me there. I've never met anyone who would take me out for coffee and a suicide tree."

"Well, you're in luck. That's just the kind of girl I am." She tossed the final clattering bag onto the pavement. "And I thought you'd appreciate it."

"Why?"

"Because you notice things."

She looked up and her eyes moved through him like a bucket through still water, churning up something shivery, deep inside. He must already know this girl. From a past life his brain had forgotten, but his body remembered.

"You want to make it up to me?" she said. "Tell me a story. Tell me one true thing."

He could tell her. He would never see her again.

"So the Buick I have, that broke down," he said. "My dad gave it to me."

"Yeah?"

"He gave it to me when he left," Lance said. Beyond the two gas pumps, a blue Geo Metro sat idling. He'd just look there while he talked. "When he took off, he left me a letter. And the keys to his Buick. One of the things he wrote was *Take my car. You're going to need it.* I keep the letter in the glove box, and the guy who towed my car almost took off with it. I had to throw a rock at his truck to make him stop. Now I'm afraid he's going to murder the Buick."

"Wow. Did you get the letter back?"

"I did," he said.

"Do you still talk to your dad?" Dakota asked.

"No. I don't even know where he is."

"Maybe that's better. Sometimes I think that would be better." She was rocking from foot to foot. He could smell her again, the spritz of an orange and a touch of something more real—sweat. What would it be like to wrap his arms around her? To bury his face in her neck and make her still?

"I wish I could read that letter," she said.

"No one's read it but me."

"Not even your mom?"

He shook his head.

She brushed her hair back from her eyes. The blue Geo puttered out of the parking lot, leaving them alone. Nowhere to look but her.

"Good secret story," she said. "Want to trade secrets?"

"Definitely."

Dakota opened the driver's-side door, reached under the seat, and came out with a leather-bound book.

"I have this book," she said. "No one sees this either."

"A journal?"

"Not exactly."

She held it so he could see. Flipped through its pages. It smelled like a used-book store, a grandpa's leather suitcase. Rough-hewn pages stitched into the spine and inked with brilliant sketches: a leaf with insectile veins, a sunset bleeding color into clouds, matchstick trees with filigreed branches. Words. Calligraphy like spikes and flowing rivers, filling every available space, squeezing between angular symbols and haunting faces and then the book was closed and she was staring at him.

Seeing the book had changed Dakota. Words and images, filling in the deep space behind her eyes and when she swung her gaze at him, he felt the full freight of her—all that thinking and intention—crashing into him. So much to see. He fought to keep his eyes level.

"You're an artist," he said.

"I draw." She covered the book with her hands, like the sunlight might cut it to ribbons.

"You're incredible. You could frame any page in that book and sell it."

She watched him. "But I don't want to sell it."

"So what's it for?"

"What's it for?" she said. "What's playing trumpet for?"

"I love music," he said.

"Yeah. I love everything in this book," she said. "All the things people should notice, but don't. Like clouds. Like tiny white flowers. The things you lose by not paying attention. I have to keep them somewhere. They feel like clues."

"Clues to what?"

"I don't know yet."

He made a brief sound, close to a laugh. No words came. The conversation should fade to black now. He could close his eyes and vanish into a dark room where he had time to crawl into his mind and unpack Dakota's drawings and words and turn them over in his hands, but they were still in a parking lot, and she was looking at him, and time kept moving.

She stuffed her book back under the driver's seat.

"Dakota," he said. "That's amazing. You should show people."

"I just did."

"I mean, people in general."

A battered pickup pulled into the parking lot, American flag in its window. New country blaring. The passenger spat a long brown stream out the window.

"Like them?" she said.

"Maybe not them."

"There are an awful lot of them."

Dakota double-checked the book's hiding place, then slammed the door. They walked toward Joe's and Dakota went around the side of the building with her cans. Inside, there was nobody behind the counter, and Lance's charger was right where he left it. He plugged his phone back in by the nachos. Outside, Dakota was playing the three-note sequence of can redemption in the key of F: Crunch, churn, *BEEP*.

Crunch, churn
BEEP

Dakota, feeding cans into a machine. He walked to a window at the end of his phone-charger tether and could see her elbow sliding backward, hand dipping into the bag, reappearing with an empty soda can. A soothing rhythm. A hypnotic elbow.

His phone jolted to life in his hand. Texts, voice messages. Words scrolling in the preview ribbon, charting the course of his absence. Questions, exclamations, all-caps profanity.

Crunch, churn, BEEP

Voice mails first.

Hey. Did your phone die? Did you hang up on me? I'm outside. Call me.

BEEP

Lance, it's Mom. Miriam says your phone is dead. I need you to call me.

BEEP

Lancelot! Our knight. Where is our sweet knight? Maid Miriam awaits. We can't hold this room forever. There is demand, Lance. Major demand.

BEEP

We are holding on to hope, Lance. We have visions of white horses. A parachute. Grand Theft Auto.

BEEP

Lance. It's me. I don't think it's too much to expect a phone call. If—

BEEP

Hey. I miss you. I'm sad about tonight, Lance.

BEEP

Miriam. He grabbed a fistful of hair on the back of his head. The Party, whooshing by in voice messages. The past catching up to the present while he stood beside nacho cheese.

BEEP

This is Jim from Bank of the Cascades. Just wondered if you had any questions about the upcoming Personal Banker orientation—

Lance stabbed his finger at the screen.

BEEP

Hi, Lance? This is William over at Goodview. We got your part in this morning—why don't you give me a call?

Lance hung up. William's voice had lacked pep. He sounded like a doctor with bad news. Outside, Dakota was still feeding cans.

Crunch, churn, BEEP

The rhythm felt endless. Like if he didn't interrupt the cycle of can redemption, he might be stuck here forever. He pressed his arm to the metal top of the nacho machine and it hissed. The sharp odor of burnt hair. A white line.

"Ouch," he said.

"Hey kid," Joe called from behind the counter. "Electricity ain't free."

"What?"

"You're sucking up all my juice through the wall."

"The charger was plugged in all night."

"So?"

"So," Lance said, "a charger uses electricity whether or not it's hooked up to a phone."

"Says who?"

"Says physics. Says the entire world."

"You best watch your mouth, son. You make your call and go."

His phone battery was still blinking red. He turned his back on Joe and dialed Goodview Towing. He needed William to get him the hell out of here. Away from bubbling cheese and grape soda cans. He needed to hear William's honeyed voice telling him it was all going to be okay.

"Goodview Towing!" William answered.

Lance took a breath. William sounded better. Chipper, even.

"Hi. It's Lance. I'm glad I caught you. How are things with the Buick?"

"Oh, well. That's real interesting."

"Interesting?"

Interesting was a blue butane flame in the pit of his stomach.

"Last night the missus and I run a few tests. We get code 254. Airflow sensor. The airflow sensor regulates combustion. If the sensor can't regulate, you can't get the right combustion." William spoke the words deliberately, like lines he was rehearsing for a play.

"I'm with you."

"'Course you are! Well, here's the thing," William said. "It ain't the airflow sensor!" His laughter rang between Lance's ears.

"My car is not running," Lance said.

"Not at all." Lance's stomach went from simmer to boil. He was being hustled. William was about to mention the check engine light. Lance could feel it coming, and heard his father's voice: *If they say "check engine light," you just run. Slap them first, if you can get away with it. Then run.*

"What about the check engine light?" Lance asked, baiting him.

"What? Check engine?" William said. He sounded thrown. "No, no. But, hey, you know that air hose? How it's got kind of an opening near the top there?"

"I don't—"

"I'm thinking that might be it."

"William. Are you telling me the car isn't going to be ready today?"

"Tomorrow's looking good for sure. You still got a room?"

Lance shook his head, denying the conversation; denying another night at the Trainsong, his broken car, the missed party. William's voice, calling up from a well.

Hello? Lance? Ya still there, bud?

Blood on fire. He needed to walk. Right now. And he did. Away from the nachos and out of Joe's with the sad clank of the bell. The bell clanked again. Joe was coming through the door. Lance turned to face him. He backpedaled, and Joe kept coming.

"What?" Lance said. "Hey, what!"

"You're not the sharpest tool in the shed." Joe pointed at his own skull. "Missing marbles."

"Excuse me?" Lance stopped. His grip was getting slippery. Like it had at The Float, when he grabbed the butter knife.

"You got a loose wire," Joe said, stepping forward. "In your brain."

Something snapped and Lance was free, floating toward Joe, riding a current of hot air.

"You think I'm stupid, Joe? You came out here to tell me that? You know what, I'm valedictorian of my class. Okay? I've got a full-ride scholarship. I got a thirty-five on my ACT!"

"Thirty-five? Sounds low."

"Well it's not. And it pretty much guarantees I won't end up pumping gas for a living."

"You pump your own gas in Washington, fool." Joe took another step forward, and Lance raised his fists. Lance wanted to stand his ground, but Joe had scars like vapor trails crisscrossing under his half-beard, like he'd been sliced up with a razor, and his head looked impossibly thick, like a triple-walled pumpkin. One hand was coming up now, giant, opening, and something black was unspooling from his fingers. Dangling like a yo-yo.

"You left this plugged in. By the nachos."

"Oh," Lance said. He slowly took the charger.

"Bad for the environment."

"Right."

He held it out toward Lance.

"You're too smart to lose this twice."

"I guess not."

Lance took the charger and wrapped the cord around the connector. "People forget behind their backs."

"What?"

"People forget what they want to forget," Joe said.

"Why would I want to forget my charger?" Lance asked.

"Oh, I don't know. You're vale-dic-torian. You tell me."

Joe looked over Lance's shoulder at Dakota. Dakota, who was watching the whole thing. Her attention was like heat on a sunburn and his cheeks were on fire. He could see The Parking Lot Meltdown playing on repeat behind her eyes. Chart-topping tracks like "I'm Valedictorian of My Class, Okay?" and "I Got a Thirty-Five on My ACT." She knew all the words, and now everyone at The Float would know them too.

She took a fistful of redemption slips and went inside.

He was alone in the parking lot.

In Bend, they'd be cleaning up Jonathan's house. Trying to mimic Ms. Davis's trademark diagonal vacuum lines. Jonathan would be frying bacon and doing impressions of whatever stupid things people had said the night before. Maybe Lance would be on the couch with Miriam. She could be running her fingers through his hair. She did that sometimes, when he asked.

The best hangover feeling. Better than bacon.

Lance ran his own hand through his hair. Once. Twice.

The clang of the awful bell pulled him back to Baring. And Dakota, in the parking lot of a service station. This girl he'd somehow known for one day and maybe forever, balancing two gleaming flats of shrink-wrapped purple soda cans.

"What's wrong?" she said.

How did she know?

"My car's not ready."

"Good thing you've got a ride."

She unlocked the doors.

The inside of Dakota's car was dark and cool. She sat beside him and leaned back to snap on her seatbelt. Her scent rolled over him and he felt submerged, like he'd been beneath the willow tree.

She was so close. His heart like a stone, skipping over water.

Dakota pulled out of the parking lot and his phone buzzed.

Miriam.

Lance bolted up straight and glanced over his shoulder. He wanted to talk to Miriam, but Dakota was sitting right there. It felt rude to answer, and it also felt wrong to decline the call. Lance looked down and let the phone buzz in his lap, over and over, until it was still.

8

The motel's air conditioner was garbage. Lance turned dials, mashed buttons, and the unit gave him nothing but a soft, warm breath. He opened both windows. The air, too heavy to move, slouched around him. Sweat dribbled down his back and ran into his eyes, and when he lay on his bed, his shirt stuck to his chest.

Since things couldn't get any worse, he called his mother.

"Are you serious, Lance? I'm too busy to drive up tonight. Do I need to send someone to come get you?"

"No, Mom."

"I'm sure David would come up if I asked him."

"No."

She gave a long, heavy sigh. He could hear everything stacking up behind that sigh. Judgments, clichés, examples. And when her dam of a ten-second silence burst, out came the flood.

This trip was senseless! People are counting on you! You're a grown-up, Lance! I'm not going to be here to hold your hand and it reminds me of the time, and how did that turn out?

Her comments sank like fists into a heavy punching bag. They didn't hurt, just gently knocked him around. He swayed from foot to foot, muttering responses until something jabbed him hard.

It's Sunday night, Lance. Your speech is this week.

Yes. The weekend was gone. He smacked his lips.

"Lance? The speech is done, isn't it?"

He eyed his orange duffel bag. It crouched in the corner, a tense little animal.

"Mr. Leeds wants to do a practice run on Tuesday or Wednesday. Can you let him know a time that would work?"

He squinted at the bag. Staring it down.

"You should pick a time in the late afternoon, so you have your morning free for enrollment paperwork. Lance?"

"What?"

"The speech is memorized, right?"

"I'm working on it," he said. "Right now. I'm working on it now. I really need to go."

Lance hung up. He took a breath and approached the orange duffel. The bag that had traveled—unopened—to Seattle, two separate coffee shops, a hotel room, his audition, and now the Trainsong Motel. Enrollment materials, honors college application, scholarship follow-up essays. His Personal Banker orientation packet. The speech.

He flung the bag on the bed.

He yanked the zipper like ripping off a Band-Aid, and a small, horrific face peered up at him. Bug eyes and claws and a mechanical laugh.

AHH-HAHAHAHA!

Lance shrieked, dropping the bag.

"Damn it, Jonathan!" he said.

He pulled out the foot-long figure. Mr. Jangles. A humanoid rat with giant fangs and claws. Taped to its head was a tiny blue graduation cap. Since middle school, Mr. Jangles had been ambushing people in showers, lockers, kitchen cupboards, and backpacks. This was his first trip out of state. Lance dropped the figure on the floor and Mr. Jangles screamed again. He called Miriam.

"Hi stranger," she said.

"Sorry I didn't call earlier," Lance said. "I've been out running around. Trying to get this stupid car fixed."

"So what's new?"

"I found Mr. Jangles."

"Nice," she said. "Jonathan was wondering."

"I didn't need that today."

"Do we ever need that? Can't you leave that thing in Washington?"

"He's wearing a graduation cap. You have to admire the attention to detail."

Mr. Jangles lay facedown on the carpet, still wearing the cap.

"When are you coming home, Lance? Is something wrong?"

"Yes, something's wrong. My car is broken and my mechanic is an idiot." He flopped back on his damp mattress. "This guy can't fix it. He might never fix it."

"Your speech is this week."

"I realize. My mother brought that up."

"She has a point."

"I'm so glad you agree. You two should hang out."

She sighed and he felt the threat of a Miriam Moment of Silence. He'd just wait. He could fall asleep, waiting for her to inhale again.

"Do you need me to come get you?" she said. "I could borrow a car."

"Really?" He sat up straight. "Could you spend the night?"

"In a motel? Ew, Lance. I looked that place up. Bedbug city."

"C'mon," he said, scratching his scalp. "It would be fun."

"What are you even doing? Do they let you practice in your room?"

"No," he said, sitting up. "I mean, I've barely practiced. It's been crazy here."

"Meth crazy?"

"Funny. No. There was a car accident last night. Like, right outside my window. And this guy was stuck in the car and I ran down to help them and then the driver, this girl—she was totally drunk—was screaming at me, and trying to pull the guy out of the passenger seat." Lance got up, acting out the whole scene. Pushing Breanna, the arrival of the police. He leapt around the room, flinging sweat. He peeled off his shirt and kept going. All the way to The Float, the cheeseburger, the knife fight.

"Isn't that wild?" he said.

"You must've been really hungry," she said. "Like when you snapped at those guys at the Fireman's Fair. Remember?"

"No," he said. "I mean, kind of. But this wasn't stupid kids. This was real. And it gets better."

He went on. The free burger. *Taking a shot! At an actual bar!* He was grinning, gesturing as if she could see him.

"Can you believe it? Miriam?"

"Wow," she said.

Wow?

This was a story. His first empirically good story. The *wow* hadn't even sounded excited and what was that noise in the background? Soup cans? Was Miriam stacking cans of soup?

"It was amazing," Lance said.

"Yes. Kind of hard to imagine."

"Really amazing," he repeated.

Lance knew he had slipped out of one of their approved conversational grooves. He was still talking, but the needle had jumped and the record was hissing along on blank vinyl. Static between radio stations. There were certain topics of conversation Miriam just couldn't hear: Seattle. Jazz. Now this. Everything here.

Lance walked to the window facing Dakota's room.

"Anyway," he said.

"I'm just sad about the party," she said. "I thought you'd be sad about missing the party."

"I am, Miriam."

"We've been waiting a long time."

"You should just drive up here."

She sighed.

"Lance."

His name, spoken like a two-week extension on his virginity.

He pushed aside the blinds. A girl who was not Dakota was

standing in front of Dakota's door. *The soda sister.* Same dark ringlets of hair, same skin tone, but her sister was shorter and sluggish. She seemed to carry extra gravity, as if the extra steps Dakota stole when she walked, this girl paced out in slow motion.

"Lance?" Miriam said.

Dakota's sister brought alternating objects to her mouth. Smoldering cigarette. Can of Moody's Grape.

"Oh, man," he said.

A snapping sound, like breaking pencils.

"Miriam? What's that noise?"

"Look," she said. "If you can get back here tonight, we could still have the room at Jonathan's."

Her voice cut through the slow-brained heat. Lance turned from the window.

"Really?" he asked.

"Jonathan's parents are gone until tomorrow."

"So this could still work? Tonight?"

"I think this can still work. Don't you?" she asked softly.

A rare flash of color in her voice, like the first time they'd kissed, when she'd whispered *Come here.* Teeth had collided. Drool and laughter and *Sorry, sorry.* Not pretty, not graceful, and exactly right. He wanted that again. To be attacked. Hip-bumped like the open drawer of a copy machine. And Miriam's *Don't you?* had sounded like *Come here.*

"I'll call the mechanic right now," he said, leg jittering.

"Good. We'll hide Mr. Jangles under Jonathan's pillow."

"Or hang him from the chandelier."

"With a note that says *Goodbye, cruel world.*"

"Oh my god," Lance said. "Yes!"

Miriam at her funniest. Her sexiest.

He was off the phone, grinning and dialing William so fast his hands were shaking. No answer. He called twice, three times. No answer.

His conversation with Miriam had felt like an inevitable 370-mile runway to Bend. A revving V-6 engine. But with the third play of *Hello, you've reached Goodview Towing,* the feeling was turning slow and heavy. Now there were two people outside of Dakota's door.

It took Lance a second to recognize Dakota. Her hair was pulled back, and her whole posture was different. Shoulders, loose and free. She looked like a kid. She was grabbing at the air in front of her sister, pretending to snatch her cigarette. Her sister ducked, slapped her arm. Dakota's laughter was choppy on the breeze.

A voice rang out, and the sisters stopped moving. The voice was similar to Dakota's. The sisters' response was fluid, as if it had been rehearsed many times. Dakota opened the storm door, and her sister set the brace to hold it open. They stood off to either side, waiting.

Lance's phone buzzed and he walked back to the bed, but it was not William. It was a number he did not recognize and a crawling in his gut told him not to answer. He stood still while the phone went silent and the caller left a message.

Lance, this is Officer Perkins with the Washington State Police. I'm calling about an accident and the hospitalization of James DeWitt. We need to ask you about your involvement. Please call me as soon as—

Lance hung up. His leg was shaking, but so were his hands. He was hungry. He just needed to eat. He grabbed his case and stepped out onto the patio. The air was cooler than it should've been in June, and there was no one left standing in front of Dakota's door. Wind whipped up in the field between him and The Float. Weeds ruffled and bowed. From where he stood, the roadhouse no longer looked fixed in the parking lot, but buoyant on shifting grasses. Bobbing on gentle waves, and drifting closer.

9

The sun had gone down, and The Float's crowd was changing along with the quality of light. Families disbanded from tables, and men sprouted up along the bar like mushrooms on a log.

Dakota was watching her mother and sister eat. Not like part of the family. Like a staff member on an outing with her residents.

"Hey Wildman," Mason called from behind the bar. "C'mere."

Lance couldn't take his eyes off the large woman. Hair like unspun steel wool. Shoulders tipping as she ate. The same terrible gravity that hung on Dakota's sister had clung to this woman longer and harder and she did not look up. Her fork moved against glass, scraping up sauce on her plate with a rapid-fire *shtikshtickshtik*.

"Good thing humans don't eat their young." Mason pursed his lips, feigning worry.

"That's Dakota's mom?"

"A rare sighting," Mason said. "Ms. Berg's as scarce as Sasquatch. Probably for the same reasons. Avoiding hunters.

Zookeepers. Kick back and enjoy the show. Try not to stab anyone tonight."

Mason soda-gunned him a glass of cola. From the edge of his vision, he watched the ordeal of Ms. Berg standing—a slow-motion eruption from the table. When she glanced in Lance's direction, he finally saw her eyes. Glassy and blank, like something behind them had snapped and could not be put back together.

"Thank ya, Mason," Ms. Berg said. "Always good."

Her smile. Her voice. Horrific in its familiarity. Dakota, imprisoned by thirty years and two hundred extra pounds, locked behind bloodshot eyes and a loose mouth. Ms. Berg's gaze slipped past Lance without stopping, but Dakota's eyes met his. Her shoulders tensed, hair shifting forward. A dark curtain. She walked away.

"Thank you, Ms. Berg," Mason said. "Anytime at all, m'lady. Bye, Dakota!"

Dakota did not turn around. Before they were out the door, Mason leapt into action, bending an invisible Ms. Berg over the bar, pumping her from behind, slapping her phantom butt.

"See, son," Mason said, still going to town. "That's why you gotta hit that now. Because Dakota is one grade-A piece of ass. Butcher's choice. Today. But one day soon, she'll be a full-grown heifer." Mason plugged his mouth with his thumb and inflated his cheeks. "Can't fight genetics, dude. Trust me. I've tried."

Lance forced a laugh, not knowing what else to do. Down the bar, Meebs and Rocco alighted like bats. Rocco shot him a solemn nod. Meebs was telling a story, hands fluttering through the air.

"So, hey," Mason said, refilling Lance's glass. "I thought you were outta here."

"Looks like one more night."

"You should hang with us," Mason said. "We'll get the whole gang together. Catch the trainsong."

"Yeah, maybe," Lance said. "I've got a lot to do."

"Uh-huh," Mason said, looking distracted. "Just be here around ten."

The Float's front door knocked into the bell, and Mason's head snapped up. A family. Two kids, a well-dressed woman, and a guy in a green polo, treading water in the entryway. They looked as if they'd peeked over the reef and were about to swim back to shore.

"Hey there!" Mason said, grabbing four menus. "Come in! Make yourself at home!"

Mason gave the kids a box of crayons and said something to make the wife laugh. He crouched down to take their order, one elbow cocked up on the table the way waiters sometimes do. Ten minutes later, the guy in the green polo was removing his shoes. Lance didn't know how Mason pulled it off. The whole family got involved, looking for a gap in the crowded rafters.

"Okay everyone," Mason said. "Let's count him down."

Three, two, one!

The whole family screamed when he let them rip, like it was the wildest thing the guy had ever done. The laces hit the beam and the shoes locked themselves around the wood. Everyone at the bar applauded.

"Spin the wheel," his wife said. "Spin the wheel."

Mason smiled and led them down the bar past the American flag, where a prize wheel hung. It was a *Wheel of Fortune* knockoff someone had probably slapped together in their backyard. Pegs and a flapper, a dozen or so colored slivers with black writing:

FREE BEER
SIDE OF BEANS
FREE MEAL AND ROUND OF DRINKS
T-SHIRT
$1000
FREE WATER
ROUND OF APPLAUSE

A thousand dollars, Lance said to himself, recounting the zeros.

Mason double-handed the wheel and gave it a good, hard crank. The flapper went *tickatickatickatickaticka.* The whole family pressed up against the bar.

The flapper stopped on a thick yellow slice.

"Side of beans!" Mason said, hands on his hips.

"Beans," the man's wife said.

The man wasn't looking at her. He was looking up at his swinging shoes, as if he'd already forgotten how they'd gotten there. Laces, swaying like willow branches.

The swift clap of a plate. Lance's dinner.

The server who brought his food had a streak of purple hair and downturned eyes and the kind of sad young face where you could already imagine wrinkles, set into the bone structure like fault lines. When she passed Mason on her way back to the kitchen, he bit his tongue and gave her butt a quick squeeze. Normal as *hello.* She didn't miss a beat on her way to the kitchen.

This place.

Lance stared down at his burger.

He'd eat this last meal.

He would go back to his room and complete the necessary forms. He would finish his speech and call William and the car would be fixed like it was supposed to be. Like he'd known it *would be* when he talked to Miriam. He pressed his shoes together, and pressed them both against the hard case of his horn.

Lance knew exactly where he was going.

And he would never set foot in The Float again.

10

Someone was pounding on his motel room door.

His mother? Officer Perkins?

Through the fish-eye perspective of the spyhole, Rocco and Meebs looked horrific. They were bent-faced creatures who'd come from a parallel dimension to bend his face, too.

Meebs pushed giant, distended lips toward the peephole.

"Open up, Wildman."

Lance turned the lock and they shoved past him into the room. Meebs flopped his hair around, walking the perimeter with canine diligence. Like he might start picking things up to sniff them. Rocco stood stock-still and stared.

"Dude," Rocco said. "Read much?"

There were books open all over his desk, on his bed. Scholarship paperwork, waterfalling onto the floor.

"I didn't know you could read, Wildman," Meebs said, peeking under the bed. "What, no fridge?"

"What the hell is this?" Rocco said, picking up Mr. Jangles by the foot. The figure screamed at him. "Are you a devil worshiper?"

"No," Lance said. "It's a weird tradition with my friends. We hide it. Like in people's houses. Or their lockers."

"Oh yeah," Rocco said. "We did that with a dead mouse. Remember, Meebs?"

"Yeah, bitch. I remember. That shit was under my seat for two weeks."

"Driving to school with your windows down," Rocco said. "Ha."

"That's funny," Lance said.

"You're funny," Meebs snapped.

"Time to go, Wildman," Rocco said. "You told Mason you were coming."

Lance's phone said it was 11:45 P.M. William hadn't called back. Three missed texts from Miriam.

"Lost track of time," Lance said.

"It didn't lose track of you-uuuu," Meebs sang. He was everywhere, rattling the broken latch on the window. Fingering the chain lock. Flipping through Lance's book on OSU campus policies. Lance moved toward the door.

"What's that?" Rocco said, nodding at him.

"My trumpet," Lance said, clutching it closer. "I don't like to leave it."

"You're bringing it to the bar?" Rocco said. "Meebs. Stop creeping around, you weirdo. Let's go."

And Lance was back like he never left. Pirate host with her dead wooden eyes and the enamel crack of pool balls. Lance followed Rocco and Meebs to a dark corner booth. People rose out of the murk. Déjà vu faces. Dakota. A boy with black eyes and a bandaged nose. A pretty girl with long blond hair. She stiffened and slapped Mason's chest.

"Mason, you asshole," she said.

"He has arrived!" Mason said, leaping up, clapping his hands. "Wildman, meet Breanna. Breanna, Wildman."

The girl he'd pushed stood and stared. Her eyes were mean. Blue little bullets. She shoved her way out of the booth. Heeled shoes went *tick-tick-tick* all the way to the bathroom. *SLAM.* Stone was standing now. Big white bandages. Bright eyes peering out from their bruised caves.

"Lance," James said.

"Wildman," Mason corrected.

"I'm James."

"Stone," Rocco corrected.

"Shots?" Mason asked. "Who wants shots?"

A cheer went up, and Mason went to the bar.

"Appreciate your help, sir." Stone extended his hand. "Apparently I had a brain bleed. I could've lost major motor skills. Shoe-tying skills. Whatever part of my brain prevents me from shitting myself twenty-four seven."

"You still got that part, right?" Rocco said, taking a step back.

"Luckily, the accident only damaged his thinking centers," Dakota said.

"Maybe." Stone shrugged. "Little foggy. Kind of like being wasted."

"Brain bleed," Meebs said, like it was a soda flavor he might want to try.

"Man still makes some mean fries," Rocco said, crunching into one.

"Shots!" Mason said. He set down a tray of glasses, golden liquid flashing inside. He picked one up, they all did. "To saving Stone's life. And knocking Breanna on her ass."

"To Wildman," Stone said.

"Wildman!"

Lance took the shot. Whisky burned a hot trail down his throat and he choked back a cough, gritting his teeth.

"What's your next adventure, man?" Stone asked him.

"Sugarville," Mason interrupted.

"We're going tonight?" Rocco asked.

"We'll see," Mason said.

"So, hey," Stone said. "Have you talked to the cops yet?"

"No," Lance said. "This guy, Officer Perkins, called. I haven't called him back."

"You heard the story, right? That I was driving?"

"Yeah," Lance said. "But Breanna was driving."

"You should've seen her last night," Mason said, a fresh shot in his hand. *"Maaaaaasssooon! They're gonna arrest me! Let me in! Oh, please, Mason!"*

"It wouldn't have killed you to help," Stone said.

"Fuck off, Stone," Mason said. "I should eighty-six her ass. She keeps crashing daddy's cars, she's gonna get us shut down. Limits, son. Learn them." Mason threw back his shot.

"Anyway," Stone said, "if Officer Friendly gets ahold of you, it'd be great if you could back up our story. Tell him I was driving." Stone looked at the bathroom. "Should I go check on her? Is that what I'm supposed to do?"

"That's the drill," Dakota said.

"But she's in the girls' bathroom."

"Want me to go?" Dakota asked. Mason made a kissing sound.

"No," Stone said. "I got this."

"You could totally be a woman under those bandages," Dakota said. "No one will know."

"Good point."

Stone left. Dakota scooted down in the booth and patted the empty seat. Lance's chest tightened five clicks, and he slid in beside her.

"Whoa, Wildman," Mason said. "Dakota's never asked a boy to sit next to her."

"Just never asked you," she said.

Meebs and Rocco gave an *oooooo,* and Lance wished they would stop.

"I can't sit because I have a job," Mason said. "You know what a job is? I could teach you." Dakota's hair came forward a little. She looked away. Said nothing.

"Ice him down," Meebs said.

"Frozen," Rocco said.

"Let me know when that seat gets too cold, Wildman," Mason said. "I'll save you space at the bar." The guys laughed. Dakota did not move.

"I don't want Stone to do time," Rocco said. "The fries will suffer."

"He's too gentle for prison. He's got a soft face," Meebs said, reaching for Rocco's fries. Rocco slapped his hand. "Ah, shit!"

"Fucking Hamburglar," Rocco said.

"I'm vegetarian," Meebs said. "I don't thieve burgers."

"Yeah?" Rocco said, pointing his fry at Meebs's face. "Fries have beef tallow."

"Tallow ain't meat."

"You idiot."

"Will he really go to jail?" Lance asked, watching the bathroom door.

"Probably," Dakota said, looking at the table. "His record isn't good."

"So why not tell the truth about Breanna?" Lance asked. "She was driving."

"She's got a kid," Dakota said.

"A future. She doesn't belong here," Rocco said. Dakota nodded.

"What's so special about Breanna?" Lance asked. In the direction of the girls' bathroom, the distant ring of raised voices.

"Breanna is Breanna," Rocco said.

"So what part of the cow is the fucking tallow?" Meebs said.

"Tell you what. I'll sell you this fry for a dollar," Rocco said, holding one up. "Look at this shit. Tender. Golden."

"Ten fries for a dollar."

"You ever seen a fry this pretty?" Rocco said. "This fry is better than ten fries."

"A dollar?"

"This is King Fry," Rocco said. "King Fry costs a dollar."

Lance had to check. King Fry looked pretty much like every other fry in his basket.

A door clapped open and Breanna, who was just Breanna, was leaving the bathroom with James, who was Stone. She was gesturing at him, still mad, jabbing her index finger as if popping invisible balloons. Lance was afraid she'd poke him in the bandages.

"Beer!" Mason said, returning to their table. Full pitcher, empty glasses. "No fighting. Free beer!"

They squeezed into the booth, which pushed Lance's shoulder into Dakota's and she pushed back a little, like she wouldn't mind if he squeezed even closer. A shoulder! This shoulder and a whole incredible part of an arm, making him tingle. Somehow he was touching shoulders with a girl who wasn't his girlfriend, drinking beer in public. And everyone at the table, even Breanna, was smiling and acting like this was perfectly normal.

"Wildman," Stone said. "What's your story?"

"Drink first," Mason said.

Mason passed him another shot, and he took it. More alcohol, lighting him up in a golden way that made the edges of the room fuzzy so he kept tapping the corner of his hard case with his toe, like his horn might get slippery and somehow dribble down through the cracks in the floorboards.

The group fell into conversation. A party next weekend at Metzger's and last week's party at VanderJack's. A raft of strange names and places: Cold Creek and The Back Field and The

Point—vocabulary he didn't understand. But he was learning their cadence. Their rhythm and sections. Who got to solo, and when. And they were singing for him:

So Stone convinces everyone to pound energy drinks before the exam. He pukes all over the backseat.

The party at Breanna's was the best. Classy. She had big ol' ice cubes.

Then Dakota tells the guy "No." Right there on the stairs, in front of everyone. So this dude shrugs, turns around, and drives all the way back to Seattle!

Bong water. All over his lap. Smelled like a dispensary.

Four guys. Just, boom. Rocco knocked them down. I'm pretty sure it was four guys.

Verses like stories, choruses repeating themes: Stone was the Dumb One, Breanna the Special One, Dakota the Ice Queen, Meebs the Burnout, Rocco the Badass. Lance paid attention, trying to learn the words. Then Dakota was looking at him with those eyes, and he hoped she'd forgotten everything he'd said to Joe. For one more night, his stories could be about evading police, pulling a knife, taking shots.

Right now, he was still Wildman.

"Let's do a fire," Dakota said, looking straight at him.

"Hell yeah," Rocco said. "Let's ride to Sugarville." He shook Lance by the shoulder. "You'll love this, dude. Right up your alley."

"Wildman's probably jumped a thousand trains," Meebs said.

"He's bored," Mason said. "He could do it blindfolded."

"No, that sounds great," Lance said. "Let's jump a train."

Was this really him? Had he just said that?

Their conversation was a river, carrying them outside and past the dumpsters to the dark edge of the parking lot. He followed Dakota as she threaded through a wall of pines. She always knew how to move. The perfect way to pick her way down an embankment, sidestepping shrubs and evergreens until the scents of cedar and damp earth twisted up around them and he was time traveling, back with his father, camping, foraging mushrooms—hearing the songs they used to sing. He was drifting downhill, riding a warm current of memories until he spilled out of the woods into a moonlit pan of a field.

They crossed a loose ring of garbage and stopped at a circle of stumps and stones surrounding a pit of char and half-cooked logs. Most of the crew went out for wood and Lance found himself sitting across from Breanna.

"Where are you from, Lance?" she asked.

"Bend."

"That's a good place to be from." She turned toward him and squinted, suddenly interested. She was pretty. Pretty in a way she couldn't shake with alcohol or bitchiness. It just clung to her. "Mount Bachelor is cool. Smith Rock. Do you climb?"

"No," he said.

Her eyes drifted over his shoulder, like he'd just gone transparent.

"I'm heading back that way," Lance said. "I just got stranded."

"That happens." She looked at him again. "A little advice: Get out while you can."

"Tomorrow," he said.

"Popular day to go."

"Monday?"

"Tomorrow," she said. "Don't you know, Lance? Everyone's leaving tomorrow."

He smiled, and he hadn't meant to smile for Breanna. Then Dakota was back, building up the kindling. She was doing it all wrong. She pushed the biggest logs together on the bottom. Then a latticed pile of sticks, twigs. Tinder on top.

"What?" she said, looking back at him.

"That won't burn," Lance said.

"Oh yeah?"

"Your fire is upside down."

"It's all perspective." She scraped up pine needles, nesting them on top. "You just have to light it upside down."

Lance tilted his head, trying to turn it upside down. He tipped and fell. Soft ground. Lovely dirt. He rolled on his back and put his hands behind his head. Better than a bed.

Dakota laughed and struck a match.

The tinder went up—a puff of white smoke and yellow fire, burrowing into orange twigs that curled like broken guitar strings. Somehow, this thing had worked. The fire sank, swallowed by the surrounding wood, puffing gray smoke. Yellow tongues darted out between the logs and everyone was back and Lance was sitting next to Dakota. Fire builder. Cemetery Girl.

Who was she?

The group felt different in that way everyone changes around a campfire. The limitless feeling when walls fall away and the roof turns to stars and conversations can spool out for hours.

"Guitar, Stone," Meebs said softly. There was a case beside Stone. It had materialized in the woods. "C'mon."

"I'm damaged," Stone said, pointing to his face.

They pleaded and Breanna leaned her head on Stone's shoulder and whispered in his ear. All Lance heard was *James*. The word flipped a switch, and he unsnapped his case and pulled out a guitar. Lance felt a sharp twinge, like he'd forgotten something. But his wallet was in his back pocket. He had his keys.

Then Stone's fingers came alive, and Stone was all there was.

He plucked and strummed and drummed his fingers on the guitar's wooden body. Pulled on the strings so notes warbled and shook out into the darkness. He sang a little. Lyrics too soft to hear or understand, more like impressions of words. The music swelled and swallowed them. They swayed and sighed and no one spoke.

When the music was done, Lance could only stare.

With that guitar, Stone had peeled off his skin and stepped out brand-new. Like Dakota, sharing her book. It was almost too much to look at him. Stone did not match their stories. None of them did. This guitar player could not be stupid, and Breanna could not be worth it, and this girl beside him with the warmest shoulder he'd ever felt could only ever be warm. And then there was something crashing through the bushes. A shaking, shambling thing that made them sit up straight and look into the pines.

"What's up, fools!"

Mason—three cheers for Mason, because he was carrying a

box of alcohol and wearing a bright smile and the whole group lit up. Clearly a hero. The only role left, because everything else had been assigned. Mason brought liquor and beer and the smell of the fryer, clinging to his clothes.

Bottles made the rounds, and everything tasted good.

"So Breanna tells me you're from Bend," Mason said. "Is that where you're heading tomorrow?"

"Bend is good skiing," Meebs said. "Been there once with my folks."

"Rich people there," Rocco said. "The richest."

"Sounds like Telluride," Stone said.

A collective moan from the group.

"Here we go," Mason said. "Jesus Christ."

"Telluride!" Dakota sang, a high, keening note.

"How do you know it's like Telluride?" Rocco asked.

"He doesn't," Breanna said. "He just wants to talk about it."

Stone shook his head.

"What's the deal with Telluride?" Lance asked.

"Finest place on earth, man. That's where I'll end up. They've got wild trails and this bluegrass festival and—"

The group protested: *No, don't ask, c'mon . . .*

"Fine. Doesn't matter," Stone said. He was done talking, but they kept grumbling—*Telluride, goddamn, fucking Telluride*—and Stone just nodded along. Smiling. Rolling his eyes. Just taking it. In every group Lance had ever been a part of, there had always been a guy like Stone.

"So what brought you out here?" Stone asked him.

"I had an audition in Seattle."

"Acting?"

Lance paused, wondering how that might be. Life as an actor. His identity felt so fluid around the fire. He could start any new life today, and they would let him.

"Music," Dakota said. "He's a musician."

Yes. He was a musician. That was exactly right.

"Wildman plays an instrument too," Breanna said. "It just never stops."

Mason snickered, a strange, low laugh.

"What do you play, man? Guitar? Drums?"

"Trumpet," Mason said.

"Yeah," Lance said. He looked at Mason. Something about the way he'd said it.

"It's a sexy trumpet," Dakota said.

"Oooo," Meebs said.

"I like trumpet," Stone said. "It just reminds me of waking up at the ass crack of dawn. Can you play 'Taps'?"

"'Taps' is more of a bugle song," Lance said.

"But can you play it?"

"Yeah," Lance said. "Since I was about eight."

The group laughed—the first big laugh Lance had gotten, and it felt good. Everyone was smiling but Stone. His eyes narrowed, skin pinching around his bandages. He shouldn't have said that to Stone. Why had he said that?

"I'll play it for you," Lance said. He reached down and grabbed smoke.

"What's wrong?" Dakota asked.

Lance spun on the log, looked behind him. Scrambled up, standing.

"Easy, Wildman," Rocco said.

"Wow!" Mason said. His eyes were wide, lit up by the fire. He clapped. "I wondered when you were going to notice."

"You have my trumpet?" Lance asked. Relief, and a twist of something else.

"It's locked up safe," Mason said. "Don't worry. You'll get it tomorrow."

"Can we get it now?" Lance asked, looking back toward the woods.

"Afraid not," Mason said. "We've got a train to catch."

11

The rails looked moon-polished and slick, but Rocco walked the left one like a balance beam and never once fell. Meebs skipped along the wooden ties. Actually skipped, but no one laughed or even seemed to notice. Mason was up near Dakota. Lance watched their shadows dance closer, farther apart.

His fingertips ached for his horn. The phantom tingle of a lost limb. Lance slowed down, letting Stone and Breanna catch up. He needed to make it up to Stone, for how he'd acted.

"I'll play 'Taps' for you," Lance said. "As soon as I get my horn back."

"Sweet," Stone said.

"Were you in the military or something?" Lance asked.

"Or something," Breanna said.

Stone's smile vanished.

"Why do you ask?" Stone said. "Do I look military to you?"

"No," Lance said. "It's the 'Taps' thing. And you"—he started, too drunk to stop himself—"you kind of look like a soldier in the zombie apocalypse right now. All bandaged up with your lady. Walking toward simpler times."

Breanna and Stone laughed.

"Simpler times," Stone echoed.

"Stone has a whole plan for when the zombies come," Breanna said. "It's pretty serious."

"It mostly involves outrunning Mason, whose fat ass could feed a horde of zombies for three days," Stone said. He mocked Mason screaming. Breanna laughed, this soft, lilting sound that barely seemed like it could live inside her. She looked up at Stone the way she'd looked at him with his guitar. A flicker behind her eyes.

"You'd save me," she said.

"I am saving you," he said.

"I know, baby."

She tucked herself under the wing of his arm, and Lance watched the rail ties beneath his shoes. Made them move faster. He stretched away from Breanna and Stone until an invisible cord snapped and he was in his own orbit, drifting past Meebs and Rocco, toward Dakota. She'd broken free of Mason and her gravity dragged his own stumbling feet forward, and she was slowing down or he was running.

Dakota. The only thing in a world of blue light.

They walked alone.

"Hey," she said.

"Hey."

"Good stars."

She took a long, deep breath and turned toward him. Eyes open wide. A look as strong as a touch, like she'd cupped his face with her bare hands. Lance's chest shook. A trembling intake of breath and Dakota smiled.

"Cold?" she asked.

"No. I'm okay."

"Nervous?"

He shook his head.

"You're smart, Lance. Valedictorian? Really?"

"Ugh," he said.

"So you have a good, important brain," she said. "You sure you want to do this with your good, important brain?"

"Is it dangerous?" he asked.

"Jumping a train? Very dangerous."

"Oh, good," he said.

"Will you let me pull you on?" she asked. "When you jump?"

"Of course."

"Of course." Nodding, smiling. "Good answer, Wildman."

Just ahead, Mason was down on all fours. Palms on the rails.

"You feel that?" Mason said. "Right on time."

"Mason, dude, you can't feel shit." Meebs hopped up on a rail, shoes squeaking.

"It's coming," Rocco said.

"I'm first up," Mason said. "Dakota, you want second?"

"I'll go right before Lance," Dakota said.

Mason gave her a look like, *Didn't quite catch that.*

"I'm out," Breanna mumbled into Stone's shoulder.

"I'll walk the lady back," Stone said, pulling her close. "She's about to Humpty Dumpty."

The train whistled in the distance. A lonely coyote.

Lance's chest got tight. His thinking narrowed to the rails and how this would work. To his left, about a hundred feet of open space before the forest choked in around a sharp bend in the tracks. The trees crowding the turn had battered branches, raw ends a luminous white. The train had done that. Like pruning with a sledgehammer.

"Two cars to remember," Rocco said, leaning into Lance, whisky thick on his breath. "Larson's Lumber. Mandalay Motors. Then, boom! Runrunrunrunrun. Don't get too close."

"Suction," Meebs said, so stoned his eyes looked bloody.

"Right," Lance said, remembering sophomore physics. "Bernoulli's principle."

"Not Bernoulli," Rocco said. "Mandalay. Mandalay Motors."

"After Larson's Lumber—" Meebs started, but someone grabbed Lance by the shoulder, pulled him backward. "Hey, Stone, let go of the Wildman. We're coaching, man! C'mon!"

But Stone was leading Lance down the slope, away from the others. Breanna was there, hands braced against a tree like a runner stretching after a sprint.

"There's a metal handle to the left of the door," Stone said, acting it out. "Right there. Grab that handle."

"I thought someone would pull me on," Lance said. Dakota was by the tracks. Mason was wrestling with his backpack.

"Yeah. Thing is, that handle doesn't move," Stone said, eyes hard behind his bandages. "Or pull back at the last second." Shot glasses. That's what Mason was after, with a chunky black slice on the bottom of each one. *Magnets?*

This advice was important, but Lance couldn't stick his thoughts to Stone's words. His attention kept skipping back to Dakota. Dakota next to Mason, Dakota taking another shot. Lance's body followed the orbit of his mind, and by the time he realized he'd walked over to her, Stone and Breanna were gone.

"Places!" Mason shouted.

They lined up in the order they would jump: Mason, Meebs, Rocco, Dakota, Lance. The train whistled. Not a coyote. A train. Pressure in the air. Shoes crunched ballast. Whisky on Dakota's breath. He could taste it. He timed his inhalations, trying to breathe her in.

"C'mon, Mason," Meebs said. "Shot o'clock."

Mason snapped the magnets onto the nearest rail. They trembled, *tick-tick-ticking* on the metal. Whisky boiled in the glasses.

"Get 'em while they're hot!" Mason shouted.

They leapt up, lined the rail, yanked the glasses up to their mouths. Lance couldn't unsnap his. When it finally jerked free, he lost half the liquid down the side of his hand. The gulp hammered him in the gut. Too much, too fast. A cold sweat broke out on his back. Someone took his glass away.

"Get ready!" Dakota shouted.

The stars were gone. The train's headlamp was the sun, dragging a world of steel behind it. Dakota grabbed his arm and pulled him, stumbling, down the slope and into the shrubs. She was saying *Remember you need to*—and the whistle blared, flattening her words. The roar rattled the hollows of his lungs and caught in his throat like something he could swallow. The beat on the track shook his clothing against his skin, and they were all standing together. A line of pale faces.

The whistle blew past, a smear of dopplered sound, a click-clack thunder.

Cars cleaved through the darkness, gray and rusted, tagged with painted words, puffy and colorful, black and jagged. The yellow flash of a car.

LARSON'S LUMBER

Dakota grabbed his arm. He bent his knees, trying to breathe away the tickle in his chest. Gray car, gray car, red car, yellow car, brown car. A silver car, coming closer.

MANDALAY MOTORS

"Go!" Mason shouted, his voice swallowed by thunder.

They charged from the ditch. The roar of breath and slip of rocks and a world gone tippy with whisky, then the rocks evened out and he was running along a train, a living thing, unfolding into the darkness—and what a sight! He was laughing, hooting. Pumping his fist.

Mason shambled in the lead, moving off-kilter, like a broken machine. He drew even with an open door in the middle of a box-car. Everyone was speeding up, shouting at Mason *Jump, JUMP!* then his pace matched the train and his knees bent and he flashed into the car like a trick of the light.

The car beside Lance was pocked with rust. Filthy. A bad way to die, coming closer, pushing toward him, tilting off the rails! The track, curving. He stumbled sideways. Easy to forget a curving track with all the noise and how running straight would put your ankle between two pieces of steel, suck you in, and grind you like hamburger under a bootheel.

The train gained speed. It tugged at him like a gentle vacuum and yes, Bernoulli's principle. Because a speeding train pulled the air along with it, and pulled you along with the air.

Bernoulli. Suction. Bernoulli! Suction!

Dakota's hair, bobbing in long, dark waves. Rocco pulled even with the open car. Mason's hand flashed out and vacuumed him into darkness. Meebs was going too fast. Half-jumped, stumbled. Something bad. Something terrible, then a hand from the car and he was okay, kicking up inside, and just Dakota now, and he could run beside this train with her forever.

The door became a real thing, with all of its parts. Metal step and a handle. Mason, Rocco, and Meebs all visible inside. Dakota angled her eyes at the step. More like a bar. Small and rounded and slippery looking. Dakota watching it. The bar, her feet, Mason's outstretched hand.

She was in the air.

Her foot tapped the step, stuck like a magnet. Mason grabbed her forearm. Maybe she didn't need him, but he grabbed and flung her backward, hard. The car swallowed her.

Hurry! Mason mouthed over the roar. *Hurry!*

Mason's hand, outstretched where Dakota's should've been. Beside it, the handle Stone mentioned, fused to the door with bubbling rust. Mason screaming. Mouth screaming, but eyes so dull. Reaching out a meaty paw.

Lance leapt.

No decision, he starfished his limbs. One hand shot for the handle, the other for Mason, feet for the step. Something had to stick. Mason's hand sealed on his like a firm handshake, gave him a quick squeeze.

Then tore away.

The violence of the move spun Lance sideways. Feet scrabbling, he grabbed fistfuls of air. A palm banged into metal, two fingers twisted around the handle. Toes mashed the rounded bar, pedaling its frozen-pond surface. The train shuddered, everything gone. Nothing to hold. Falling through the pond. Then a flock of hands grabbing his shirt and pants and neck, and he was in the air, then grounded. A bone-shaking hug from the car's wooden floor.

He took a breath.

The beginning of his second life was a dusty landscape of plastic soda bottles and a gray penny. He tapped his hands and feet on the wood, ensuring they were there. One, two, three, four. Okay. He loved that gray penny. He wanted to kiss it. Swallow it.

Around him, an argument.

"I was supposed to pull him in," Dakota said.

"Whatever. You were busy falling on your ass," Mason said.

Lance stood, shaking with the shuddering train. Everyone looked at him, like it was his turn to talk.

Ca-LACK, Ca-LACK, Ca-LACK

"Why did you let me go?" Lance asked Mason.

"What?"

A sudden stillness.

"You grabbed my hand," Lance said. "Then you pulled away."

"What the fuck are you talking about?" Mason said. "If I'd let you go your ass would be in the ditch."

"You made it, man," Rocco slurred, shouldering into him. "S'cool."

"Yeah," Mason said. "You made your train, Wildman!" He was smiling a true smile. Then everyone was cheering and slapping his back and of course Mason had tried to pull him in.

Why had he said that to Mason?

Blue light flooded the car. Lance's heart bobbed in his chest, trying to find a rhythm in a flood of adrenaline and whisky, the *ca-LACK* pounding in his belly. Then Dakota was touching him. Pinching his middle finger and dragging him toward the boxcar's open door. Trees, a blue-black flicker. The scent of damp wood. Summer air was alive and raking through his hair and brushing every strand from Dakota's face so she was unhidden, eyes and lips.

She leaned close, then grabbed his chin. Turned his head and put her mouth to his ear. Her breath was warm and said:

Moonflowers.

The trees shrank back and away, melted into tall grass. A meadow. Perfect and wide in a way that made Lance want to jump and fly and run and run until he tumbled down into soft blue grass. The sharp clack of the train struck out like a bell, and flashes of the white flowers speckled the earth, building in number, mottling the field like raindrops on a clean sidewalk. There were hundreds of them.

Dakota held him by a fingertip. Time was rushing, slowing. He could not tell.

The flower droplets evaporated, then someone said *Sugarville* and the train shuddered and slowed. Dakota let him go when Mason, Rocco, and Meebs squeezed into the door. They would have to jump, of course. He wondered how he should tuck his body when they leapt and tossed themselves into the field like dice. Should he protect his head? His kidneys?

Brakes squealed. Couplers braced. A tin-shed rattle, and the train was still.

All they had to do was step down.

Lance's legs were still rubbery. He almost slipped when he dropped onto the ballast. They walked into the weeds, then the woods. Empty bottles and cans lined the single-file path like mile markers. The air felt flat without the rush and beat of the train. Mason led the group—the only one still drinking—taking big pulls from a fifth, haphazardly whacking branches with the bottle.

Dakota was walking close to Mason. Lance's arms were swinging freely at his sides. Hands empty.

"When do you think I can get my horn, Mason?" Lance asked.

"What horn?" Mason called back.

The group laughed.

"Better watch it, man," Rocco said. "Wildman will knock you down."

"I'd like to see that."

"You didn't see him at the accident," Meebs said. "He's a kung fu fighter."

"Yeah," Mason said. "I heard he knocked down a girl."

More laughter. Lance was glad for the distance between him and Mason.

"What happened to Stone?" Meebs said. "Where'd Stone go?"

"You're just noticing this," Rocco said.

"He'd better be on time tomorrow," Mason said. "Or his ass is going to be unemployed."

"C'mon, man. Dude's brain was bleeding," Rocco said. "Yesterday."

"How can something bleed," Mason said, "when it doesn't... even... exist?"

Meebs burst out laughing.

"Stone's not the one who left the fryer on last week," Dakota said. "I'm just saying."

"Oh, that's true," Rocco said.

"He poisoned my thinking," Mason said.

"Oh yeah? Is that why you banged Mandi on Friday night?" Rocco asked. "Hooo."

"Yeah!" Meebs said. "Now you got a poisoned *dick*."

Dakota laughed, then Mason's bottle exploded against the trunk of a maple. Everyone stopped. Mason kept walking. He gripped the stem, holding jagged glass in front of him like a torch. Everyone walked behind him and was quiet.

The group shook free of the trees and passed the fire pit, embers still glowing a candied orange. Mason finally dropped his bottle on a stack of empties. They made it back to The Float's parking lot and everyone was just kind of loose there, under a streetlight. Except Mason was cornering Dakota. If there had been a wall, he would've been leaning on it, but there wasn't so he was just looming. Talking too low for Lance to hear.

Dakota was shaking her head, smiling. Shaking her head again.

Lance's leg was a jackhammer, pounding a hole in the pavement. He stared at Mason and Dakota, trying to pry them apart with his eyes.

"Got any weed left?" Meebs asked no one in particular.

"Aren't you assholes going home?" Mason said. "Last call was seven hours ago."

"I'm out," Rocco said, walking toward Meebs's car. "Meebs."

"Meebs can give you a ride," Mason told Lance.

"The motel's right there." Lance pointed across the field.

"Meebs. Give him a ride."

"Yeah. *Meebs, give him a ride.* Always driving bitches," Meebs said, shuffling off.

Dakota, Mason, and Lance watched one another.

"I'll walk," Lance said.

"We can walk, Mason," Dakota said. "It's right there."

"I know you can walk." Mason's eyes went glassy. "Lance. Tonight's it, right? You're off to Bend tomorrow?"

"Yeah," Lance said. "It's been great, though."

"So great." Mason gave Lance's hand a single pump. "Nice knowing you."

"See you, Wildman!" Rocco called.

"Yeah buddy," Meebs said. "Look us up next time you're in the middle of fucking nowhere!"

Dakota was leaving, so Lance followed her into the field. The walk happened too fast, breezing past, and he was suddenly back in the Trainsong parking lot with cars as still as stones and curtained windows and Dakota.

"So, how was it?" she said.

"What?"

"You know," she said. "This part of your life."

"Fun," he said.

"Yeah?" She laughed. "Fun."

"Also, I think this might be the best night of my life."

She laughed. "Yeah! It felt big, didn't it?"

"Totally big. The biggest."

"Thank you for seeing the field with me."

"Of course. I can't believe you can see that field whenever you want."

"Tonight was the first time I really saw it," she said.

There was a question he should ask, only he did not know how to ask it, then she reached out and cupped his cheeks with her hands. Actual hands! How could they be so warm? How could they be touching him? Then those hands dropped and they were hugging like they were in an airport—like when you won't see someone for a year, or ever again. She turned her face into his neck. The tip of her nose. A brush of lips. She breathed in, inhaling him.

"Goodnight, Lance," she said.

"Goodnight."

He was shaking so hard. He twisted away from her and crossed the parking lot. Walked up painted blue steps.

He hadn't done anything wrong. A hug. A pinched finger. He was trying to open his door, key pecking the knob like a nervous bird. He could not look back. It was so dangerous to look back, so he went inside and turned up the heat and lay on his bed and closed his eyes, trying to tighten his grip on the memory of tonight. Hold it close. Her smell, her skin.

Already slipping, but two words he could keep.

Goodnight, Lance.

His name, like a word that had been invented for tonight.

A word he'd never really heard before.

12

Lance was out of clothes.

Heaped in the corner were khaki pants, button-down shirts, a few pairs of underwear, and jeans, baking like compost. He'd woken up with the heater on. His room stank like an old toaster and his tongue was dry. His teeth felt furry.

Lance wanted to be clean like enamel after a mirror-and-scalpel scraping. He rubbed the stubble on his cheeks and chin and smelled the horror of his armpits, then picked through the pile of clothes for something to salvage. The shirt from the accident, splattered with blood. Last night's jeans stank like beef jerky. He shook out a blue-and-white-striped shirt and a pair of khakis.

He brushed his teeth twice and did the best he could with no razor and no iron. When the steam cleared from the bathroom, he looked like a fair approximation of Lance from Bend. He struck his best pose of respectability in the mirror, but something was missing. He replayed his mantras:

You are valedictorian.

You are the first-chair trumpet player.

You have a full-ride scholarship.

Miriam Seavers—

Miriam. Had he really forgotten to call Miriam? And his trumpet!

A low throb in his skull, carrying a single thought:

GO HOME.

Things were slipping away. Hours, days, mantras. He'd pile everything in this room onto a tarp, drop it over his shoulder and run. He was valedictorian. He could figure this out. But Mason had his trumpet. The cold sweat of panic and Lance was pulling on shoes, out the door. Walking across the parking lot, there was only The Float and his horn. And a voice that said:

"Hey you."

Dakota, on her front patio. Kicking back in a green chair.

He mumbled something back. Too early for Dakota. Too early to be a person. He hadn't digested all their memories from last night, and here she was again, piling them on.

"You're in a hurry," she said.

"I need to get my horn."

"Mason won't be up," Dakota said, glancing at The Float. "I wouldn't go over there. He's not good in the morning."

How did she know Mason wasn't good in the morning? Lance kept looking from Dakota to The Float, trying to make his brain do something. According to his phone, it was 10:26 A.M. The backs of his eyes ached. Hollow stomach. An incoming hangover, getting worse by the minute.

"Wow," Dakota said, looking him up and down.

"What?"

"Are those clothes serious?"

"What do you mean?"

"Are you seriously wearing them?"

Lance looked down.

"Yeah," he said.

"Those are pleated khakis."

"They're wrinkled."

"Wrinkled and pleated."

"What the hell is a pleat?" he said.

Dakota pinched a fold just above his knee. His skin tingled. A lightning bolt, skittering up his thigh. He stepped back and looked down at the crease.

"What's wrong with pleats?"

"Nothing. If you weigh four hundred pounds or have grandbabies."

Lance sighed. He did not understand pants. He didn't understand what made them cool and what made them uncool. He was unclear how a bootcut differed from a straight fit and how a guy's ass was supposed to look in jeans. He'd look over his shoulder in the mirror, but his ass remained cryptic. Beyond comprehension.

"My mom buys my pants," he said.

"Yes. That is obvious. You need a new wardrobe consultant," she said. "You have a reputation to uphold, *Wildman*. C'mon."

Dakota's car relaxed him. Her scent dropped his shoulders below his ears, and he sank into the car. The hug of a seatbelt and he was breathing, wind whipping through the windows, making his head less sticky.

"I could just do laundry," Lance said.

"There's no Laundromat for twenty-five miles."

"How do people get clean clothes?"

"That's what thrift shops are for."

"Oh, man. I need my car." Lance pressed his palms to his eyes. "I need my horn."

"There will be time." Fifteen miles away, Last Chance Thrift was the only operational business in a withering strip mall. Hollowed-out storefronts: A Stitch in Time, Buzzers, Pridays— windows dark and plastered with advertisements, posters, lost-pet flyers. But plenty of cars in the parking lot.

Apparently Last Chance Thrift was a happening spot.

Dakota led Lance through a crowd of elderly clothes-pickers to a back corner of the store labeled VINTAGE THREADZ. The place smelled somewhere between an antique bookstore and a day-old bakery outlet.

"Vintage Threadz. With a *Z*?" Lance asked.

"Oh yeah."

Dakota rifled through the racks, plucking shirts and jeans from their hangers, each with a single, clean jerk, like a seasoned fruit-picker. In under a minute, her right arm was a bolt of denim and fitted T-shirts.

"Those look nothing like me," Lance said, pointing at her arm.

"No," Dakota said, pointing to his pleats. "*That* looks nothing like you."

Lance could not come out of the fitting room. The jeans rode low on his hips. Torn at the knees, ostensibly on purpose. The gray-and-black T-shirt flared at the shoulders and narrowed at his waist, like a *V*. Or maybe his body did that. The material hugged his chest so he could see the outlines of his pecs. Man boobs. But they didn't look bad. Or maybe they did.

"Weird," he said.

He took a breath and stepped out of the dressing room.

Dakota spun. Her eyes widened.

"Holy shit," she said.

Lance leapt back and slammed the door.

"Hey, hey," she said, tapping at the door. "Open up."

"What," he said, cracking the door. She wedged her hand inside, pulled it open.

"You look great," she said. Her eyes were sparkling. A new kind of smile. "Damn, boy."

"I'm changing back."

"Don't you dare put those pants back on," she said. "I'll make you walk home."

"You won't."

"Don't test me."

His rumpled khakis and stripes lay in the corner of the dressing room, like he was a snake who had just molted. He gathered everything up and stepped out into the shopping area. People were staring. One graying woman with a plume of purple hair looked him up and down like a piece of furniture she wanted to take home and sit on.

"What do you think?" Dakota asked her.

"Mmm-hmm, girl," she said, and winked. "You'd better get him home."

"Oh my god," Lance said. He stalked straight out through the front door and stood waiting beside Dakota's car. No sign of her. Two minutes. Three minutes. She finally came outside, grinning.

"What took you so long?" he asked.

"You forgot to pay for your clothes, Wildman. You a shoplifter now, too?"

"Oh man," he said. He searched his jeans for a wallet, then burrowed into his khakis.

"Don't worry," she said. "The pleasure's all mine."

In Dakota's car, Lance didn't know what to say. His new clothes were tight and squeezing him in strange places. Thankfully, she had stopped looking him up and down. He didn't know how he'd react, and these jeans couldn't keep a secret. He could plainly see the rectangular outline of his phone bulging up from his thigh.

When the phone started buzzing, he couldn't get it out of his pants.

"Ah, jeans!"

He twisted and arched his back, writhing against the seat. He had to turn himself sideways to get the right angle. Dakota was still laughing, crying apparently, by the time he finally answered.

"Hi, William," Lance said, out of breath. "How do things look?"

"Hey, Lance. Why don't you just come on by."

"What? Come on by where?"

"The shop."

"Can't you just tell me what's happening?"

"I'd rather show you, if it's all the same."

William gave directions, Lance repeated them back, then hung up. Dakota pulled onto the shoulder.

"So?" she asked.

"He wants me to come to the shop. He won't explain why."

"Sounds like a trap," Dakota said, looking at her phone. "His shop is way out on Deathmurder Lane."

"He killed my car," Lance said. "I'm next."

Dakota pulled a U-turn and hit the gas.

"You're taking me?"

"Oh yeah. Horror movie rule number one. Never split up."

"Right," Lance said. "What are the other rules?"

"No smoking. No going in basements. Virgins tend to live until the end."

She looked at him. Lance kept his legs still, and his mouth shut.

13

On Lance's phone, the destination dot for Goodview Towing sat on a nameless gray line that intersected with a state highway Dakota had only been on once before. They left the highway and climbed into forest. A steep one-lane road bent around hairpin turns, the shoulder narrowing until pavement met cliffside at a ninety-degree angle.

Without a word, Dakota twisted the car into a gap in the greenery. They rattled down a long gravel drive to an open gate laced with barbed wire. A wooden sign, painted with elegant black letters:

THE BONEYARD.

"Not a great name," Dakota said.

"No. Not great."

They got out of the car.

Walking into the Boneyard was like entering the climactic discovery scene of a true-crime movie. The killer's corpses were on display, as if there was some pride involved: A Ford truck with eviscerated hoses splayed across its hood. An '80s-era Celebrity, compacted and blackened like an overcooked potato. An accordioned convertible. Others, jacked up, stripped of their tires, and left in the sun to rot.

But no Buick. Maybe it wasn't too late.

"Where's his shop?" she asked.

"No clue," Lance said.

Dakota whistled something scary, probably from a horror movie.

"Can you please stop?"

Lance led the way, feeling slightly more rugged in denim. Cars, everywhere. A hedge maze of metal and broken glass. Vehicles without doors, spray-painted silver. A radiator. Pile of tires. Dakota was close behind him. Maybe he should hold her hand.

A sudden motion to Lance's right and he leapt back, fists flying up to defend himself. A beast! A creature! A very small dog, leaping onto the hood of a Crown Victoria. The cocker spaniel growled, baring its teeth.

"Daisy! Goddamn it!" Lance said.

"Hey there!" William said, jack-in-the-boxing into view. "Glad you found us." He came around a pile of crushed bumpers and introduced himself to Dakota, then led them through the Boneyard.

"That guy's your mechanic?" Dakota said.

"I don't know if he's *my* mechanic. He's *a* mechanic."

"Let's hope so."

William was waiting for them outside a squat, gray building. He smiled.

"Where's the shop?" Dakota said.

"You're looking at it," William said. "Just me and the missus."

William's shop was apparently a single-stall residential garage illuminated by one halogen lamp clamped to a steel shelf. Rusted blue toolbox on the ground, scattered parts.

And what was left of the Buick.

The doors were wide open. Hood up, insides gutted. Hoses, wires, and cables draped over its sides. Someone hunched in the driver's seat. A flash of orange hair and weathered cheeks briefly conjured William's evil twin—but no—this was a woman. Small flashlight in her mouth. Face slick with sweat.

The Missus.

"Hey there," she mumbled around the light.

"What's going on?" Lance asked.

"That's what we'd like to know!" She cackled at her own joke. William, too, roared with laughter, and the sounds ricocheted off the tight concrete walls, making the garage sound like an asylum.

"Mary, tell him what you found," William said.

"I had to go into the dashboard," Mary said, shaking her head. "Whole thing is dead. Speedometer. Gas gauge. Nothin' works!" Wires spilled out beneath the dash.

"Lance, c'mere." William stepped to the side and aimed a flashlight into the guts of the engine. "See that little wiggly wire? That little one. You see that?"

"Yeah."

"Looks wiggly, don't it?"

"It does."

"See, I don't remember them wires being that wiggly. Could be somethin' there. See, babe? That wiggly wire?"

"Lance, get in," Mary said. "William will show you how she starts up." Lance switched places with her. The interior reeked of Old Spice and motor oil. This car had spent the night with someone else. He tried to ignore the conduit spilling around his ankles. Fragments of plastic and clipped wires that did not look like they could be put back together. William stood beside the engine with an aerosol can.

"Now grab that key and get ready," he said, eyes dancing with glee. "Crank it!"

Lance turned the key.

"Keep going! Keep cranking!"

Lance twisted until the Buick was grinding. Squealing. Begging him to stop. William sprayed a stream of oil from his can. The engine popped like a firecracker, then died.

"See how it starts?" William said.

"Yeah," Lance said. The word tasted like lead.

"That's encouraging, ain't it? Go on and crank it again. Hard."

"I don't think that's good for the car," Lance said.

"Probably not," Mary said.

"True. Probably not," William said, nodding. "So how about that wiggly wire, Lance? What do you think?"

Lance did not attempt to see the wiggly wire. Instead, he looked back at the dash and remembered preparing the Buick for a trip with his grandmother a few years ago. His father had removed a fuse to make the check engine light go off.

That'll kill the dummy light. Let's not give Grandma anything to worry about.

"Have you checked the fuses?" Lance asked.

Mary and William stared back at him. Then William dug in his toolbox and came out with a handful of green and yellow fuses. Lance thumbed them in while Mary turned the key, feeding whatever juice the battery had left into the dash. After the third or fourth fuse, she cried out.

"Hallelujah!" Mary said. "Let there be light."

"Nice!" Dakota said.

Lance sat back and smiled. The check engine light was on.

"Seatbelt light's on too," Mary said. "Battery light. Lookee."

"Still empty on the gas gauge," William grumbled. "Speedometer shows zero."

"Well the car ain't movin', William."

"Have him crank it again."

Lance tried. The engine grunted, choked.

"Go on. Fire her up!" William lifted his can with a wild-eyed grin.

"I think," Lance said, forming his words carefully, "we should bring the Buick to a specialist." Dakota nodded.

"Specialist?" William said. "So, wait. You want to go somewhere else?"

Lance pulled out the key and stared at the dashboard.

"I told you not to bring him here," Mary whispered.

She led Lance and Dakota into their office, more art gallery than repair shop. The walls were crammed with half-finished oil paintings. A crusty loaf of bread, perfectly textured and lying on a pencil sketch of a table. A crow leaving its invisible perch. The largest piece was a wall-size rendering of the seashore at night: craggy cliffs and sparkling seafoam under a white canvas sky.

Mary rifled through a drawer, then pushed a form across the counter.

Lance paused and read the numbers twice. "One hundred eighty-seven dollars?"

"Yup," Mary said.

"But you didn't fix anything!"

"Diagnostics," Mary said, tapping the invoice. There it was. Circled. Underlined. DIAGNOSTICS. Lance felt the loss of the $187 like the removal of a kidney. He shook his head, denying it.

"Just a minute," Mary said. "I'll bring you the keys."

Lance stepped outside with Dakota. Opposite the Boneyard, a line of hedgerow evergreens caught his eye. Flashes of silver-blue flickered between their branches and without a word, they were walking in that direction. Grass rose from ankle to knee until they reached the living wall and saw, beyond it, the lip of a water-worn ravine. A slope of ferns dipped, then rose and broke off into a wide and wild ocean view.

"Whoa," Dakota said. "Good eye!"

"I thought there might be something here," he said.

On the horizon, a small blue suspension bridge.

"Hey," Lance said. He grabbed his wallet.

"What?" Dakota asked.

He held up the Goodview Towing business card.

"Whoa. Who made this?" Dakota asked.

"Had to be William," Lance said.

A sound like broken wind chimes. Car keys. It was Mary, walking a deliberate, crooked path in their direction.

"Well there you go," Mary said, slapping the keys in his palm.

"Thank you," Lance said.

"Nice view," Mary said. Her eyes, so blue. Lance hadn't noticed them before. She glanced back toward the office. "Told him not to let you in the garage. People don't want to see garages. Kitchens neither. They want it all to be magic."

Past her, beyond the Boneyard, stood a bigleaf maple. Leaves flapped like green flags and William stood in the shade, smoking a cigarette. His posture was fixed straight up and down. "So why did he want me to come?" Lance asked.

"He said you had the charm." Mary looked him up and down. He followed her eyes, freshly startled by his clothing. He smoothed out his T-shirt.

"Yep. Will's old man just *charmed* them. Had that magic up his sleeves. Couldn't always tell you what was wrong, but could always make her run. Every time."

"And William thinks Lance has the charm?" Dakota asked.

"That's crazy," Lance said.

"What's crazy about that?" Mary said. "You got your dash working in five minutes flat."

"That's just a trick my dad showed me." She fixed him with those eyes, like she was reaching under his dashboard and grabbing out *his* wires. Then she turned toward her husband.

"William don't have it," she said plainly.

William had refreshed his cigarette. So still, as if sunk in the earth up to his ankles.

"But, boy," Mary said. "You should see him paint."

She walked back through the grass, stalks whispering against her legs.

"What now?" Lance asked.

"I'd call for a tow," Dakota said. "Maybe get a different driver this time."

"I feel bad taking my car somewhere else."

"Don't feel bad," Dakota said. "He's not a mechanic. He's an artist."

William hadn't moved an inch, yet he was transformed. Dakota's words had changed his appearance the way a photographer might, by adjusting the angle of the camera or the quality of light. His downturned eyes no longer looked defeated, but stoic. He was not lamenting the Buick, just considering colors. Dreaming up his next masterwork.

"You could draw him in your book," Lance said.

"Oh yes."

"If he's an artist, then what are you?" Lance asked.

She smiled like she'd just been caught at something. She looked him over.

"Wardrobe consultant."

Dakota moved her hair forward a little, curtaining off her eyes.

"Really," he said. "It just hit me—I have no idea what you do all day."

"I know," she said. "Isn't that nice?"

"Why?"

"Because then we don't have to talk about it."

She took a deep breath and patted her pockets, searching for something. He'd said it wrong, and now the answer was locked up inside her. The breeze blew salty-cool air across the field. The leaves chattered and Lance felt a sudden emptiness. There was so much he would never know about her. A sudden feeling of loss, wrapped up in his own name, and the way she'd whispered it the night before. He'd leave this place, and would never stop checking the rearview mirror. He'd be a thousand miles away, ten years older, looking back and asking a question that would not be *What do you do all day?*

It would be: *Whatever happened to Dakota?*

14

The lobby of Macland's Auto Repair reeked of stale popcorn and burnt coffee baking on a hot plate. Off to one side there was a giant Plexiglas window where customers could ostensibly stand and observe auto mechanics in their natural habitat. Lance and Dakota decided to keep a field journal of their social and dietary habits. This blue-suited tribe communicated with grunts and profanity. Hierarchy was determined by tool size. Grooming habits, nonexistent. They subsisted on beef sticks and cans of carbonated corn syrup.

The guy assigned to work on Lance's car was chugging on a Moody's. They weren't sure of the flavor until he picked up a clipboard and, deep in thought, stuck out his tongue. Purple. Bright as a permanent marker.

"It's over," Dakota said. "Get out now."

"Maybe he just likes grape soda."

She shook her head. "Lance. A purple tongue is the sign of the beast."

He and Dakota were laughing too hard to notice how long things were taking. When Lance finally pried his phone out of his jeans, it was six P.M. and Miriam had called twice.

"Go ahead and call," Dakota said. "I'll watch the Buick. I will be strong and vigilant."

Lance stepped outside. The hard afternoon light had gone a soft orange, and the windshields of cars shone like burnished copper. He took a long, deep breath. After his time in Macland's, the air tasted sweet.

He'd come out to call Miriam. He dialed Jonathan instead.

"Well, hello there," Jonathan said.

Jonathan never answered his phone. Lance waited, making sure this wasn't a clever voice mail prank.

"Lance? Are you breathing at me? Or is this his murderer? You'll never get away with this."

"It's me, man. Couldn't hear you for a second."

"No. Wait. Is this *the* Lance Hendricks?"

"Yes."

"I mean, the *one true* Lance Hendricks?"

"Okay, enough."

"Lancelot. Dude. How are you not back?"

That's right. He was Lancelot.

"The car's not fixed."

"Really?" Jonathan said. "Still? I can't believe you missed The Party! Such a riot. And the things I found in my parents' bedroom getting it ready for you. I can't unsee those things, Lance. My parents are perverse people. I can no longer look my own father in the eye."

Lance laughed. "Sorry, man."

"Really, I don't get it. What's going on? Are you hooked on amphetamines?"

"No."

"Did your dad get ahold of you?"

"No, Jonathan."

For any other friend, that would've been the end of the phone call. But Jonathan had been there the afternoon at the creek, the day his father had gone. When Lance kept breaking off to examine river rocks, any reason to stand alone and look down, so he could cry and not be seen. And Jonathan had seen him. He had put a hand on Lance's back and had said *It'll be okay* and *You'll get through this,* and he had never told anyone about that, not ever.

"Do people think I'm with my dad?" Lance asked.

"There are some pretty wild stories."

"Like?"

"Whisky shots. A knife fight. Did you hear me, Lance? A knife fight."

"I just pulled a knife. I didn't fight with it."

Miriam. She'd told them. How long had they all laughed about that? His stomach was folding over, contracting. And he suddenly knew why he'd called Jonathan. He'd wanted to talk to someone who knew him. Really talk. About the train, the cemetery, The Float, Dakota. These jeans, and how it felt to be called Wildman. How crazy it all was! But Jonathan couldn't hear him either. Like Miriam and his mother. The wrong groove. The same empty hiss.

"I should really call Miriam," Lance said.

He made his excuses and got off the phone. In his chest, a

feeling that said this was a bad time to call Miriam, but there he was, making the call. She answered right away, on the second ring. He wasn't ready. He could've used one more ring.

"Lance?"

"Yeah, hi."

"Well," she said.

"What?"

"What happened last night? Did you forget your charger?"

"Miriam, I—"

"Seriously, Lance. Should I be moving on? Is that what you're trying to tell me?"

"Moving on?" he said. "I've only been gone three days."

"I haven't heard from you in twenty-four hours."

"We've been together two years!"

"Where are you now?"

"Another repair shop. The first one was a total disaster."

"Yes," Miriam said. "This has been a total disaster."

"You know," he said, "I don't appreciate you telling all our friends I'm making up stories." He inhaled. Exhaled. He needed to breathe.

"I didn't say you were making them up," she said. "I let the stories speak for themselves."

"Well guess what? I got wasted and jumped on a moving train last night. What do you think of that?"

Silence.

"Is that true?"

"Who knows, Miriam? Who knows."

"This is dumb," she said.

"Yes."

"It's dumb that you're choosing your car over us."

"It's not," he said. "Don't you want us to have a car next year? Don't you want to take weekend trips?"

"Yeah, but we're going to be busy, Lance. College isn't like high school."

"Yeah? College sounds boring." The word *boring*, which he had not expected to say, crystallized the deep, impalpable dread he'd been feeling all year. More tests, more teachers, more deadlines. Oregon State University sounded boring. And yet, all these words he'd been tossing out like candy from a parade float:

I'm really looking forward to it.

It's great. I can live at home a few years, so I don't have any debt when I graduate.

My girlfriend is going to OSU, which is perfect.

"College sounds boring," Miriam repeated.

"Yeah," Lance said. "That's right." Silence. Across the street, a crow settled on a power line. There were five lines total, parallel and evenly spaced. One black dot of a crow. The bird ruffled its feathers and scolded him. A small flock landed. A dozen small bodies, staggered in a way that looked familiar.

"Are you having a midlife crisis?" Miriam asked.

"I'm eighteen."

"I know. But you've always been advanced." Beyond the crows, spires of evergreens, ferns on a hillside. There were people living behind those trees, down that road, beyond where he could see. Hundreds of thousands of lives tucked back in the bushes, in places he'd never even thought about.

"You're scared," she said. "You're running away."

"I'm not running," Lance said.

"Yes, Lance. You are."

"Miriam. Please."

"It's like something your dad would do." Lance spiked his phone into the grass. Miriam had never met his father. She'd only heard stories. He walked to the nearest smallish tree. He grabbed it, throttled the trunk, kicked bark until it chipped. He was sweaty, breathless.

In the grass, his phone vibrated. He went back into Macland's without it.

Dakota was standing, waiting for him.

"You okay?" she said.

"Yeah. Why?"

"That little tree must've said *something*."

"Right," Lance said. "Funny."

"But I've got bad news."

"What?"

"There are at least five more little trees out there. I think they just showed up."

Lance looked outside. There were a lot of them.

"We'd better make a break for it," Lance said.

"About that," she said. "More bad news."

"What?"

"Your car's not ready."

Back in the shop, beyond the Plexiglas, the lights were off. Mechanics, tucked somewhere out of sight.

"That figures," Lance said.

They left and Macland's door locked shut behind them. The sun had just vanished, and the air was already cooler.

"Hey." She took a deep breath, looked up. "Does this mean we get one more night?"

"Yeah." Lance smiled and looked at her. "One more night."

"Okay. You get your phone. I'll get my car. We'll meet right here." She pointed to the ground.

"Right here," Lance said, pointing.

Lance picked up his phone from the grass. The tree's bark, scuffed and chipped. He was no longer angry. He couldn't even *remember* angry. Every poisonous, simmering thing in his blood had gone tingly, and waiting for Dakota felt like warming up in the orchestra pit on opening night. The tuning up of instruments. That awful, giddy flutter before a show.

Dakota's engine fired and her headlights swung around. She was coming. Twenty minutes alone in a car with Dakota, about to happen. This rare gift of a moment. She was a silhouette when she parked. She popped open the passenger door and the dome light turned her three-dimensional. Eyes, electric. Hair, spilling down.

"Need a ride?" she asked.

One more night.

15

Dakota, on the other side of the console.

Breathing, like it was something people just did.

Normally, he would've talked about his plans, logistics, what he needed to do next—the way his mother and Miriam liked to talk—but being with Dakota was like dreaming. Different things mattered in dreams. So he didn't talk about his plans at all. Words vanished with the click of the car's locks and the shiver-making smell of her neck.

He just wanted to look at her.

Dakota turned out of Macland's, heading toward a dark wooded road. The sun was down.

"Hey," she said. "Is anyone worried about you?"

He took a deep breath. He was worried about him.

"My mom," he said. "And my girlfriend is freaking out."

Dakota nodded. "She misses you?"

"Maybe," Lance said. "I don't know. More like she's mad I'm not there."

"My mom hates it when I'm gone," Dakota said. "But it's kind of how you'd hate to lose a good refrigerator. You don't really love a refrigerator. You just hate it when it breaks."

Lance laughed and looked at her. "You're funny."

"Really?" She smiled a full smile. She turned onto an unmarked road. Pressed on the gas. "That's so nice. No one here thinks I'm funny."

"You're obviously funny," Lance said. "You're empirically, scientifically funny."

"Can we do an experiment to prove this to them? Are marshmallows involved?"

"I wish," he said. "None of my friends believe I actually jumped a train. Or did a shot at a bar. Or would wear these," he said, pointing to his jeans.

"They have a lot to learn, Wildman."

He laughed. Dakota's mouth was a line. Her eyes somewhere far away.

"I thought Macland's might fix your car. I was getting ready to never see you again."

"Yeah," he said. Her eyes now on him. Not watching the road at all.

"Don't go to business school, Lance."

"Really? That's what you want to tell me?"

"Yes. Don't land there and die."

"*Don't land there and die?* I'm more afraid I'm going to die right now." Dakota cranked the wheel into a turn. His hand pawed for a handle above the door—nothing to grab. Her headlights carved out a small pocket of light. Trees hurtled past.

"Relax. I could drive this road in my sleep," she said.

"Like Breanna?"

"No," she said. "Don't worry. I'm the one trying to save your life."

"And my wardrobe."

"It's all related, Lance."

He smiled at the sound of his name and pressed his hand against the car's cool window. Trees and sky. The first pinpricks of starlight, threading through his fingers.

"I could be a mechanic," he said. "William thought I was charmed."

"You are charmed," she said. "What do you think about William? What's his story?"

"I don't know," Lance said. "Crazy, right? I can't stop seeing him under that tree. All that art in his office. Did it look good to you? Was that good art?"

She looked back at him, like she was surprised he'd asked. "Yeah," she said. "His business card should be hanging at the Frye. And that voice!"

"Totally an opera singer. I wanted him to belt out 'Moon River' for me."

Lance started to sing with William's voice.

Moooooooon river—

She laughed. "Don't stop!"

"I'm not a singer."

"How do you know?" she asked.

He said nothing, because Dakota wouldn't care about his reasons. Reasons like *he'd never done it before* and *people told him he wasn't a singer.* She wrapped a finger in her dark hair, twirling it over her ear. Her earlobe was not loose and dangling like Miriam's. It ran straight into a soft curve in her neck. He wondered how it would taste, then she was looking straight at him.

"What?" she said.

"I want to know more about your journal," he said. "The clues."

"Oh, man," she said. Her jaw tightened. He wanted to lean closer. Put his head on her shoulder. Where were these thoughts coming from?

"C'mon," he said. "What clues did you see today?"

"Really?" she asked. "You want to know?"

"Really."

Her gaze drifted to the top of the windshield, something building in her eyes. Excitement.

"So many clues, Lance!" She pounded the steering wheel so hard he jolted in his seat. Relief, plain on her face, like she'd been holding her breath for years. "William under the maple was a huge clue, right? The way that little blue bridge looked over the water. I mean, you get it. You actually see things. You're the first person to ever see that field with me. That was a clue."

"Yeah," he said. He locked his teeth together. "But a clue to what?"

"I don't know," she said. "They're all the things that wake me up and make me feel alive. That's what's important, right? I just can't figure out how to pull them all together. Or turn them into something real, that people understand. Like a job. Or a degree. Or whatever bullshit thing. And I can't even talk to anyone about this, because all people want to talk about is *my day*."

"Oh, man. I hate talking about my day."

"I know, right? It's just a stupid list. I woke up. I ate breakfast. I vacuumed. I drove from here to here. And then—I'll see something just perfect. Like, a droplet of rain rolling down the window. Or I'll be driving and suddenly the air will smell like being seven years old at my grandmother's farm. Or the sunrise hits a tree and makes it look golden and perfect. Like the only tree in the world."

"God waving," Lance said.

She chewed her lower lip. Those lips.

"What do you mean?"

"My dad. He had this thing about God waving. He'd always point out leaves in the late afternoon and how the sun hit them. When they were bright and flashing he'd say *There it is. God waving. Better pay attention.* He'd always drag me outside to see the sunset, or watch morning fog roll in. He was good about that stuff."

"So where did he go?" Dakota asked.

Another curve. She took it slow.

"North." Lance stared out the window.

"That's a story," she said. "Will you tell me?"

This pocket of time. It was okay. This was barely real.

"He used to take me camping all the time. He taught me the difference between true north and magnetic north. Do you know?"

She shook her head.

"So, most people navigate by magnetic north," Lance said. "That's how compasses work. But magnetic north isn't a fixed thing. And it's changing all the time. As much as forty miles a year. It'll be over a Canadian island one year, then Russia the next. Every once in a while it flips poles completely. So your compass would point north but you'd be walking the exact opposite direction."

"Crazy."

"I know, right? But true north never changes. It's always right under Polaris. So when the sky was clear, my dad would always say *Make sure you're navigating by true north, Lance.* He'd say it in this really annoying way, and I kept using the compass, because I didn't get what he meant. One night he kept repeating his stupid true-north line and I snapped. I said *What the hell do you mean, true north?* And he grabbed my chin and pointed it up at the sky and said *Your eyes, Lance. Trust your own damn eyes.*"

"That's intense. So can you find it?"

"After that little episode? Oh yeah. It's the last star on the handle of the Little Dipper. If it's clear enough, I could show you." He bent his head, trying to see out the window. "Anyway, that's where he said he was going. To find true north."

When he turned back, she was looking at him the same way she had when he'd stepped out of the changing room, wearing new clothes.

"Wow," she said. "But how do you just leave your kid like that?"

"I don't know," Lance said. "Can't really ask him."

She nodded.

"It sucks when they go," she said.

"What's the story with your dad?" Lance asked.

"Oh. He took his car with him."

Pines closed in on the road, swallowing the shoulder.

"That's the problem," Dakota said. "He left. But he's still the same. Another wife who looks like my mom. She drinks the same damn soda, Lance. He'll just have to run away again. He never figured it out."

"Figured what out?"

"The clues," Dakota said. She ran a hand through her hair, bringing it down. Just a nose now. A sliver of cheek. "What they mean."

"And you haven't either?"

"No," she said. "That's why I'm still here."

He sat up straight. "But you can't just wait around at The Float, right? What if it takes your whole life to figure it all out?"

"I don't need to figure it all out," she said. "Just one true thing."

"One true thing," he repeated.

"One thing in your life that makes you stop and say *This! This!* No doubts. No wondering. Isn't that how music is for you?"

"Maybe," he said, but the real answer was *almost*. Music could be real, but wasn't yet. The notes had been sneaking out in Seattle. A kind of music he'd never played before. Notes that he had been hiding from Jonathan and Miriam and his mother. The kind of music that never felt closer than it did beside this girl, when she looked at him that way.

"I can't talk to anyone like this," he said.

"Me neither."

And now Dakota was watching the road. And so was he.

"I can tell you anything, you know?" he said. "Because it doesn't really matter."

The comment didn't land how he expected. Dakota tightened her lips. A hard silence. The forest darkened. Trees turned to brittle shadows and the car took a quick bend in the road, skirting the edge of a rushing river. Froth churned a luminous white.

"You know what I mean," Lance said.

"Yeah," Dakota said. "You mean knowing me won't have an impact on your real life."

"That's not it," he said. "This whole thing just feels like a dream, you know?"

She smiled a little, and the acoustics straightened out. Lance wanted the drive to never end. He wanted to keep the windows up and seal in the moonlight. The look and feel of a small, tight place with Dakota inside. But they were already in the Trainsong parking lot. Their hands were opening car doors, because that's what hands did when cars stopped, and when they stepped outside, the magic of the ride washed out around their ankles.

They stared at each other across the hood of a Ford Focus, and Lance felt like he'd just woken up.

"Oh damn," he said. "My horn is still at The Float."

"Should we head over now? Or would you prefer to change into something pleated?"

"I'm ready now, thanks."

"Okay, Wildman," Dakota said. "Let's roll."

16

Outside The Float's back door, an exhaust fan exhaled warm grease. A muffled pounding, like fists on a wall, was coming from inside. A double-time, irregular meter. Maybe a 2/6 with a 3/4 signature. Lance almost had it figured out when someone screamed:

You fuckers! Let me out!

"Mason's got someone in the walk-in," Dakota said.

She led him through the back door, past a rack of canned beans to where Mason stood with a small ring of servers and cooks in striped pants. Someone had shoved a broomstick through the walk-in freezer's *U*-shaped handle. More pounding. Wood jumped and rattled.

"Time for Quiz Bowl, Freezer Edition!" Mason shouted.

"Damn it, Mason!"

The captive beat the door.

"Nice threads, Wildman," Mason said. "Got a date?"

"Hey!" The captive's voice was familiar. "I just dropped three orders of fries. You're going to burn your damn restaurant down."

"Stone," Mason said, shaking his head. "You have the power here. Only you can save you."

So it was Stone.

"Hey, Mason," Lance said. "I wondered if I could pick up my trumpet."

"Trumpet," Mason said. "Hmm. About this big? Black case? Spit-polished and called the Wild Thing?"

"Exactly."

"Never seen it." He turned back to the walk-in. "Hey, Stone. Bonus question: Where is Wildman's trumpet?"

"How the hell should I know?"

Mason made a buzzer noise. Stone charged. The broomstick shuddered. Servers giggled, but the cooks looked nervous, like they might be next.

"Mason," Dakota said. "He's injured."

"He's fine. We were having a civilized discussion about the word *emanciated*," Mason said. "Stone needed a time-out."

"*Emanciated*?" Dakota said.

"It means really skinny, right?" Mason whispered. "Little African kids."

"Emanci-PATED!" Stone shouted. "It means free, idiot!"

"Wildman?" Mason asked.

"*Emancipated* means free," Lance said. "*Emaciated* means really skinny."

"Yeah. Skinny, Mason," Stone said. "Like the opposite of you."

Mason gasped. "Stone."

"Open the door, or I start breaking glass. I'm not fucking around."

"After hearing testimony from our judges," Mason said, "we'll call it a draw."

Mason yanked out the broom and the door blasted open. Stone whipped past them. The draft from the freezer frosted Lance's arms.

"Want to step inside, Wildman?" he said. "Cops will never find you."

"Funny. They called me earlier," Lance said.

"I heard. They were here looking for you," Mason said. "Perkins the Prick said he's left you three messages. Don't worry. I told him you were the Wildman. You have too many outstanding warrants to give a shit about his podunk jurisdiction."

"Thanks, Mason. That's helpful."

"I figured you'd be back in Bend. Now this could get awkward."

"Yeah," Lance said. "So, hey. Before I get arrested, do you think I could grab my horn?"

"We're slammed, dude," Mason said, suddenly frantic. "It's dinner rush. Go have a drink, and I'll be out in a second."

Dakota tried to say something, but Mason was already walking. Out in the bar, Rocco and Meebs had pinned down their usual table with a half-empty pitcher. Meebs gave Lance a high five. Rocco slapped his back. Apparently, in these parts, it was easy to go from someone whose ass people wanted to kick to someone they couldn't wait to see. You just had to stick around a few days.

"Return of the Wildman!" Meebs said.

"Fugitive," Rocco said. "When they start offering a reward, I'll turn you in. I'm just saying it now, so there's no weirdness between us."

"What do the cops want to know?" Lance asked.

"Just that Stone was driving," Rocco said. "That's all."

"Breanna was driving," Lance said.

"Not according to expert testimony," Meebs said, tripping over the word *expert*.

"You guys told him Stone was driving?"

Meebs and Rocco simultaneously raised their glasses for a sip, like their arms were connected to the same lever.

"We've been over this," Rocco said. "Breanna is going to be a lawyer. Stone got discharged from the military, man. Like they discharged *him*."

"He's a stoner," Meebs said. "Wildman, look. The guy's name is literally Stone."

"It's not," Lance said. "His name is literally James."

"Not around here," Rocco said. He filled three glasses with beer and pushed one toward Lance.

"I just don't see why you guys give Stone such a hard time."

The table went still. Dakota, Meebs, and Rocco were all wearing the same expression. Like he just admitted he'd never seen *Star Wars*.

"He plays guitar well," Lance said. "Has a decent vocabulary. You know?"

Meebs buried his head in his hands. Rocco rubbed his eyes.

"I mean. Should we tell him about Purple Passion?" Meebs asked. "Or the Russian girls?"

"More pregnant," Rocco said. "That's the best story."

"Yeah, yeah!" Meebs got all animated, like someone just dropped a quarter in his slot. "Okay, so Breanna goes off to school and gets pregnant."

"With Stone's kid?" Lance asked.

"Nope," Meebs said. "Knocked up by a rich frat boy. So now she's getting laid and getting paid!" He did a finger snap.

"Anyway," Dakota said.

"Anyway," Meebs said. "We're at the campfire and I say, *Hey, Stone, you should give Breanna a call. Nine months free birth control.* And he gets this look. Puzzlement."

"Pure puzzlement," Rocco said.

"He says, *Why wouldn't I have to use protection?*"

"Oh, man," Lance said.

"Wait, wait, wait," Meebs said. "So Stone says, *Well, couldn't she get* more *pregnant?*"

"No."

"*Like pregnant again?*" Rocco said, doing a pretty good Stone impression. "*Like, with twins?*"

"Oh," Lance said. "Yikes."

He looked back at the service window, trying to make this story fit with Stone. But Stone wasn't there. Behind the bar stood a man Lance had never seen before. He was in his early sixties, cheeks like jowls, head shaved to gray stubble. His mouth gave him away: thin lips touched by a sour smile.

This man was Mason's father.

"Anyone seen Mason?" Lance asked, scanning the room. But the server came before anyone answered—the same girl Mason had grabbed the day before. She took their order in a small voice. Just over a whisper.

"Who's Renee banging these days?" Rocco asked, when she was maybe out of earshot.

"I think she's onto the old man," Meebs said.

Mason's father was fully grinning now, shoulders back, chatting up two young couples by the prize wheel. His whole body had changed. He looked like he'd been built with rusty metal but had somehow turned himself elastic, cheesy grin snapping all over his face. One of the girls had a foot up on a barstool, unlacing her white sneaker.

"Girls would sleep with that?" Lance asked. That got Meebs. He snorted beer up his nose, coughing it out.

"Can't get a shift at The Float without giving it up," Rocco said. "Isn't that right, Dakota?"

"Wouldn't know," Dakota said. "I don't work here."

"*Yet*," Meebs said. "You don't work here *yet*."

"No escape," Rocco said.

At the bar, the blonde was in her socks. Her friends watched as she hauled back with her sneakers and tossed them into the rafters. They caught and did a limp little dance around a wooden beam. Mason's father led the bar in applause, then cranked the prize wheel, which *clickclickclicked* and stopped on: FREE MEAL AND ROUND OF DRINKS.

The bar cheered. Mason's father struck a bell by the service window.

"Winner!" he shouted.

"Decent prize," Rocco said.

"Blondes tend to do well," Dakota said.

The girl was laughing, hopping up, high-fiving her friends.

"But she's got no shoes," Lance said. "What is she going to do without shoes?"

"Go barefoot," Rocco said.

"The prizes don't seem worth it," Lance said, looking up. An uneven ceiling of treads and laces. Some of the pairs looked brand-new.

"You could get a thousand bucks," Meebs said.

"Has anyone ever won?" Lance asked.

"Hell no," Rocco said. "Those assholes don't even have a thousand dollars."

"They do," Meebs said. "They got five grand hanging behind that flag. That's Mason's retirement plan."

"Thanks for your contribution, son," Rocco said, slapping Lance's shoulder. His cheeks burned. His name in black letters. One day, Mason would spend his money.

"Seriously," Lance said. "Has anyone ever won a thousand dollars?"

"Totally," Meebs said.

"Bullshit, Meebs." Rocco turned to face him. "It's rigged. Everyone knows it's rigged, idiot."

"How's it rigged?"

Rocco stared at the wheel. "Magnets."

"Fucking magnets," Meebs said. "How do they work?"

"Here we go," Dakota said.

"That couple in the Chevy Malibu—" Meebs started.

"—couple in the Chevy Malibu," Rocco cut him off. "Those were Mason's cousins, you stoner. And they didn't win."

"They did!" Meebs said. "I was sitting right here, eating my motherfucking grilled cheese—"

Lance's phone buzzed in his pocket. His mother.

"Whoever it is, take it," Dakota said. "This conversation lasts exactly seven minutes." The call went to voice mail, and Lance got up and walked to the parking lot. The humidity was thinning in a cool early-evening breeze, fresh scents unraveling in the air. He closed his eyes and breathed deeply, hoping to ride something into memory. His phone buzzed. His mother, angry and shaking in his pocket.

"Lance," she said.

"Yeah." She took a long breath.

"Are you ignoring me?"

"No."

"Are you trying to make it so I can't sleep. Is that on purpose?"

I'm not calling the police back either, he thought. *Don't take it personally.*

"Mom."

His mother hadn't cried the morning his father left—not in front of him. But her words were trembly now, and the warble in her voice put a lump in his throat.

"I should've called," he said. "Miriam and I had a fight."

"I know," she said. "She's worried about you."

"Why are you two talking all the time?"

"Lance. Because we care about you. When are you coming home?"

"The car's not fixed."

"You know, I think it's about time to say goodbye."

"To what?"

She sighed. "Campus is only three miles away. Miriam will be close."

"Oh yeah. Life will be great, unless I actually want to *do* something."

"Like what, Lance?"

"Like road trips. Like anything that matters."

"I'll try to not be offended by that," she said. "Listen. Tomorrow is Tuesday. We have our campus tour at three P.M. Wednesday is your Personal Banker orientation."

"At the bank?" he said. "I thought I didn't start until next week."

"It's just orientation."

"I don't want to be a Personal Banker," he said. "I'll have to work with Creepy Bill."

"You'll be an associate. It's good money."

He sighed. "I'll be home by Wednesday."

"You need to be home tomorrow. Mr. Leeds is concerned."

"Mr. Leeds?"

Lance pictured Bend High School's football-coach-cum-guidance-counselor hunching over his computer with bent little arms, like a Tyrannosaurus rex on a tricycle. Jonathan did a good impression.

"Everyone is now aware of your little episode, Lance."

"So now it's an episode."

"Well. I just don't want you to miss any major opportunities because you're off having an adventure in the woods."

Possible comebacks tangled in his brain. A jumble of live wires.

"How is my speech a major opportunity, Mom? I'm already valedictorian. I already picked my school. It's done! Finished! There are no opportunities."

"What are you talking about, Lance?" she said, putting giant pauses between her words. "You have a great summer job. A full-ride scholarship. A wonderful girlfriend."

Yes, all the things. Like a musical stave barnacled with notes. Pages of dried ink to be played through. And the best you could do was play the notes exactly as they'd been written. Because everyone was counting on you. Because you had your assigned part, and your job was to play it perfectly.

"Yeah," Lance said, looking up. Breathing away the pressure behind his eyes. "Life is great, Mom. There are just no opportunities."

"Lance, have you been drinking?"

"What—no!" But there had been two beers. Maybe two and a half. "You think if I have something real to say, I must be drunk. Awesome."

"I'm going to send Dave up tonight," she said softly. "He's happy to make the drive." Dave was his mother's smarmy real estate partner, with whom she'd had far too many late-night phone calls. Once, after a few glasses of wine, Dave had tousled Lance's hair. That asshole was probably tooling around in his sporty new Subaru right now, listening to smooth jazz and cruising up Highway 97, wind flopping his comb-over all over the place.

"If Dave comes here, I swear to god I'll break his windshield with a baseball bat."

He didn't know where he'd get the baseball bat. Mason, maybe.

"Excuse me? Did I hear you correctly?"

"I'm just telling you what to expect. If that man values his Subaru, he will not show his face here tonight."

"Is that so? Let me tell you what to expect," she said. "You'll be paying for this little trip out of your own pocket. Including the repairs. So I hope you have it covered."

"Fine," he said. Him and his three hundred dollars. He glanced down at his shoes, and considered the prize wheel. He wondered who was right about the couple in the Chevy Malibu.

"Listen," she said. "If you're not home by tomorrow, I'm calling the administration."

"You're calling the president of the United States?"

"Don't be an ass, Lance."

"You don't be an ass."

"You do *not* talk to me that way."

Lance pulled his phone away from his ear and looked at it. A harmless piece of plastic. Already cracked. He lifted a finger and hung up on his mother. He imagined throwing the phone. The satisfying crunch of pavement; tinkling circuitry, scattering like fairy dust. The phone buzzed. He swiped his mother into voice mail. Then again. Texts:

If you don't answer, I'm calling the police.

Lance tried to respond, but his hands were shaking too hard. He could barely get the letters out.

Don't be nad itiotn I'm fine

He scowled at his phone. Put his mother into voice mail again. Another text.

Lance, please come home.

He took a deep breath, trying to shift the tremors from fingers to legs, where they belonged.

Tomorrow

He paced. Above, shadows shifted through the parking lot's

floodlights. Jagged shapes, like flakes of sky, scattered in the breeze. Bats. Once he noticed, he couldn't stop seeing them. They mingled with his eyelashes when he blinked. His phone hummed.

I trust you Lance. See you tomorrow.

He exhaled. Turned off his phone. Moonlight washed over his face. Bats swarmed. Inside, an empty seat next to Dakota. Waiting for him.

One more night.

17

Back in The Float, Breanna had taken Lance's seat.

"Hey Wildman," she said, hitting him with her tractor-beam smile. "Who were you talking to?"

"My mom."

"Whoa," Rocco said. "Wildman has a mom."

"Crazy," Meebs said, chewing fries. He'd ordered a grilled cheese.

"Let me get you a chair," Breanna said. She grabbed one from a nearby table and wedged it between her and Rocco. Lance sat. He did not want this chair.

"Thanks."

"Yeah," she said. "Got to work together, right?" She poured him a beer, slid it over. Lance did not touch it.

"I just want to make sure our stories are straight," she said. "With the police."

"Goddamn earthquake," Rocco said. Beer sloshed in his glass. Silverware pecked at the sides of plates.

"Hey." Breanna planted a hand on his knee. "Relax."

Lance felt every one of her nails through his jeans. Tingling raced up his thigh in a warm, pleasant way. He wished it hadn't felt like that.

"C'mon," Meebs said, reaching for his wallet. "Let's bully the jukebox."

"Good plan," Dakota said.

The two of them slid out and stacked up a playlist and everyone drank more. Another few pitchers and the whole crew was laughing. How could he be afraid of Officer Perkins? Or anything at all? He'd hide in the walk-in. Jump a train. And how could he stay mad at Breanna? She was pretty and quick and kept saying *Wildman*. Dakota was talking to him, looking at him. Music played, and the latest in a string of '90s pop ballads faded out on the jukebox.

"Hey," Rocco said. "Did you just *ugh*?"

"Ugh?" Lance asked.

"Oh yeah," Dakota said. "Just then, you said *uggggggghh*."

Breanna laughed.

"Oh, right," Lance said. "That song."

"Hey! I love that song," Meebs said.

"Just the ending," Lance said, raking a hand through his hair. "Songs should end." Fingers against his scalp felt good. He ran his hand through his hair but wished the fingers belonged to someone else. He stared at Dakota.

"Don't all songs end?" Dakota said.

"Oh no. Not in the twenty-first century they don't. Songs don't end anymore. They just fade out!" His hand struck the edge of a plate, catapulting his fork. It crashed into Meebs's water glass.

"Hey-ooo," Meebs said.

"I've seen that look before," Rocco said. "When I stepped on his cheeseburger."

"It's lazy," Lance said. "A song should end on a specific series of notes. You put together a whole composition. Hook, verse, chorus, bridge, and then what? You just repeat yourself and turn down the volume? It's not an ending. It's lazy."

"Hey everyone," Rocco said. "Lance cares about this."

"I mean, would you do that in a book? Just write the same last sentence over and over again? And what about art? Like a painting—"

"Art," Meebs said to no one in particular.

"Play us a song," Breanna said, leaning forward.

"Yes," Dakota said. "Please."

"I need my horn," Lance said, pounding the table.

Mason was behind the bar, filling a pitcher.

"Mason!" Lance shouted.

"Hey," Meebs said, tapping his arm. "Don't get eighty-sixed."

"Wildman." Rocco chuckled.

"Mason!"

Hearing his name, Mason jolted to attention. Then he saw Lance and went languid. Slow and floating. No rush. He sauntered toward their table with a fresh pitcher. Lance tried to meet his eyes.

"Check out that table," Mason said, pointing to the two young couples from earlier. Their pint glasses were empty, plates cleared. "Check out their *feet*."

Under the table, their shoeless feet looked like strange little animals, huddled together for warmth. The group looked full and a little sick.

"Mason," Lance said.

"Dude. If you ask me about the horn again, I'm tossing it in the dumpster. You'll get it."

"I wasn't even going to ask you about the horn," Lance said. "What horn?"

Rocco's first real laugh broke free. Lance had never heard him laugh like that.

"Yeah?" Mason said. "So what do you need to ask me, *Wildman*?"

"Has anyone ever won a thousand dollars?"

"Who wants to know?"

"Everyone," Lance said.

"You want to spin the wheel, ace? Take off your shoes."

"No. I'm good."

"*I'm good*," Mason said, then laughed. "You could win a thousand bucks. That would leave you up nine-ninety."

"Yeah," Lance said, looking at the American flag. "That stupid bet."

"What?"

"The shoe bet," Lance said. "I mean, *I can tell you where you got your shoes?*"

"Is it stupid? Or are you stupid for taking it?"

Mason's voice, tangling with something red and fibrous, tightening down over his temples. Mason stepped closer, towering, eyes small and dark.

"You got an answer for me, buddy?"

Lance's thoughts, skidding on adrenaline. A little math. Rough calculations.

"I'll make you a bet right now."

"Yeah?" Mason said, eyes shining. "Let's hear it."

Lance reached across the table and took Breanna's wineglass.

"Hey, there's still—" she started. Lance gulped the last of her wine and set the glass in the center of the table.

"I'll bet you I can break this glass without touching it," Lance said. "And without touching the table."

"I could do that," Rocco said. He threw Lance's fork, which struck the glass with a clang.

"Jesus, Rocco!" Breanna said.

"And without throwing anything," Lance said.

"You're going to break this glass," Mason said. He picked it up, looked it over. "Without touching it. Without touching the table. Without throwing anything."

"Yeah." Lance nodded, considering micrometers of thickness, the mouth's circumference, the strength of the stem. It would be close.

"Bullshit," Mason said.

Rocco and Meebs got excited and set some rules. Lance couldn't leave the bar, nor use anything that wasn't already in The Float. If there was a question about the winner, the group would vote.

"Okay," Mason said. "How much do you want to bet?"

"Ten bucks," Lance said. "I want my ten bucks back."

The whole table laughed. Strangers were stopping mid-conversation and coming closer. An audience.

"Ten bucks?" Mason said, puffing up. "How about a thousand?" Lance's heart stuttered. Throat clenched. People were watching now, and the attention of the crowd trapped him and Mason like two bugs in a jar.

"I don't have a thousand dollars," Lance said.

"Bet your car," Mason said.

A mosquito whine in Lance's ears.

"It doesn't run," Lance said slowly.

"I'll take it as scrap." Mason's little smile. Those eyes. No real color at all. The surrounding faces were like tiny spotlights, heating him up. Burning his cheeks.

"It's on," Lance said.

Applause, hoots. Meebs drummed on the table with his hands.

"Bring me my trumpet," Lance said.

"What?" Mason asked.

"I'm allowed to use anything in the bar. So bring me my trumpet. Now."

Mason argued, but the group forced him to go. Rocco went along, *Just to be sure.* Everyone in The Float had circled around their table. Their mumbling spun around words like *thousand* and *car* and *Wildman*, then the world narrowed to a tulip-shaped wine-glass with lip prints like tiny pink tire treads. A good target.

He hadn't done this in two years. The first time, it took over an hour. He'd blown the Wild Thing in Jonathan's basement until his cheeks were puckered balloons and his bottom lip was stretched and screaming, ready to pop and wreck his embouchure for life. Those long, high notes. They could do that.

Lance reached for the glass.

"Hey," Meebs said. "Can't touch it."

"I haven't started yet." He held its base against the table, dipped his index finger in beer, then traced the rim until it made a bright, metallic squeak. He pressed harder, listening, curling his fingers forward and back around the lip until the sharp sounds smoothed themselves into a long, resonant ring.

The glass trembled at C-sharp.

"Hands off the glass," Mason said.

"Hands off my horn," Lance said.

He snatched the horn from Mason, just like that. A coolness washed over him, pouring down his neck and shoulders, opening his lungs. His horn. That familiar weight. He unsnapped the case and it was fine, everything fine, polished and ready.

"Wild Thing," Meebs said. A statement of fact. No one laughed.

The instrument snapped into Lance's hands. His thumb, clicking into the saddle; second finger, snug in the ring. Perfect. He touched his lips to cool brass, angled the bell toward the wineglass. He blasted a quick test note. The stem trembled like a nervous dog.

"He gets a minute," Mason said. "That's the rule."

"There's no time limit," Lance said.

Mason was talking, then Lance blew and kept blowing. His horn was the only sound. Brass and hot air, lips buzzing, stinging, lungs squeezing air through the leadpipe and slipping around the scale until he found C-sharp, already panting. Too much beer. He pulled the mouthpiece away, remoistened his lips.

"No way," someone in the crowd muttered.

Impossible.

Forget it.

Voices. He'd erase them by playing harder. His lips buzzed. He hit C-sharp right away and rode the note hard, until the glass was singing back. A high-pitched, warbling cry—a summer cricket, a broken refrigerator. Lips throbbed, glass singing louder. Blood burned in his face and his knees went slack and a dark tunnel squeezed in around his eyes. Floating, falling.

The glass popped like a rifle shot.

Shattered glass pinging off flatware, spraying pebbles all over the floor. He was breathing, trying not to faint. Swimmy in the room and oh the screams! Applause! Shaking, and it was people shaking him. Hands on his back. Cheers and ringing between his ears. He opened his eyes. Mason, shaking his head. Mason, saying:

"No way. Nice trick, but no way."

"What do you mean *No way*," Rocco said.

"He touched it," Mason said.

"No he didn't," Meebs said.

"Yeah he did," Mason said, standing tall.

"Touched it with what?" Rocco asked.

"With air waves."

"Air waves?" Stone said, squeezing in. "Air waves, Mason?"

"Let's vote on it," Dakota said. "Who thinks Lance won the bet?"

Dakota, Meebs, Breanna, Rocco, and Stone raised their hands.

"You weren't even here, dumbass," Mason said, punching Stone in the chest.

The group stared at Mason, a hard ring of faces.

"Okay," Mason said. His brow smoothed. He snapped on a smile. "You win buddy."

He gave Lance's hand a swift pump.

Another round of cheers, hands slapping Lance's back and shoulders. He could pay for his car! He could stay at the Trainsong! He'd use the Wild Thing to shatter his phone and do whatever the hell he wanted!

"Pay up, bitch!" Meebs said. He was bouncing, hair flopping. Ready to drop on all fours and gallop around the bar.

"I will," Mason said. "But there's no time limit on the money either. Right?" Mason squeezed Lance's shoulder. A sticky, unpleasant feeling. Then he wove off through the crowd. Disappeared behind the bar.

"He'll pay," Rocco said.

"Has to," Breanna said. "Too many witnesses."

Breanna touched Lance's back and everyone was happy, sitting around the table together. Faces, so bright. And all these people, their glances and congratulations charging him up until everything was so smooth and light that he could tip off his chair and drift through their warm current and never touch the ground. Then the bar was closing, and Lance was outside.

They were all bunched together by the front door, waiting for Stone.

"Leave his ass," Rocco said.

"His brain," Meebs said. "He has problems with his brain."

"I'll get Stone," Lance heard himself say.

That might've been a mistake. Back inside, the wooden floor was uneven. He tried to hold steady. Neon lights floated in red, gold, and blue slashes, scribbling the air like fluorescent markers, wobbling around the face of the man behind the bar. Mason's father. Mason's father, now talking to him.

"What?"

"I'll bet you ten bucks I can tell you where you got your shoes," he repeated.

And for a startling moment, this man was Mason and Lance had been trapped. Time had flung itself forward thirty years, and he was still at The Float. Lance looked down at his hands. Not wrinkled. He looked past his hands to his shoes.

"Baring, Washington," Lance said. "I got my shoes in Baring, Washington."

"Okay, wise guy." His mouth puckered. "What do you want?"

"Can I talk to Stone?"

"Stone's working."

But there was no one in the service window. Just a to-go box in a plastic sack. The front door rattled. Coming in behind him, two women. One was tiny, bird-boned with a gray thimble of a head. The other was overweight, an avalanche of orange hair, thick arms and legs. They looked like a pair of comedians, except neither one was smiling.

"We're closed!" Mason's father shouted. "Closed, ladies!" They kept shuffling forward, like they couldn't hear or didn't want to. What was wrong with them? Mason's father stalked down the bar and disappeared, leaving Lance alone. The women were coming straight for him.

"Stone!" Lance called into the kitchen. "Stone!"

Stone's face popped into view. The bandages were gone. The skin around his eyes was purple and wet-looking, but he was smiling. In the little rectangle of the service window, he looked like a tragic theater puppet.

"What's up, dude?" Stone asked.

"We're heading over to Meebs's place. Everyone's ready."

"Excuse me," Orange Hair said, suddenly at the bar. "Do you mind if we see a menu?"

"It smells delightful," Bird Bones said, leaning into view.

"Kitchen's closed, ladies," Stone said. "Sorry."

"Could you even do a sandwich?" Orange Hair asked. "We're starving. There's nothing out here."

"Everything's sanitized," Stone said, looking uncomfortable.

"Anything?" Bird Bones asked.

"I can make you a few Bloody Marys," Stone said. "They've got a lot of stuff in them. Celery."

The women exchanged a chilling look. An *aw-shucks* look, but not the aw-shucks of stepping in a puddle with new shoes. The conclusive aw-shucks when, after a series of flight delays and poor beverage service, the 747's last engine blows and you're headed straight into the Pacific. This was the end of a capital Bad Luck Day. The kind of day that can kill you. Bird Bones was wringing her hands, which Lance had never seen anyone actually do.

"No, just all day," Bird Bones said to Orange Hair, a little gasp of a sound.

Something rustled, violently. Lance turned his head. Neon swam. Stone was gone and so was the to-go bag. In the kitchen, clanking flatware. He came out with two steaming plates of corned beef and cabbage. The women blinked at the food like they'd just woken up and were still trying to figure out what was real.

"Look what turned up," Stone said.

"Goodness," Bird Bones said, staring at her plate.

"How much—?" Orange Hair began.

"On the house," Stone said, then to Lance, "Let's go."

On the way out, Lance glanced back at the ladies. They both looked small from the other end of the restaurant, and they hadn't started eating yet. They were still. Staring down at their food.

One movement: Orange Hair reached out her right hand, and Bird Bones took it.

18

Outside, Dakota was the only one left.

"What happened?" Stone asked.

"Mason got pissy," Dakota said. "They went to Meebs's place."

"You stuck around for the handsome ones, eh?" Stone said.

"The parents'-basement scene is played out," Dakota said.

"Really?" Stone said. "I thought that scene had maybe a year left."

"Nope," she said.

"And he's got pizza."

"His parents' pizza," Dakota said. "Those are his parents' special pizzas. He made a point of that. No one is getting pizza."

"Can we go for tacos?" Stone said. "I'm goddamned starving."

"Tacos are far," Dakota said.

"Ah. Tacos are far," Stone said. They laughed at this, a joke between them.

Dakota drove and Stone rode in the front. He didn't even ask if Lance wanted shotgun. As they pulled out, Stone lifted his right foot and crossed it over his knee. A big black boot, tattered around the heel. Its chunky sole was plastered with food scraps: lettuce, bits of cheese. Angled straight at Dakota.

"Ah! Stone! *Wuuuuug!* Boot! Boot!" Dakota screamed. Stone dropped his foot.

"Sorry. Forgot about the sludge. I'll have to hose 'em down at home."

"Looks like you've had those a while," Lance said.

"Yeah?" Stone said. "So?"

"I just meant you've never thrown them."

"Oh, hell no," Stone said. "Never will. That wheel is rigged."

"Can we not talk about the wheel?" Dakota said.

"That wheel is gonna be your world, sweetheart," Stone said. "Wheels and shoes."

"Maybe for a few months," Dakota said.

"That's what I said. *A few months.* Now, two years later."

"Good thing we're not the same person."

"Yeah," Stone said. "Good thing." He rubbed his sinuses, breathed in.

"Where's home tonight?" she asked.

"Randall's."

She shook her head. "Your dad's such an asshole."

"Mmm-hmm."

Lance's head was still warm and buzzing from the beer. It was hard to hear from his position in the backseat, so he just leaned back. Stone cracked a window to smoke and wind whipped around him, the scent of evergreens mixing with cigarettes. Streetlights painted their faces white and yellow, and Stone was sitting so straight, chin out and grinning. Dakota put on the same ghost song she'd played for Lance the day before. Maybe she played that song for everyone.

Twenty minutes later they pulled into a fiesta-colored drive-through and Stone ordered a giant sack of tacos. He was a buck short on his order, so Lance covered him.

"Careful," Dakota said. "He's like a dog. Feed him once and he'll never go away." Stone muttered *thanks* under crinkling wrappers and Dakota pulled out, leaving the sad island of a strip mall. Tacos had been far. Far from The Float. Farther from Bend.

"Stone," Lance said, leaning forward.

"Yes, Wildman," Stone managed through his tacos.

"What should I tell the cops?"

"About the accident?" he asked. "I was driving."

"That seems like a bad plan."

"Why?" Stone asked.

"You'll go to jail."

He shrugged. "Better me than her."

"I don't think so," Lance said.

"You don't? Why the hell not?" Stone said, half turning in his seat.

"You play guitar. Breanna doesn't play anything."

Stone laughed. Dakota looked straight ahead. They passed a final cluster of streetlights. Darkness solidified, swallowing their faces. In the faint glow of the dashboard, Dakota's and Stone's hands were almost close enough to touch.

"Plus, you make good fries," Lance said. It came out like a hiccup. He didn't mean to say it. He hadn't liked it when others had said it. But they laughed and Dakota put both hands back on the wheel.

"He does make good fries," Dakota said.

"Damn straight," Stone said. He half turned again. "Why do you care what happens, Wildman?"

"I saved your life," Lance said. "I feel responsible for you."

"Uh-oh," Dakota said. "That's why he bought you a taco."

"That's going to be a bitch," Stone said. "You'll have to send a lot of care packages when I'm on the inside. Bake me cookies."

"Conjugal visits," Dakota said.

"Desperate times, Lance," Stone said.

"I'm telling the cops the truth," Lance said.

"Naw, man. Think about it. Small-town kid drops out of high school, gets discharged from the military and kicked out of his house. He then works as a fry cook. He drinks too much. Hangs out with unsavory characters. Goes to jail. Fade to black. That's the story."

"That's the wrong ending."

"What? That's the perfect ending!"

"Not for you. Your story ends in Telluride," Lance said. "That's what you told me."

Oncoming headlights flooded the car. In the wash of light, Stone looked like one of those old photographs, a young picture of someone's grandfather. The car went black.

"Telluride," Stone said. "So let's go."

"To Telluride?" Dakota asked.

"Yeah," Stone said. "We've got a half tank of gas and two packets of hot sauce."

"I'm in," Lance said.

"Don't tempt me," Dakota said. "My bag's packed. We just have to swing by the Trainsong."

"Nope," Stone said. "Can't swing by anywhere. It'll break our momentum. We have to go right now, or we'll never make it."

"Just like the hot springs," Dakota said.

"Yeah!" Stone said. "Exactly! Oh, man. What a trip."

The idea flared in the dark car and suddenly everything was possible. Plans came rapid-fire. Dakota plunged them down back roads, hugging curves and listing the highways that could tie their trip together across four states—perfect-sounding numbers—the 90 to the 80 to the 70, like a countdown to destiny, and Stone was chopping the trip into shifts and Lance was organizing snacks and coffee breaks and the idea had taken hold.

Telluride!

And it was going to be like this one trip they'd taken, and this other trip they'd talked about, and this other trip they should've taken, but didn't. Then Stone leaned back and sighed and said:

"It would be amazing."

And the word *would* hit the atmosphere like air hissing from the tires. Dakota relaxed her foot on the accelerator. The conversation slowed and the car was drifting back to the place it had come from, rolling downhill toward The Float, then past it to a series of empty lots. Clusters of trailers. A maze of steel siding and small yards and, yes, they would drop Stone here.

Dakota parked outside a blue double-wide. The light fixtures looked like they'd been cobwebbed for Halloween.

"Hey," Stone said. "This doesn't look like Telluride."

"Must've made a wrong turn," Dakota said.

"Well, hell."

Stone climbed out and paused by the front door. Then he disappeared around the side of the trailer.

"Will he be able to get in?" Lance asked.

"We'll wait," Dakota said. Lance got out of the car and took Stone's place, riding shotgun. A new experience up front. Just a few inches closer. But like distance from an open flame, inches mattered.

Dakota breathed a heavy sigh. She set her eyes on him. "Hey."

"Hey," Lance said.

He had to ask. The question was ricocheting in his brain, doing damage.

"Did you ever have a thing for Stone?"

"Stone!" she said, not quite rattled enough. "Maybe. Just for a minute though. No longer than a minute. When he was still James. Lifetimes ago."

A light went on inside, and Lance exhaled. It didn't matter. They were alone now.

She drove. The smile hadn't left her lips and her hand was on the console between them. It was just resting there, fingers gently parted, and one of two things was certain. Dakota either:

1) completely, desperately wanted him to hold her hand; or

2) just liked to put her hand on the console.

He stared. Four fingers and a thumb. Ratios and probability. Harder than a multivariate equation. Worse than a story problem. The Sphinx's riddle: a girl's open hand on the console.

Lance's hands were still folded in his lap when they pulled into the Trainsong parking lot. He'd blown it. Ruined the whole night, his whole life, by not holding this girl's hand on the way home from tacos. But Dakota didn't say goodbye or go inside. She grabbed two plastic chairs from her front patio and walked them to where the parking lot's edge crumbled into weeds.

"C'mon," she said. "Let's catch the trainsong."

The ground was uneven. They had to work to find a place where the chairs' wobbly legs would hold steady in the dirt. They stuck the chairs side by side with a view of the treed slope and the tracks, silver lines under moonlight. The train was coming. They sat, Dakota on his right.

"Almost," Dakota said. She turned and dark hair spread over her left cheek, stirring her scent into the air. Lance's legs shook. The plastic chair jumped, trying to buck him down the hill.

He should think about something else.

The physics of a plastic chair, of a train. The approaching *calack*, a broadband noise caused by vibrations of the wheels on the railheads, the irregularities of running surfaces. According to his AP science textbook, millions of dollars and decades of research had been unable to silence the sound of an oncoming train. Compressions and refractions, closing in, shaking Lance's chest as if they were coming from inside. He could pop, like the wineglass.

He was sitting next to Dakota in the dark.

"Almost," Dakota said. "The light will come just there."

She pointed with one hand, the other open and still. Time thickened and Lance looked down. Her hand, dangling in the space between chairs. Fingers curled slightly, as if being trailed through a stream. In his chest, a hammer striking steel. His hand crossing through still time—this impossible distance. Fingers brushing Dakota's. Clasping.

Holding her hand. Those eyes.

"You," she says.

She squeezes his hand and the train's light pricks the darkness, its horn screaming across the field: a giddy, nauseating sound. Blood beats in his temples. A bone-shaking rhythm. He lifts Dakota's hand to his lap as if it will run away. Vanish with the train. The sound bears down and the train is passing, a drumbeat, a strumming, a whisper, suggestion. Gone.

But this hand. This impossible thing.

He cannot look back at Dakota's eyes, because he has never seen a hand before. Never knuckles. Never the half-moons of nails, the crisscrossing in the folds of skin. To touch her hand freely this way, not brushing, not accidental, is the first real thing he's done in his life. The rest of the world will bend around this hand.

Dakota shifts in her seat. Her eyes are hungry. Alert. He can't look. The weeds are papery in the moonlight, and the trees are standing still and THIS HAND! Crickets and toads pile their voices into the darkness, filling the hollow of silence the train left behind.

"No one has ever held my hand before," Dakota says. She lifts their clasped hands up between them, so they can both see. "God, it's so nice, isn't it?"

He looks at her blankly, hears her words. How can she talk about this while it's happening? "I was afraid to sit next to you," Lance says. She is stroking the flesh of his palm just above the wrist, and he can't stop telling her things. "I was afraid to touch that tree."

"Yes," she says, nodding.

Her fingertips send shivery bolts up his wrist, all the way to his shoulder. She presses her thumb into the center of his palm, massaging it. Loosening his whole body through his hand.

"Are you glad you stayed another night?" she asks.

"So glad," he says. He's shaking. Hard to smile. Sensations all twisted together. He wants to cry and laugh and shiver and scream.

"Are you happy here?" Lance asks, watching her fingers.

"I'm happy now," she says. "What about you, Lance? Are you happy?"

"I don't know."

"I think happy people mostly go to bed before midnight," she says. "We're up with all the other ghosts."

And this is just hands. Nothing wrong with touching hands. But it's delicate work, holding hands with Dakota. Like crossing a room with an overfull glass of water. The rim of the liquid curves up, suspended by pressure, trembling with each step. So you just keep walking, hoping you can keep it all nice and even and slow.

"Hey," she says, pulling his hand close, right against her leg. Her leg. He is touching her leg. "Are you sure you're real?"

"Yes," he says. His teeth chatter. All this trembling.

She opens her lips to speak. A creak of moisture. "Not a ghost?"

He's holding this glass, moving so slow, so careful—but now

their foreheads are nearly touching. Frozen time thaws to a rush and they're running downhill, the ground tipping forward, still tipping, and Lance's feet pedal air, and his stomach drops and he loses the Earth and presses his lips to hers. Their mouths open to receive each other and everything is spilling, everything, everywhere.

19

The kiss is music when notes disappear. No beginning or ending or wondering or stopping. The kiss is its own thing, and the only thing. His neck and shoulders relax and he and Dakota pour into one another until everything is humming. He is breathing for the first time in eighteen years and thinking:

This can happen. This is possible.

20

The kiss vacuums away space and time and crashes them raw and squinting into the sunrise. The daylight is stealing their shadows. Scooping out the deep black corners and glazing the world in silver.

The sun wasn't invited.

"Sorry," he says.

"For what?"

For stopping. For being human. For the sun.

"I don't know if that was supposed to happen."

"That's the only thing that's supposed to happen." She clutches his arm. "Ever."

They hold hands. They each grab a chair and carry it back to the Trainsong. Everything is grayed by the dawn. He does not want to say goodbye in this parking lot.

"Your goodbyes keep getting better," she says. "Maybe I'll slash your tires."

"Be careful. I know where you live."

It's too small and plain. He should be shoving off from shore. Climbing into the belly of a helicopter, shouting over chopping blades. Instead, she's bouncing back and forth on the balls of her feet, and they aren't looking at each other anymore. Their hug is quick and awkward. Too much light. No time left to kiss.

Lance crosses the parking lot and walks up the wooden steps to his room. He takes out his keys and looks back. Dakota is still outside, looking up at him.

"I don't want to stop looking at you," he says.

His voice strikes the early-morning stillness like a stone in a pond. Was that actually him speaking? Could other people hear, or only Dakota?

"You don't have to," she says.

She has her keys out. She is standing beside her door.

"How do we do this?" he asks.

"Get your keys ready. We'll go on the count of three."

Lance slips his key into the lock. Braces his shoulder against the door.

"One. Two. Three!"

They open and slam their doors in unison and he has woken up from his perfect dream to find himself in a motel with crumbling drywall and the smell of toast and two angry cats.

A different place from three seconds ago. A different planet.

He wants to sleep. Slip back into this dream of Dakota. But the things in the motel walls are scampering and chewing. Teeth on wood. Again, he closes his eyes. He tries to hear the scratching differently, like soft footsteps, coming up the stairs. He can almost convince himself, repeating the words. A new mantra:

It's her. It's her. It's her.

21

Heavy feet, pounding up the steps.

Lance bolts up in a panic. It's too bright. Sunlight, baking him in his bedsheets.

What time is it? What day is it?

Whoever is coming sounds like they have cinder blocks strapped to the soles of their shoes. Slow, clomping footsteps, like when his father used to play bogeyman. Memories flare up from the night before. A shattering wineglass. Green plastic chairs. Those hands. Dakota's mouth.

What have I done?

Whoever is coming knows. Miriam knows. Everyone knows. Somehow there are pictures, and everyone has seen them.

Leaping out of bed, he bolts to the bathroom. Checks his face for evidence: lip prints, hickeys. His cheeks and lips are clean. His face says *nothing happened last night.* He looks at his ears, remembering. His neck, remembering. Oh, his neck. He runs his tongue over the back of his lips.

Evidence!

His lip tissue is pulpy. Tastes like iron. His mouth hadn't been used so hard since his first kiss with Marcia Buckman in the tree house by Fireman's Park. They'd mashed faces, trapped as if by electrocution, teeth and tongues banging with desperate violence.

THUMP THUMP THUMP

Pounding on his motel door—a staccato arrangement of fist and wood.

"Lance Hendricks?" A man's voice.

THUMP THUMP THUMP

Lance drops to his belly. Face to carpet. Breathing odors of mud and cleaning solution. He makes certain promises. He will never kiss Dakota again. Never kiss anyone but Miriam. He'll marry her, in fact. He will go home immediately, apologize to his mother, and propose to Miriam.

Just as soon as this man goes away.

Creaking wood. Rustling papers and the crackle of a radio. Steps, clomping across the landing, moving downstairs. Lance tiptoes to the window and sneaks a glance through the blinds. A police cruiser is angled in front of Cheri's office.

"Holy shit," Lance says.

He freezes. The tabby cats stare, anticipating his next move. There are mysterious, small-town forces at work here. Police involvement. He's all tangled up with Stone. He's gone too far with Dakota. She belongs to this town, and this town will have its revenge. He pulls on his thrift shop clothes and stares at the mirror.

He needs to be The Lance Hendricks Machine. The machine

that plowed through six AP classes and hundreds of hours of pep-band practice, endless disappointments in Miriam's basement, lectures from his mother. A machine that gets things done, and runs on a few simple truths:

You are valedictorian.

You are the first-chair trumpet player.

You have a full-ride scholarship.

Miriam Seavers is in love with you.

And nothing is different. Only the days have changed. It's Tuesday instead of Saturday. His speech is in three days instead of six. This is now a story problem, and all he needs are the right numbers. Phone numbers, road numbers, bus route numbers, dollar numbers.

He will solve this equation for home.

The number 5 bus can drop him on Route 2. It's a 25-minute ride, then a 10-minute, half-mile walk to Macland's, *X* dollars for the repair, 17 miles back to the Trainsong, 400 miles to Bend.

He has the figures, and The Lance Hendricks Machine is moving. He is across the empty parking lot before anyone can see him. He is waiting 17 minutes for the number 5 bus and 47 minutes later he is standing outside Macland's.

But his car is not there.

Not outside, where it should be. It's still inside. Behind the Plexiglas, on a lift. No one is working on his car. The smells of popcorn and burnt coffee. The mechanics are wearing the same clothes, drinking the same soda. Only without Dakota, it's no longer funny. Standing at the counter is the man from yesterday. The one with the purple tongue.

"I'm the owner of the Buick," Lance tells him.

"Yeah? Lucky you."

"I really need my car today," Lance says.

"We're working as fast as we can, kid." His mouth makes a tight purple *O* when he purses his lips. The white badge on his blue uniform reads: CLEM.

"What's wrong with the car, Clem?" Lance says.

"Plenty of things," Clem says. "It won't start."

"I'm aware of that."

Clem's eyes shift, and Lance can hear it coming. The approaching sentence, like an atmospheric pressure change and then he actually says it:

"We've also noticed the check engine light is on."

Check engine light. The words echo with Clem's voice. In Lance's head, the pop of a broken lightbulb.

"You know," Clem continues. "That little light on the dash."

Nails dig into Lance's palms. He has two fists. Targets include Clem's big jaw and a plastic cup of pens. Lance swings hard and smashes the cup. Pens scatter. The cup does a limp cartwheel across the floor.

"Hey!" Clem says. "Those are our pens!"

"Check engine? The dummy light, Clem? Do I look like a dummy to you?" Lance chokes back the words *ACT score. Valedictorian.*

Clem shrugs.

"Get my car off the lift. Now."

Clem mumbles something and walks away. Fifteen minutes later, the Buick is coming down and Clem has an invoice with him, bright yellow paper with perforated sides and a bold black number in a box.

"Five hundred and fifty dollars?" Lance says. "For what? What did you even fix?"

"Your starter."

"There was nothing wrong with my starter!"

"It was blown. Looked recent, too. Someone had been cranking on it pretty hard."

Just crank on that real hard.

"You're kidding me," Lance says. "Three hundred dollars for diagnostics? I'm not paying that."

"Then you're not getting your keys." Clem lifts his chin a little, as if inviting someone to punch him there. Another blue-suited mechanic walks up behind him. A show of force.

"And we're gonna need you to pick up those pens," the other mechanic says.

Lance stares at them, and a sudden coolness washes over him.

"That's it," Lance says.

"What?" Clem says.

The red lever. Break glass in case of emergency. Lance withdraws his phone from his pocket.

"What are you doing?" Clem asks.

"I am calling my mother."

"Oooo," Clem says. The other mechanic laughs.

Lance will pay the price for pulling The Mom Lever. She interrupts his *hello,* and her opening salvo has all the words: *responsibility, ungrateful, loyalty, disaster, ruined.* But he can endure. This is not about words. It's about numbers. Minutes and dollars. And she will only talk so long before he can explain that her only son is being taken advantage of by cruel small-town mechanics.

"Now what's going on?" she finally asks.

He tells her.

"So let me get this straight," she begins softly. She repeats back the details, then Lance stands up and gets ready for the show. Clem does not hear his ringing phone the same way Lance does. Clem even answers with a smirk, as if his world is not about to end. It takes his mom about ten seconds to shatter his smirk all over the floor. Poor Clem's smirk may never be the same again. It only gets worse. Clem, not knowing Lance's mother, attempts to speak. He jerks and sputters. He twists his head one direction, then another. He makes the mistake of saying *Listen, lady.*

Lance flinches, and Clem goes pale. His eyes widen with horror. He looks out the window, over his shoulder. Like someone is coming for him. Lance can't watch. Quietly, he walks over and picks up the pens.

His mother calls him back with that straight-out-of-combat edge in her voice.

"That's it for the Buick. I'm having it junked out."

"Mom—"

"I've had it, Lance. Your car is off life support."

"How am I supposed to get home?"

"I've made all the arrangements. Just get yourself back to the hotel."

"Okay, but—"

"And now I understand there is a police officer looking for you?" She laughs, not a happy sound. "Why didn't you tell me about the accident?"

"I didn't really have—"

"You just need to get home. Immediately. That's what needs to happen. Get yourself to the hotel."

"Okay, Mom."

Back at the counter, Clem pushes some papers at him.

"Special lady you got there," Clem says. "I'd be doing you a favor, keeping you here."

Lance thinks about this. Stares at the counter. "Is there another mechanic in town?"

"For this car? No."

"What about—is it Robert? Robert's Auto Repair?" Lance remembers the bizarre advertisement from the phone book. *A REAL MECHANIC.*

"Robert!" Clem says, suddenly coming to life. "That guy? Yeah. He'll take your car as a down payment. If he'll take your car at all."

"Is he good?"

"He's good with problem cars." Clem chews the inside of his cheek. "He's the best."

"Maybe I'll go see him," Lance says.

"Your mom had better be rich, kid. And you'd better not pull any of your grade-school b.s. over at Robert's. He'll feed you to his fish."

Outside, the air is quivering with a grass-crackling, sticky-tar-bubble heat. The tow truck his mother called is waiting for him.

A bleak shade of green, like something decommissioned from the military. The driver has a wattle chin and nicotine-stained teeth. Instead of *hello* he says:

"Junkyard?"

His eyes are small and dark, buried in the folds of his face.

"How much to go to Robert's?" Lance asks, tapping his wallet.

"Robert's Auto Repair? I got orders to go to the junkyard."

"How much?" Lance asks, heart pounding.

"How much you got?"

Lance has thirty-three dollars. The man takes the money without counting it and Lance climbs into the cab, which is neat, but rank. Stale fries and wet laundry. No air-conditioning. No identification in the truck. No pictures, no stitched oval name tag. The man says nothing, and turns onto the highway.

Hot pavement stretches out like a quivering blue ribbon. Miles later, the driver twists the truck onto a narrow lane that winds through tall walls of ferns and blackberries. Sun filters down in blobs and the sky has a silver tint, like they've traveled into a new layer of atmosphere. A gap opens in the vegetation, and they're crunching down a gravel road.

The truck idles in front of a two-story cyclone fence. Concertina wire spools around the top. Blades like silver butterflies. The driver stares at Lance.

Small, dark eyes.

"What?" Lance says.

The driver rolls down his window, leans out, and punches a code into a keypad. The tall gate splits, swinging inward without a sound. A flawless mechanism. They pull inside, cresting a hill. An industrial maze sprawls below, a factory that manufactured something, maybe aluminum. They descend and are lost in tight gray corridors. Steel shutters and shop doors. They drive to a dead end, then make a hidden turn.

The driver stops. Stares.

"What?" Lance says.

"End of the line."

The driver points a meaty index finger. Like a horror movie. Like he might open his mouth wide and scream. Lance jerks back, looks over his shoulder. A small yellow awning over a gray door.

ROBERT'S AUTO REPAIR

Lance exhales.

"What?" the driver says.

"I wasn't sure where we were going," Lance says.

"I went where you told me to go."

"Right," Lance says. "I'm just glad to be here."

"Are you?" A hiss, and the Buick's wheels touch the ground. "That's because you haven't met Robert."

22

Robert's office is sparse and neat. A well-lit collection of ninety-degree angles. A giant wooden desk. On the desk, a single black portfolio. And a wall-size aquarium at the back of the room with the biggest fish Lance has ever seen.

The fish is several feet long with scalloped silver scales like layers of freshly minted dimes. It has a blade of a lower lip, protruding at a forty-five-degree angle. The fish doesn't swim. It *paces*. Like the grizzly Lance once saw at the zoo with his mother, the day he came to understand the word *cagey*.

A door bangs open.

The man stepping inside looks ready for a postapocalyptic gunfight. Torn leather jacket, bounty hunter sunglasses. Black hair combed in neat, greasy rows. He shoves the sunglasses up on his forehead and his dark eyes roll around the room like overlubricated ball bearings. Those eyes will not stop.

"I'm Robert," he says. "And that's my platinum arowana." His voice is rough. Words crumble out of his mouth.

"Beautiful fish," Lance says.

"Ha!" Robert says, crossing behind the desk. "They call them monkey fish. Want to know why?"

"Yeah."

"Because they *eat* monkeys." Robert stares at the fish as if he hates it. "Solitary son of a bitch. Can't put another fish in there. Just try."

The front door bangs open again and a young man enters with a clattering steel box. Robert jolts, his tattered coat ruffling like plumage.

"Shit, Douglas!" he shouts. "Way to make an entrance."

"Sorry, sorry." Douglas is just a few years older than Lance. He carries a stack of papers to a filing cabinet.

"So what brings you here?" Robert says, turning his wild eyes on Lance. "That Buick out back?"

"Yeah," Lance says. "Macland's said you're good with problem cars."

"Oh, that's what they said, did they?" Robert throws himself into the leather chair behind the desk, rocking backward. "What they *meant* was, I actually fix things. What they *meant* was, I don't sit around giving grandmas lube jobs all day. What they *meant* was, I'm a *real* mechanic."

"That's great," Lance says. "I was—"

"I'll tell you something else," he says. "I expect to be paid for my work. I'll tell you—I'm not doing this for fun. Am I doing this shit for fun, Douglas?"

"No sir," Douglas says.

"No sir," Robert says, leaning forward. "I'm a rabid capitalist businessman. I'm here to make money. Right, Douglas?"

"Right," Douglas says.

"Kids don't feed themselves, do they Douglas?"

"Nope."

"Now let's get out and see that car."

Robert's garage is a two-story cathedral. Only five vehicles inside: gleaming, foreign things, tiny and colorful, more candy than car. Two are up on giant lifts bookended by machines the size of mainframe computers. And there's space. So much space. Lance's Buick is in the middle of it all. Isolated as if contagious.

Robert walks up and pops the hood, exposing the engine.

"Are you kidding me?" he says, a vein near his left temple suddenly visible.

"What?" Lance says, peering over his shoulder.

Robert reaches into the engine block and plucks out a chunk of yellow glop. "You see this?"

Lance nods.

"Insulation. Some sonofabitch squirted insulation on your hose." He flicks the chunk against the wall like a cigarette butt.

"And this!" He backhands a limp piece of plastic, then tears it off.

Lance flinches. "Is that—"

"I'll tell you what that is," Robert says. He flaps a wide palm in front of his cheek, like a leaf. "Some shade-tree bullshit. This is out under the maple with your football buddies and a case of Oly."

Lance almost laughs, but Robert is tearing into the guts of his engine block. He twists his wrist and yanks out a giant piece of metal, like pulling a tooth.

"And this?"

"Airflow sensor," Lance says.

"Sure, if you're driving a Dongfeng in Beijing, goddamnit!" Robert says, spittle flying. "But we're not in China, are we? We buy American here, don't we, Douglas?"

"Yes sir," Douglas calls back.

"I won't put this part back in your car," he says. "You could beg me. *Pweese, Wobert. Pweese give me a cheap Chinese part.* Why? So it can break in six months? So we can buy more shit parts from China? No!" He thrusts the part at Lance's chest.

"I think the original airflow sensor is still on the backseat," Lance says.

Robert glances in back. "Yeah, good."

"Any idea what's wrong?"

"You got two issues." Robert's hands writhe like mice in his jacket pockets. "You got what was wrong in the first place. Then you got what's wrong now that a couple of grease monkeys have been jerking off on your engine block."

"Geez," Lance says. "I can't believe this."

"Hey, hey," Robert says, clapping him on the back. "Don't go to the dark side, kid. Look. This is an amazing car. A '93 Buick Century, V-6 Custom? You kiddin' me? American made. Bulletproof."

His eyes were fixed, reverent. "Hell. If I had to peel out of here in any one of these pieces of shit and drive cross-country, I'd do it in this car."

"It was a gift."

"Well," he says, "someone must love you. Let's sort this out." Back in his office, Robert pulls out a black calculator, a fountain pen, and a neatly lined sheet of paper. He works with horrifying delicacy. On the wall, beside the aquarium, a framed picture Lance hadn't noticed before. A family photo crammed with at least a dozen faces. An attractive, red-haired woman stands beside Robert. Lance recognizes Douglas as the oldest kid in the picture.

"Here it is," Robert says. Lance's eyes skip to the bottom, ink figures so neat they might've been typewritten.

$1,500

"Fifteen hundred dollars?" Lance stops breathing. He touches his empty wallet.

"Just the advance authorization," Robert says, shuffling papers.

"Authorizing what?"

"Diagnostics." Lance hears himself *ugh*.

"Look," Robert says. "I can't work on a meter, kid, coming out to call you every hundred dollars' worth of work. I need full trust. I work with a clear head, and it takes as long as it takes."

"Is the car even worth fifteen hundred dollars?" Lance asks.

"Is it worth it to you?"

Lance nods. "Yeah."

"Then you just answered your own question. Sign right there, and there." Lance signs his name twice and Robert tucks the papers in a desk drawer. "Now, where do you need to be?"

"The Trainsong Motel," Lance says. "Is there a bus stop nearby?"

Robert scoffs and picks up the phone. He calls someone named Bea and asks her to *scoot right over.* About five minutes later, the red-haired woman from the picture shows up. She and Robert kiss, then she looks Lance up and down.

"The Man With The Buick," she says.

"That's me."

Bea is sweet. She has attitude, but none of the googly-eyed madness of her husband. She drives a Buick, too. A much newer, much nicer Buick. On the way to the Trainsong, Lance tells her the story of his breakdown and she really seems to listen. Her hands are small and pale and delicate on the wheel. He tries to imagine those fingers locking up with Robert's greasy metal-ripping talons and can't quite make the pieces fit.

"How many kids do you guys have?" he asks.

"Twelve," Bea says with a proud smile.

Kids don't feed themselves.

Twelve kids. Which part of their family will Buick diagnostics finance? One meal for fourteen? Robert Junior's braces? Bea drops him at the front office and gives his shoulder a squeeze.

"Robert will fix you up," she says. "He's the best."

Bea's confidence lights him up, but the feeling vanishes the instant he opens the door to his motel room. That smell. And the place is just as he left it. A wreckage of dirty clothes. Scattered papers and the awful orange duffel. He's just starting to straighten up when his phone rings.

A Bend number. And a voice from another dimension.

"Hey Lance?" the man says.

"Yes?"

"It's Mr. Leeds. Just wanted to do a quick check-in on your speech."

Mr. Leeds. The absurd voice of his guidance counselor rips him out of Washington, sucks him through the receiver, and jams him into a tiny, windowless office with the smell of sour gym clothes. He feels dizzy.

"Everything's fine," Lance says. "The speech is almost ready."

"Sure, Lance. I'm not worried, personally." Mr. Leeds is talking casually, with an under-the-breath familiarity. Like they're old buddies, just shooting the breeze. "I told your mom I'd call. You know how it is."

"Yeah," Lance says.

"So what are the chances you'll have it memorized?"

"Still working on it." Lance tries to envision a single sentence from his speech. Just one word. All he can picture is the page of required administrative signatures and student witnesses. Three peers who had attested the speech was *representative of the character of both school and speaker.*

"Hey. One thing, buddy. Please remember the part about the kids not throwing caps at the end of the ceremony. It's just chaos, you know?" Mr. Leeds laughs.

"Right. Tell them not to throw their caps."

"It's better, coming from a peer. If I were you, I'd end your speech on that note. So that's what they remember."

"I can do that."

"Great. I knew you wouldn't mind. So how did your audition go? Seattle, right?"

"It was a really good audition." Saying it, he realizes it's true. It was the best he'd ever played. Probably the best audition of his life. He looks at his horn, and his eyes sting.

"I did already send your transcripts to OSU. That's where you're headed, right?"

"Yeah. That's right." Lance squeezes his hands shut. Nails bite into palms.

"Okay, Lance. You sound kind of busy. I'll let you get back to it. See you Friday, bud!"

Many times, Lance had needed Mr. Leeds. He'd queued up to get into his office, to pore over schedules and test scores, cozying up to his desk for a peek at the roster of students to see where he fell in the rankings. Mr. Leeds had given him the special green folder where he was told to keep his speech. Another composition to memorize and play perfectly.

Lance opens the green folder. Stares at the speech.

Three knocks at his door.

TAP TAP TAP

Lance shuts the folder and drops to the floor. *Police!*

TAP TAP TAP

"Lance? Are you there?" Not the police, but he's shaking. He stands and makes the doorknob work and it's her. Dakota. Somehow Dakota, wearing a white sundress and smelling the way she smells, is right there in front of him.

"No way," she says, leaning forward. "You. Is it really you?"

"I was about to ask you the same question."

She's holding two glasses and a bottle of white wine. The glass is sweating, dripping onto painted blue wood. Her toenails, a few shades lighter. Blue like the sky.

"Can I come in?"

"Do I have to invite you?" he says. "Are you a vampire?"

"Maybe," she says.

"Then yes."

The wineglasses touch like soft chimes as she crosses the room. She sets them on the green folder, using it like a coaster. Lance laughs.

"What?" she asks.

"That's my speech. My guidance counselor just called me."

"Oh my god," she says.

"I know. It's in three days."

"No. Oh my god you have a *guidance counselor*. What am I doing?"

"Corrupting a minor."

"Guilty," she says. She twists off the bottle's cap and pours a few generous glugs in each glass.

"You're not wasting any time."

"No," Dakota says. "This is all stolen time now. We have to spend it all."

They touch glasses and drink. The wine is crisp and grassy and delicious. He's never had white wine before.

"So, this is your place," she says, pacing around the bed. "Nice."

"I've been here so long. I feel responsible for the decorations."

She laughs. "I love what you've done with it. The sailboat says

I'm a dreamer and into craft sales. While these cats say *I'm weird and maybe don't have any friends.* It's a great balance." She's looking straight at him. Not hiding. A fresh heat flushes her cheeks, like she just spent a week in Florida.

"You look different today," he says.

"Yeah?" she says. "Good different?"

"Glowing different."

"I am different today," she says.

They both drink. He's grateful for the wine.

"Not a vampire," he says, looking in the bathroom mirror. "I can see your reflection."

"Disappointed?"

"Kind of. I've always wanted to see a vampire."

"I'm over vampires," she says. "You know what I want to see?"

"What?"

"A ghost," she says. She sits on the bed and crosses her legs. The dress slides up just above her knee. "Not a little orb in a photograph, a real one. I've gone to every haunted house within a hundred miles. I've been to Aux Sable a hundred times, but it's never happened."

"That's probably good."

"Yeah. I'm not sure what I'd do."

"Run away screaming," he says.

"But I mean afterward," she says. "How could I go back to my regular life? How could I ever think about life and death and science and religion the same way? If you really think about what it means to see a ghost—it would make you a different person. It would change everything."

"So what would you do?"

"Become a Believer."

"With a capital *B*."

"Yep," Dakota says. "Like those people who see Bigfoot on a camping trip, then quit their jobs and buy an RV and recording equipment. And waders. That's all they can do. Drive around and try to see Bigfoot again."

"There are worse ways to live."

"Yeah."

"So are you shopping for RVs?"

She finishes her wine. She looks up at him.

"Nobody kisses like that, Lance. They just think they do."

Between his ears there is a white-noise seashell sound, like a long hush, and Dakota is sitting on the corner of the bed in a dress, too close and too far away. Springs tighten in his knees and calves. He could leap and crash into her body and tumble into the bed and roll into a brand-new life that would not have to be here nor Bend nor anywhere he ever dared consider. It's suddenly possible. The full freight of his life, balanced on one corner.

And his phone is ringing. Still ringing. He looks at the number and suddenly the phone is ringing at a different pitch, vibrating in a new way.

"A Seattle number," he says. "My audition."

"No," she says, clenching her hands. "Take it! Take it!"

TakeitTakeitTakeitTakeit!

She's still telling him as he walks out the motel door, closing it behind him.

"Hello?"

"Hello, Lance? This is Mr. Kay, from the Seattle School of Music."

He must breathe. Must unclench his throat.

"Oh, hi. I was really looking forward to hearing from you."

"This an okay time?"

"Perfect time." He smiles at the door, Dakota beyond it. "It's a perfect time."

"Well bud, I'm sorry to say we don't have room for you this year."

Lance tries to translate the words. A cliff, coming toward him in slow motion. Brain skidding sideways, no surface to grip.

"Excuse me."

"We're full up. Only ten spaces, you know?"

"What?"

"Sorry, my friend. You blew really well."

"How—but how did I not get in?"

"You were great, Lance. Really great. The improvisation got you, just a little bit."

"I can improvise for you right now," Lance says. "I've got my horn. Let me just—"

Mr. Kay laughs. "I'm sorry, man. We can't do that."

He could make this right. Had to make this right.

"Is there a wait list?"

"No one really gets in on the wait list. You were close, you know? A lot of people play out a little. Take a year, then c'mon back next fall if—"

A loud ringing overtakes his voice. Panic alarm. The red lever. He'd break more glass, pull it again and his mother would go over Mr. Kay's head to the person with the big desk and plush chairs who hired and fired people like Mr. Kay, and that person would get A Serious Phone Call and Lance would end up in Seattle where he was meant to be.

Except his mother does not want him there. The lever will not work. And in the place where her help has always been, there is a void. There is nothing. And all he has for Mr. Kay is goodbye.

His phone is a block of ice. He puts it in his pocket, stares at the door.

She can smell his failure through the wall. He'll drink wine. He'll walk in and gulp a glass because the Seattle School of Music doesn't matter. It never mattered. He was never going to Seattle, and so he enters the room and Dakota looks up at him and flinches. She has never looked at him this way before. Because she knows.

Or because the green folder is open on her lap. His speech.

"What are you doing?" he says.

"Did you get in?" she asks.

Dakota has flipped past the page of teacher and student approval signatures. She is two pages into his speech, which means she has read past the introduction. The words of his speech, so elusive up until now, crystallize in his brain with uncanny clarity:

As we graduate from Bend High School, it occurs to me we will all be stars. Each of us, in our own way. And in the galaxy of our shared futures, we will shine brightly. We'll drift apart and become our own suns, lighting our own paths. Finding new planets in the orbits we choose.

Words he is responsible for.

"That's private," Lance says.

"Aren't you giving this speech to a thousand people in three days?"

"Well, I mean, if I just left my journal laying out on a table, would you read it?"

"Maybe." She shrugs. "Probably."

"Well, that's wrong."

Outside, a car thunders into the parking space just below his window. Doors clap open and shut. Young voices. Laughter. Hair raises on the back of Lance's neck.

"Okay. But how is this private? There's a hundred signatures on the first page."

"They're teachers."

"And three student witnesses. Whatever that means." She puts it down. "Oh. I get it."

"What?"

"This is from your *real* life. Right? I'm not allowed to see it."

"Dakota."

His phone is buzzing. Mr. Kay! He fumbles for his phone and hope leaps in his chest, a flood of endorphins and forgiveness. *Don't worry, Dakota, it's okay, and guess what, I did get in! There was a terrible mistake!*

But it's not Mr. Kay. It's Jonathan. Lance doesn't answer.

His throat is tight again and the voices outside are swelling, ballooning up in the air and pressing against his window. An icy-hot mixture sloshes in his gut. His body knows something his brain does not.

Lance walks over to the blinds, parts them with a finger. There's a Mustang. A white Mustang with Oregon plates. His molars lock. He stops breathing. Dakota is saying something underwater. Something he can't hear.

"Lance?" she says, breaking through.

In the Trainsong parking lot, figures from another life: Jonathan. Darren. Miriam. Miriam is in the parking lot. He pinches his left forearm. This fails to erase his friends. He bites the palm of his hand.

"What are you doing, Lance?"

"You have to go," he whispers.

"What?" she asks. "Why?"

"You have to go right now."

This girl. This perfect girl. Her brow knit. Startled eyes, like she's just been stung. It was the way she looked at the bag of soda cans in the parking lot, only this time it's him. She turns away and cuts across the room.

"Dakota," he says.

"Laaaaa-aaance!" someone calls from outside.

Dakota stops, hand on the doorknob. "Who is that?"

"Lance!" Jonathan screams from below. "Where are *youuuuuuu*!"

Lance finishes his wine. He can barely speak.

"Bend is here."

23

They're coming.

His room is a crime scene. A ten-by-twelve-foot glossy photograph of him cheating on his girlfriend. He had snipped out Dakota but could still see the scissor lines. Sharp edges where she'd just been. The wine bottle. Two glasses. Her shape, pressed into the bed.

The Bend Parade is coming upstairs. They'd gotten to Cheri. They are coming for him. Lance runs a series of wall-to-wall sprints—a human pinball, bouncing off corners, snatching up wineglasses, smoothing bedsheets.

Fists on his wooden door. Shouting.

They've come for the Wildman.

"Lancelot!" Jonathan says. "Open up!"

Lancelot. His nickname does it, turns a final gear in his head that automates his elbow and hand and causes him to unlock the door, and in rolls the storm.

"Whoa!" Darren says. He fills the door frame—life-size, freckled, with dark hair twisting up behind his neck. Miriam dubbed the look *shaggy chic,* but Darren was clearly flirting with a mullet. Darren, looking him up and down, soaking up information. Lance looks at himself. Fitted T-shirt. Tattered jeans. It was as if he had carefully hidden all evidence of his criminality, then answered the door in an orange jumpsuit.

"Whoa, Lance. Are you wearing a costume?" Darren asks.

"Let me see."

Miriam. There she is. Miriam. A real person.

"Hey," he says.

"Well, look at you," she says. He can't tell exactly what she means. They hug, tight and close, and the essence of Miriam whips up around him: her perfume like fresh-cut grass, the familiar press of her body. They're on an early-morning bus to a concert, side by side on her basement sofa, talking beside her locker. Laughing. Two years in a flash, slapping him awake.

She smiles at him and it feels good.

"So are you going to invite us in?" Jonathan asks, squeezing around Miriam. His perfectly square jaw. A blond sweep of hair over his eyes. Lance reminds himself: *This is your best friend.*

"He doesn't have to invite us," Darren says, shoving past him. He carries a giant red cooler. Duct tape letters on top spell B-E-E-R. They're inside. Reflected in the mirror. And Lance sees his room through their eyes. The muddy path worn into the beige carpet. Giant box of a television. Gray fur on the lampshade.

"I've always wanted to get wasted in a seedy motel room," Darren says. "Beer me."

"I don't know if this qualifies as seedy," Jonathan says, tossing Darren a beer. Lance catches the next one.

"Are you kidding?" Miriam says. "I would rather pitch a tent than sleep in here."

"It's the cat picture," Jonathan says, handing Miriam a beer. "It shows a certain attention to detail."

"How did you get here?" Lance asks Miriam.

"We drove," she says. "It's not that far."

"We're on a mission from God," Darren says.

"Your mother," Jonathan says. "Close enough."

"She bought gas. Meals. Snacks," Darren says, grabbing up a paper sack. It was from *Oodles!*, his mother's favorite grocery store. "She's so nice, that Mrs. Hendricks."

"Generous woman," Jonathan says.

"And we drove the whole way without opening a beer," Darren says. "Mission accomplished."

They knock beer cans, pop them open. Foam dribbles onto the carpet.

"Looks like Lancelot's already started," Jonathan says, pointing to the wine bottle. "Drinking alone, are we?"

An eel slithers in Lance's stomach. He glances at the bathroom, where he hid Dakota's wineglass. He closed the cupboard beneath the sink, right? He must've, but can't specifically remember doing it.

"Not alone," Darren says, crossing the room. Lance's heart jolts. Darren is walking to the TV, reaching behind the TV. What has he found? Dakota's keys? Her book? He must tackle Darren before he can show anyone.

"Lance has been hiding something from us," Darren says. With a flourish, he holds up Mr. Jangles.

AHH-HAHAHAHA!

Lance shudders.

"Jangles is a whisky man," Jonathan says.

"How do you know he's a man?" Miriam says.

"Please put that thing away," Lance says.

"Speaking of whisky, we're going to that bar," Darren says. "And my ass is getting served."

"Well—" Lance starts.

"As long as someone can drive back to Bend," Miriam says.

"Why do you think we brought you, Miriam?" Jonathan says.

Ooooooooo. Laughter. Miriam punches him.

"Dude," Darren says. "What's up with not answering texts?"

"No service," Lance says.

"Well look," Darren says, staring at his phone. "I have perfectly good service."

"Most of the time," Lance says. "It's in and out."

"How about you, Jonathan? You got service?"

"Yeah."

"Miriam?"

"I'm good."

"Lance, let me see your phone."

"Piss off, Darren."

"Language, Lance!" Jonathan says.

"You'd better be careful when you give your big speech," Darren says. "Don't let any of that Redneck Washington creep in."

"Is Leeds completely losing his mind?" Jonathan asks. "Your mother and him have been talking. Quite a little consortium." Jonathan squares his shoulders and pulls his arms into his shirt so only his hands show—doing his best Mr. Leeds impression: "Way I see it, graduation is the most important event of your young lives. What I can't understand is why some of you haven't been measured for your gowns yet. Your arms. They may not fit. Look at me. Just look at me!"

They laugh. Lance drinks more and they're relaxing into the room until it's no longer there, talking like they've always talked. A conversational jam session with the band who taught him how to play. He knows the rhythms and the tempo, how to hit the right notes. Darren, loud and blustering. Jonathan on the quippy interludes. Lance lays down a steady, agreeable beat, and Miriam tosses in a laugh when they need it most—the perfect high-range melody.

They haven't practiced for days, but you'd never know it.

"I can't believe you've been here four days," Darren says. "Noble Lancelot, holed up in a shitty hotel room. Practicing your trumpet."

"Jumping trains," Jonathan says with a smirk.

"Knife battles," Miriam says.

"Be honest, dude," Darren says. "Did that happen?"

"Yeah," Lance says.

The band stops. Lance has just taken an unauthorized solo.

"Yes. I actually jumped a train," he says, trying again.

But did he? Sitting here with his friends it's almost hard to believe.

"I did," he repeats, trying to make it real.

"What about getting served at that bar?" Darren says. "Bullshit, right?"

"No. It's real."

"So let's go." Darren pounds his beer and wipes his mouth with the back of his sleeve. "Let's get out of this shithole and have an experience."

"I don't know if they'll let us all drink," Lance says.

"So it *is* bullshit," Darren says, crossing his arms. "That's what I thought."

"Fine," Lance says. "Let's go."

"Really?" Jonathan says.

"Yeah. Right now." Lance sets his drink down. He opens the door to the balcony and maybe The Float will be gone. Like it never existed. Just a field, overgrown with blackberries. But it's still there for his friends to see. Neon flickers in the distance. Lance is dizzy, but not from the wine. Leaving his room is an out-of-body experience. He drifts along the length of the balcony, down blue steps, into the dark sea of the parking lot, walking an unsteady tightrope to The Float.

"Hello, stranger," Miriam says, at his elbow. "How much wine did you have?"

"I'm okay," Lance says.

But the tightrope is creaking as they pass Dakota's door. Iron hooks in his lungs, dragging on his rib cage. He's going to fall. Can't breathe.

"Aren't you glad to see me?" Miriam asks.

"Of course I am." He smiles. Humid air sticks in his lungs like paste.

"Have you had a good time out here?" Jonathan asks, falling into step with them. He gives Lance a strange look.

"Yeah," Lance says. "I've had a good time."

Lance runs his tongue over the backs of his lips. Still raw. He wants Jonathan to stop looking at him, but Jonathan is staring like he has X-ray lip vision. Like he's waiting for Lance to admit something. They finally reach the edge of the field.

"We should have walking sticks," Jonathan announces. "I'll round some up."

"We don't need walking sticks," Lance says. "I've walked this path a million times."

"I'll make a path," Darren says. "I can already smell the whisky."

Darren plunges into the field. Miriam follows, laughing. Then Jonathan. Lance brings up the rear. He's always last. Always following Jonathan's eager, pigeon-toed walk. Those leather shoes, which have clomped down an endless number of school hallways and rehearsal spaces, chewed through riverbanks and lawns.

When Jonathan crushes the first moonflower, the word STOP catches in Lance's throat.

They appear suddenly, and they're everywhere, dotting the weeds underfoot. Jonathan doesn't notice. Neither does Darren, nor Miriam. They're busy talking, kicking their way down the path. Miriam crushes two flowers with her right foot. Darren lets his walking stick swing like a scythe, shredding one. Another. Maybe on purpose.

Lance stands still, letting the distance grow between him and his friends. He can't tell them to stop. Not after white wine and new jeans. He can't afford to be off-key again. And these flowers shouldn't matter to him.

How long had he lived without seeing them? Forever. His whole life. They probably grow wild in Bend. He has probably already stepped on a thousand of them. He will just go back to the way he was before he noticed.

He raises his shoe over five rounded tips. A perfect star.

He drops his foot. The crunch of its stem rides up his leg. That sensation. He can't stop feeling it. But he's just taking another step. Just putting one foot in front of the other, and following his friends to The Float.

24

The pirate is there to greet them.

Jonathan grabs the hilt of her sword to make sure it's real. Darren honks her wooden breasts.

"Good job, Darren," Miriam says. "You guys are definitely old enough to drink."

His friends are talking to the pirate, saluting her, but Lance is watching the rest of the bar. A few bearded truckers by the door. A table of farmers with John Deere caps, bills flat as dinner plates. A family of five with giant teeth, eating meatloaf. All of them, eating meatloaf like it's their job. And a dark corner booth with familiar faces. A guy with floppy hair. Another one, short and tough-looking.

Meebs and Rocco.

Does he actually know those guys?

"Darren, chill," Jonathan says. Darren is dancing for the pirate.

"Why?"

Jonathan has also noticed the rest of the bar.

"Deene ne nee ne neee ne ne neeee." Jonathan plucks a tiny, invisible banjo.

"Stop it," Miriam says, slapping him.

"What?" Jonathan asks.

"They'll get the joke," she says. "These people speak banjo."

"Can I help you?" a voice booms. "C'mon in. Step right up!"

Mason's father, behind the bar. He reels them in. Jonathan and Darren exchange a nakedly excited look. Mason's father Frisbees a fresh pair of coasters onto the bar.

"I'll do a Jack and Coke," Darren says, tossing his words at the floor like it's no thing.

Mason's father looks them over. The man's eyes settle on Lance, his thin lips curling into a smile. He nods and turns toward the bottles. The group breaks into a silent celebration. Darren pumps his fists and Jonathan does a tap-dance shuffle. When Mason's father turns around, they snap back into nonchalance.

"What about the rest of you?"

They all order. They're all served.

"Cool, Lance," Miriam says. Her biggest smile.

Mason's father stands tall over the drinks, like he hasn't quite parted with them. He grins and says: "How would y'all like to make a little bet?" Mason's father winks at Lance, who steps back.

"I'm going to push some tables together," Lance says. He turns to the corner booth. Dakota. She is there now. Watching him, something new and shaky behind her eyes. He walks toward the booth and the floor stretches out, becoming the distance between worlds. Everyone is there, all watching: Dakota, Breanna, Meebs, Rocco, and Mason.

"Look what just blew in," Mason says.

"I can't believe he acknowledged us," Breanna says.

"Your friends are so pretty," Rocco says.

"Like a commercial for fine hair products," Breanna says.

"I want to hit them," Rocco says. "Not hard, though. Just like, *pop*."

"Totally," Meebs says. "Especially her. I'd hit that."

"Easy," Rocco says. "That's Wildman's girl."

"Wildman has a girl?"

"Oh, you think?" Rocco says. Just then, Miriam looks over in her most girlfriendy way. Soft eyes, little smile. Behind her, Mason's father is holding a ten-dollar bill up to the light.

"Want to save them some money?" Rocco asks.

"I don't know," Lance says as Darren hands over a ten-dollar bill. "I'm kind of enjoying it."

"Welcome to the dark side," Meebs says, raising his glass.

They toast, and Mason's father is taking a black marker to his friends' money. He's pointing at the prize wheel and Miriam is grinning, nodding vigorously.

"So *Wildman*," Mason says. He makes a show of turning his head in this regal way, like a king addressing his subjects. "We were just having a discussion about your other life. Your real life."

"Yeah?" Lance says.

"We're trying to decide if Wildman really fits."

Lance's right leg pops into action. Trying to carry his whole body away.

Dakota told them about his speech. His ACT score. Everything.

Dakota won't look at him. He should grab her hand, down

Mason with a punch, and blast through the front door of The Float. That's what Wildman would do. Bend is watching from the bar, and Mason just keeps talking.

"You're not a stoner," Mason says.

"No smoke breaks," Meebs says, raising a finger.

"Probably not a rebel," Mason says.

"Pleats," Breanna says. She snickers, tries to catch Dakota's eye.

"I said loner," Rocco says.

"But look at his friends," Mason says. Rocco shrugs. "Not a stoner, not a loner, not a burnout, not a rebel. Too small for football. Not much left. Except nerd."

"Band geek," Rocco says.

"Exactly," Mason says, clapping. "He talks to his mom on the phone. Plays the trumpet. I mean, who plays the trumpet? Is that *wild*?"

Lance chokes back names: Lee Morgan. Chet Baker. Bix Beiderbecke. All wild. Murdered or overdosed on heroin. But this knowledge will not help him.

"And look at his girlfriend. Homecoming queen." Miriam was *not* homecoming queen, but she was on the homecoming planning committee. Also, not helpful.

"I got it figured out," Mason says, putting a hand on Lance's back. "Your new name."

And under the weight of Mason's hand, Lance's shoulders tighten with his awareness of what's happening. He failed to notice the posturing. Somber expressions. The ceremonial markings. This is a ritual this group has performed before. For Meebs. For Stone.

A Nicknaming.

"He'll be gone tonight," Dakota says. "Don't waste your time."

"How much you want to bet he won't be gone, Dakota?" Mason says. "I think he'll stay as long as you'll keep him around. Only he's not going to be Wildman anymore."

"Okay, Mason. What's his new name?" Dakota says.

"Wait for it."

Rocco does a drumroll on the table.

"Blower," Mason says, beaming.

"Blower?" Breanna says.

"The trumpet," Mason says. "Blower."

"Oh," Breanna says. "He doesn't like that. Look at him."

"Dumb," Dakota says.

"Not your decision," Mason says.

"Who decides?" Dakota says. "You?"

"That's my job."

"Here we go!" Mason's father shouts from behind the bar. Darren in his socks, holding his blue high-tops. The bar crew cheers and Darren slings his shoes into the rafters, where they knock around and hang. Mason's father cranks the prize wheel and the colors blend to gray.

"Free round of drinks!"

A cheer goes up. Miriam wraps her arms around Darren. Just for a second. But it happens.

"I tried to give myself a nickname once," Meebs says. "Didn't work."

"That's because you called yourself *The Cool*, you jackass," Rocco says.

"The Cool?" Breanna says. "Why?"

"Because I *am* cool," Meebs says.

How had he become Meebs? How had James become Stone?

"I can't wait to meet your friends, Blower," Mason says.

Blower. Five minutes ago, he was still Wildman. And Wildman, as a nickname, could've smoldered and died in the wilderness. But not Blower. Blower was a name mean enough to catch fire. Darren will fan the flames and Blower will come raging across four hundred miles of fields, mountains, and streams. Blower will follow him back to Bend, all the way to OSU. It will burn him to the ground and be spray-painted on his gravestone when he dies. And he can't stop it.

Bend is coming toward them, holding drinks.

This collision is inevitable. Darren is first, and gets right in his face.

"Dude! We got served! Twice!" Darren holds up his drinks. He is shorter than usual.

"Darren," Lance says. "You have no shoes."

"I've got shoes at home. These are your friends?"

The groups are mixed-pressure weather systems, swirling together. Lance stands in the awkward center, and Mason steps in to join him.

"So you guys are friends with Blower?" He slaps Lance's back, as if hanging a KICK ME sign. Confusion hovers a moment, then the realization curls up behind their eyes like smoke.

"Blower," Darren says, testing the word.

"Blower?" Jonathan says. "We call him Lancelot."

"We call him Blower," Mason says. "He plays trumpet, right?"

"And the skin flute," Darren says.

"Ow!" Meebs says, snapping his fingers.

"Nice one." Mason's hand continues to press on Lance's back, burning a hole.

"Blower," Miriam says, looking disappointed.

"To Blower, everyone!" Darren says. They toast. They drink.

And The Nicknaming is complete.

The groups are mixing, laughing, bonding over Lance. An unsteady, seasick feeling. He's being tossed between Wildman, Lancelot, Blower. People stand around. There are not enough seats.

"Do any of you want to sit?" Dakota offers her side of the booth.

"Just Lance?" Rocco asks. "Or anybody?"

Dakota ignores him. The comment could slip by, but Mason has to laugh. Forced laughter, trying to catch peoples' eyes.

"Oooo," Mason says, looking from Lance to Miriam. "Oh, man."

"Dakota doesn't want to sit with the townies anymore," Breanna says. Mason nods.

"She wants a taste of the high life," Rocco says.

"She's trading up," Meebs says. "Icing us *doooow—*"

Dakota knocks a glass of ice water in Meebs's lap.

"Shit, Dak!" Meebs scrambles out of his seat. "Ah!"

The group is laughing—both groups. Meebs is flailing and gets Rocco wet. They shove each other, piling out.

"Booth's open," Dakota says.

Rocco and Mason move a table over. Miriam touches Lance's arm.

"Want to sit next to me?" Miriam asks.

Where can he sit? Where is Dakota? She is not at the table nor the booth and when he turns she is walking away from them, dark hair swinging. She walks straight out through the door. He needs to scream her name. Run after her. And he cannot. His feet are stuck to the floor. His expression, frozen at indifferent. The only expression he's allowed.

"Who was that?" Miriam asks.

"Dakota."

It's hard, speaking her name. As if saying *Dakota* will force him to explain things. They sit down and Miriam holds his hand on top of the table. Her fingers are loose against his fingers, resting on a glossy menu.

"So what do you think?" Lance says.

"Of Dakota?" Miriam smiles.

He squeezes her hand a little too hard. "No. This bar. This whole experience."

"Classy." She raises her eyebrows, like she just smelled something foul.

Darren says, *"Hey Blower, pass the salt,"* and Miriam laughs a genuine laugh for Darren. This laughter. Those raised eyebrows. And what if he'd been wrong about Miriam all along? About all of her hidden depth and insight and hunger? Holding her limp hand on this menu, she suddenly seems more pond than ocean. Like if he tried to dive into her with his whole self, he'd break his neck.

Lance looks at the floor and whispers: "Dakota."

"What?" Miriam asks.

He takes another drink of the whisky in front of him. He's getting drunk, and he doesn't want to be drunk. The groups mix like oil and water all shaken up. Droplets in suspension. Too many stories, crashing together. Most of them about the accident.

"So Wildman clocks Breanna," Rocco says.

"Pa-kow!" Meebs says. "Knocks her flat on her ass."

"Stone was wasted," Meebs says. "Of course."

"He shouldn't have been driving," Miriam says.

This is the story. Stone was driving. Stone was not actually driving, but that's not important. The story is what matters. The story is what's true. And now they're telling stories about Lance.

Blower.

Lancelot.

Wildman.

These names, closing in. Miriam asks if he's okay and he nods and stares at the sugar cubes on the table. They are perfect. White and solid with clean edges. Knowable mathematical units.

"Earth to Lancelot," Jonathan says. "Is that story true?"

"Which one?"

"You actually jumped a train?"

Lance nods.

"Who are you, man?"

Lance stares back at his best friend and has no answer. Meebs and Darren are at the jukebox, pumping out classic rock. Mason is laughing, and now Jonathan is removing his shoes. His friends are in socks and Mason has so many stories. The stories sew them all together.

Two groups becoming one.

He can't listen.

He plays John Cage's *4'33"* in his head and takes out one sugar cube and tries to remember one true thing. He can remember

Dakota's hand. The rest of the room is starting to slip. He needs Dakota's hand. Her hand would not slip away. It would not pull back at the last second. He could hold that hand and feel something real and make himself still.

And there is stillness all around. Friends carved from stone. No one is moving. No one is speaking. Lance is the only one who can move, because a stiff hand on his shoulder is pulling him up and out of his chair. This person coming to collect him from frozen time is a giant with a club and a gun and a bright silver badge.

The officer squeezes Lance's shoulder harder than he needs to.

"You must be the Wildman," he says. "Come with me."

25

The booth wraps around them like wooden curtains. There is no one else: just a salt-and-pepper mustache and brown eyes and a painfully bright badge that reads OFFICER PERKINS. Lance tries to feel sober, but his focus keeps coming unglued from this man's face, like eyes too tired to keep reading.

"Why have you been avoiding my calls?" he asks, leaning forward.

"I didn't mean to."

"What's your relationship with James DeWitt?"

"Who?"

"Back there," Officer Perkins says, pointing at the service window. Stone is there, head wrapped in a bandana. Eyes looking a bit better. He sets down a plate of fries, rings a bell. "They call him Stone."

"I just met him," Lance says.

"So you don't know him?" He'd already forgot Stone's real name. The repetition of these stories. *Stone, Stone, Stone.*

"No," Lance says. "I don't know him."

"Okay," he says, flipping out a notepad. "I understand you were first on the scene at the accident Saturday night. Is that correct?"

"Yes."

"Can you tell me who was driving the vehicle?"

"Stone," Lance says, because that's the story. His eyes sting. A prickling up his back, but no time to think. Questions come rapid-fire from behind the mustache.

"And Breanna was in the passenger seat?"

"Yes."

"Do you believe they were intoxicated?"

"Yes."

"Was Stone unconscious when you arrived?"

"Yes."

"Well, you just confirmed what everyone already knows," he says, flopping his hands on the table. "You've single-handedly held up this investigation. And wasted my time."

"I apologize," he says.

"Sure you do," he says. Very slowly, he closes his notebook. "There's more to discuss here, *Wildman*. We have confirmed reports of an assault at the accident site. Pushing. That's simple assault. And someone matching your description pulled a knife right here at The Float."

"Pulled a knife!" Lance says, shocked. But, right. That was him.

"I could haul you in for any one of those things. Understand? Would you like to explain?"

"I think I haven't been myself lately," he says.

"You think? You're not sure?"

"I don't know." His answer isn't winning him points. Jail is suddenly plausible. Lance Hendricks could go to jail tonight. No speech to worry about. No choices. A few square meals and a cell. He nods to himself, thinking it through.

"I've spoken to your mother." Officer Perkins smiles, proud of his achievement. "And some folks from your school. I understand you're valedictorian."

"Yes, sir."

Officer Perkins leans forward. The table creaks. "So which track do you want your life to be on, son? You want to be successful? Or you want to end up like those losers?"

Back at the table, Rocco is holding up a french fry.

"Your whole life can go off the rails, just like that." He snaps his fingers. "I see it all the time. It just takes one bad decision."

"I understand."

"See that you do." He gets up. "You might want to think that over in the next ten minutes, before my partner and I circle back and start asking for IDs. We clear?"

"We're clear," Lance says. He stands and Officer Perkins offers his hand—a bone-crunching grip.

"Good job at the accident scene by the way," he says. "You probably saved Stone's life. Whatever that's worth." He winks, then walks away. The breeze from the closing door brushes Lance's face. Outside, the crackle of a police radio. Information moving from here to there.

Whatever that's worth.

Stone stands behind the bar, framed by the service window.

Lance tries to hear James, but it's *Stone, Stone, Stone.* The song is finally stuck in his head. Stone looks at him. They make eye contact and Lance nods and Stone nods back, like they've just reached an agreement.

Lance stands up and walks back toward his friends, wondering which name they'll let him keep.

26

The campfire seems like a good idea.

Mason swears Officer Perkins won't come back, but no one is buying it, so five minutes later they're spilling out into the parking lot. When they hit gravel, Darren and Jonathan start screaming about their feet. Their elbows and knees are popping up in the air, and Meebs is beatboxing, imitating their movements—*the Shoeless Shuffle.*

It's great.

"Assholes!" Darren takes a step and shrieks. "Urchins! There are goddamn urchins in these rocks!"

"Hey Mason," Jonathan says. "Any chance we can grab our shoes? Just until we leave?"

"Sure," Mason says. "As soon as you give me back those beers you drank."

"Dude," Darren says.

"You will never get those shoes back," Rocco says. "Stop crying."

"Hop on," Mason says, turning his back. "Ride the Mason Train. C'mon, Rocco. Take a passenger."

"You kidding me?" Rocco says.

"I got Mason!" Jonathan says. He leaps onto Mason's back, latching on like a monkey. Darren fumbles his way up Rocco's back and shoulders, which is awkward, since Darren is taller. The pairs move at an unsteady canter down the switchbacks, bickering.

"Watch the branches, damn it!"

"How much do you weigh, man?" Rocco says. "Did you eat like six cheeseburgers?" Everyone is laughing too hard to walk. They keep stopping, letting the piggybackers go ahead. When they finally reach the fire, Dakota is there. Already beside the pit, stacking wood. There is a rhythm to her movements, a soothing percussion.

tick—TACK—tick—TACK

Big logs, little logs. A nest of tinder.

"Dakota's interesting," Miriam whispers.

"Yeah?" Lance says. The construction of the fire looks perfect.

"She keeps looking at you."

Lance freezes, eyes on Miriam. "What?"

"Not that I blame her."

"What?"

"I like your jeans," she says. She pulls his hand closer, puts it on her thigh. Tingling. He looks at her. "Are you excited to come home with me tonight?"

"I am."

"You are," she says. He has not sounded convincing.

"But the car isn't fixed. It'll be fixed tomorrow."

"We can't stay the night, Lance. We already missed the campus tour. Your orientation is tomorrow."

"Orientation?"

"At the bank?"

Miriam is squinting, her angry look. Dakota glances up. She might be looking at them. Her face is blank. He needs to know what she's thinking. She strikes a match and her fire catches. Flames pulse in the glass bottles around the fire.

"Nice work," Darren says, nodding his approval. "What's your name again?" Darren is talking to Dakota. Otherwise, the groups have separated. Breanna, Mason, Meebs, and Rocco on one side of the fire; Lance, Miriam, Darren, and Jonathan on the other. Everyone but Jonathan is drinking. He looks itchy, and keeps checking his phone.

"Let's tell ghost stories," Breanna says. "Dakota, tell the one about the hitcher."

"No," Dakota says. "Too scary."

"C'mon, Dakota," Mason says. "It's your best story."

"Can't," she says. "Just can't."

She is wistful. Slow. The way she was in the cemetery, after he wouldn't touch the tree.

They begin to chant: *Hitch-ER! Hitch-ER!* The Bend crowd picks it up, and Dakota tosses her hair back, chin up. She leans forward.

"Okay. It was two years ago. I was coming down Highway 2 through the Wenatchee Wilderness, twenty miles from the nearest gas station."

The Baring group cheers like they just heard the opening chords of a favorite rock song. Dakota keeps talking, weaving something.

A tapestry, wrapping them up in her words. Firelight flickers across her cheeks and dances in her eyes and it's finally okay for him to stare at her. For once, everyone is staring.

"I only picked him up because of the storm. The sky to the west was a big black sheet of rain. But when he got close to the car I almost floored it. I should've. This guy was scarecrow-junkie thin, carrying this little green backpack. I could see his joints through his jeans. And I could smell him halfway to the car. That street smell, you know?"

"Oh man," Jonathan says.

"So he got in, and the guy wouldn't talk to me. I kept asking *Where are you going? Why are you out here?* Dead quiet. He just kept shoving his green backpack under his seat. It was really quiet, so I turned on the radio. The guy reached out. Turned it off."

"No!" Darren says. "He turned off your radio? End of the ride."

"Before I can say anything, he starts messing with his little green backpack again, so I ask, *Hey, what's in the bag?*"

"What did he say?" Darren asks.

"He looks at me with his big, junkie eyes and says, *None of your fucking business.*"

"What!" Jonathan says.

"So, okay. I keep driving. We go a little farther, and he's back at it again, tapping the side of the bag, messing with the zipper, and I say, *Look, man. I'm cool. I smoke and do whatever. Is there something you need in there? I'm not going to judge you.* And he looks at me again, straight on, and says *None of your fucking business.*"

"Oh my God," Miriam says, clasping Lance's hand.

"So I know I got to get this guy out," Dakota says. "I start messing with the clutch. Tapping the brakes. Making the car all jerky, like the wheel's flat. I pull over and tell him there's something wrong on the passenger side. And I need him to get out and take a look. Guy just stares at me. This cold stare."

Jonathan shifts on his log. Wood creaks.

"He won't leave the car. He just kind of puts one foot on pavement and leans partway out. And I say, *I think you need to get all the way out.* And he looks down at his bag and says, *Like hell I will.*"

"No way," Jonathan says.

"So BOOM—I floored it."

"While he was stepping out?" Miriam asks. "What happened?"

"The door banged into him and he hit the concrete, screaming. Just kept screaming. God. I can still hear him, you know?" She closed her eyes. "Then the storm blew in. Rain and wind and hail. I was so freaked-out. I didn't even pull over to close the door until I was back in town."

"Whoa," Darren says.

"Did you ever see anything in the news?" Jonathan asks.

"Nothing," Dakota says. Miriam's hand tightens. In the distance, the white-noise rush of the highway. Sputtering Jake brakes.

"What about the bag?" Darren asks.

"Excuse me?" She looks up from the fire.

"The green bag," Darren says. "Did it fall out with him?"

"No," Dakota says, lowering her eyes to the fire. "It was still in the car."

"Wow," Jonathan says.

"So what was in the bag?" Darren asks. The fire crackles and Dakota stares at him blankly, her eyes like polished stones.

"What was in the bag?" she says slowly.

"Yeah," Darren says.

She stares back. *"None of your fucking business."*

Darren's mouth drops open. Goosebumps race up Lance's arms, breath catching. Then Meebs claps. The other side of the fire erupts. Wild applause.

"Holy shit!" Darren says, leaping to his feet. "Did you make that up?"

"Gotcha," Dakota says.

"No!" Darren says. "You're evil!"

"That's my girl," Mason says.

Everyone is howling. Everyone but Miriam. She's quiet, watching Lance. Giving him the same look she gave the copier drawer at Bend High, right before she knocked it shut.

"I need a drink," Darren says. "C'mon, Jonathan."

"Okay," Jonathan says. "Just one."

"I'm in," Lance says. He walks with Jonathan and Darren to the stump where Mason has arranged the bottles.

"What should we do next?" Jonathan asks, grabbing one bottle by its neck, tilting it.

"I want to do that hot little number back there," Darren says. "Da-ko-ta."

"Oh my," Jonathan says, and he can tell Jonathan is watching him. He tries to keep his face blank, listening to Darren talk.

"Oh yeah. She's got that country thing. The way she says *got.* I *got* to get this guy out. And concrete. Like *kahn-crete.* That's hot shit."

"You okay, Lance?" Jonathan asks.

"Yeah," Lance says, trying to soften his eyes. "What?"

"Aw. Did I offend you, Blower?" Darren asks. His high, drunken giggle.

A hot pounding in his temples.

"Shut your mouth, Darren," Lance says.

"Oh, wow. Look at you, *Wildman*. What are you gonna do with those tight jeans? Make me sorry?"

"Guys," Jonathan says. "Have a drink." Lance had hit Darren once before, after the seventh-grade Sweethearts Dance. It involved a girl, and he'd punched him square in the nose, knocked him on his back.

"Don't tell me what to do," Darren says.

"I'll tell you whatever the hell I want." Lance's hands are fists. Eyes wide and straining in a crazy way. He can't make them go back to normal.

A commotion by the fire. Stone has appeared, white apron slung over his shoulder. They both look. Jonathan hands them each a drink, and they drop their conversation at the stump. When they reach the fire, Rocco has launched into the *more pregnant* story. Lance can't believe they haven't all heard it yet.

"Someone remind me why I hang out with you assholes," Stone says. He sits between Rocco and Breanna, rolling a joint. He nods along as they tell the story, keeping time to a familiar beat.

"So Stone says, *Can't she get more pregnant?*" Meebs breaks in, capping the story.

The group howls. His friends clap. All but Stone and Miriam.

"More pregnant," Darren says, shaking his head. "Awesome."

"That's funny," Miriam says to Dakota. "But you know it's possible, right?"

"Sorry, what?" Dakota says.

Stone straightens sharply, like someone just jerked him up by the hair.

"What do you mean *it's possible?*" Mason says. "I thought Bend had good schools." People laugh.

"It's called superfetation," Miriam says, meeting Mason's eyes. "It happens in people and animals. It has to do with hormone levels. A female can actually release another egg during pregnancy. Sometimes two kids are born, but only one is full-term."

"Really," Dakota says. "Our bodies can do that?"

"Uh, yeah. It's science," Miriam says. "You can look it up. Or I can." Miriam takes out her phone. Lance stares at the fire.

"It's science," Meebs says to Rocco, making his eyes big.

"Whatever," Breanna says.

"As if Stone knew about superfrutation," Rocco says.

"Exactly," Mason says.

"I did know, you idiots," Stone says. "That's why I said it. So it doesn't matter if it's possible. Is that what I'm hearing?" He looks at Mason, then Breanna.

"More pregnant," Darren says. He and Mason laugh. Jonathan is itchy again. Back to looking at his phone.

"All right," Jonathan says. "I can drive in half an hour. Lance, do you need to pack up?" He sees Dakota, and there is a flare behind her eyes. Alcohol mixed with something he hasn't seen before. Miriam keeps patting his thigh. Softly. *Not now, Miriam,* he wants to tell her. *Please don't touch me now.* But she's patting harder and harder. Painful.

"What?" Lance says.

"Your leg. You're going to roll the log into the fire."

"Mr. Jumpy Legs!" Meebs says.

"It's restless legs syndrome," Miriam says. "It's really great."

"Sorry," Lance says, locking his feet to the dirt. The thing inside him pulls marionette strings in his calves, cords pulling taut.

"You know there's a cure for that," Dakota says. "I meant to tell you earlier."

"I don't think so," Miriam says. "We've tried everything."

"Sex," Dakota says. "That's the number one cure for restless legs syndrome."

"I don't think so," Miriam says, stiffening.

"Yeah. It's science. You can look it up." Dakota takes out her phone. "Or I can."

Howling, around the fire. A pack of wolves.

"On that note, time to go," Jonathan says, standing. "Lance, let's go."

"But my car's not ready."

Meebs throws another log on the fire. Sparks shower the dirt. Mason tosses a bottle of whisky over the flames and Rocco catches it, hops it from hand to hand, pretending he's been burned. People are drunk.

"So wait," Jonathan says. "You're not coming back with us?"

"I can't leave without my car."

"What's the deal with your car, Blower," Mason says. "Do you have a physical relationship with your vehicle? Something we should know about?"

"My dad gave it to me," he says, bracing for a joke. But Mason's face slackens and his lips draw into a line. He nods and says nothing.

"You should go tonight," Breanna says with a grin. "If you stay, you'll never leave."

"True," Stone says. "Escape while you can. Last chopper out."

"You can always come back," Rocco says. "We aren't going anywhere."

"I am," Meebs says.

"Where, Meebs?" Rocco says.

"Somewhere."

"Meebs, you will die in your parents' basement playing Xbox," Rocco says. He mimes a corpse, rigor-mortised hands clutching a controller. Everyone laughs but Mason. That quiet look, still sinking in. Cheeks hanging like jowls.

"After a while you can't leave," Mason says, like he's speaking someone else's words. "A place gets into your bones."

"You can always leave," Dakota says.

"Agreed," Stone says.

"Oh yeah?" Mason says. "So why are you here? Nursing school, Dakota? Waiting around to sell more shitty sketches at the King County Fair? Or, no. It's because you love your families so much. Right, Stone? Dakota?" They don't answer. Everyone is watching the fire.

Miriam puts a hand on Lance's leg.

"C'mon," she says.

Firelight gives her eyes a frantic look. Miriam saved his life once. During a school trip to Eugene, she pulled him back from the path of an oncoming bus. Lance could still taste the exhaust as it came whooshing past, horn ringing in his ears. Miriam's clear blue eyes, telling him he was still alive. And her eyes had looked just like this.

"I'll make it to Telluride," Stone says. "You can do that trip in one long day."

"Yeah," Rocco says. "On the back of a unicorn."

The group snickers. Darren and Jonathan too. Lance stares at his friends, trying to make them stop. But they can't see how Stone looks, holding that bottle. He takes a long pull of liquor.

"You couldn't even get a ride from your cousin's trailer this morning," Mason says.

"So?"

"So you'll never make it to Colorado."

"He could jump a train," Meebs says.

"Right," Rocco says. "Because he's so good at that." Rocco mimes Stone trying to grab someone's hand, slipping. Screaming. More laughter.

"You don't know," Stone says. He's only talking to Mason now.

"I know you can't get there in jail."

"Yeah? What else do you know, Mason?"

"I know your ass works for me, and I'm not opening a franchise in Telluride."

"You couldn't drive there anyway," Darren says. Giggles around the fire.

"Darren," Lance hisses. Stone is gripping the bottle with both hands, searching for Darren's comment like a fly buzzing near his ear. But Darren only notices the laughter.

"You might make it," Darren says, "as long as you don't get anyone *more pregnant*." He stumbles up on a log, pumping his hips. "Triplets! Quadruplets! Quintuplets! Boom! Boom! Boom!"

A dry whoosh tears through the air. A hot wave and a fireball swallows Darren's face. The odor of burnt hair. People scream and leap up. Everyone but Stone.

"What the hell, James?" Breanna says, standing over him.

"Just a little splash," Stone says.

He's wearing a small, impenetrable smile.

"I'm burned!" Darren is standing in his socks, covering his face. "He burned me."

"What the hell was that?" Mason says, towering over Stone. "Answer me! Get up!"

"Is that an order?" Stone says. So quiet Lance can barely hear him.

"What?"

"Is. That. An. Order."

"Yeah, it's an order, dickhead. Now are you—"

Stone whips the bottle at Mason's head. He ducks and the glass thunks onto the grass. Mason freezes, then steps forward. Swelling in size.

"What the fuck did you just do?" he says. Lance steps back. Mason is terrifying.

"Just responding to orders, sir."

"Get the fuck up!"

"I will not," Stone says. "What would you like to do about that?"

"Get up or you're fired." Mason stomps the dirt. "You hear me?"

"Yes."

"Stone, don't be stupid," Breanna says. "Get up. He's serious."

Stone doesn't look up. Or even move.

"You think I'm bullshitting you?" Mason says. "If I count to three, you're fired. One. Two." Stone motions for Mason to continue. "Three. Fine, fucker. Take the week off. The whole year. Have fun in jail, you piece of shit."

Mason is shaking. Breanna makes a choked sound and turns away. Then Jonathan is grabbing Lance by the arm, dragging him into the shadows with Miriam and Darren.

"Nice friends," Darren says. He has red cheeks and watery eyes, but the burn doesn't look serious. "Thanks for standing up for me, man."

"You were kind of asking for it," Lance says. He feels completely sober all of a sudden. He could play a perfect high-range solo. Run ten miles.

"You're saying he deserves to get his face burned off?" Miriam says.

"He's fine," Lance says. "It's not that bad."

"Lance," Miriam says. "It's not like you have formal medical training."

"I'm first-aid certified," he says. "I have a card. How formal does it need to be?"

"I want Jonathan to look," Darren says.

"Fine," Lance says.

"Where are you going?" Jonathan asks.

"I'm going to check on Stone."

"You're helping that asshole?" Darren says, shaking free of the huddle. "Hey. Get back here!"

Lance is walking when Darren jerks him back by the shoulder, spinning him around.

"Your ass is staying right here."

"Touch me again and I'll kill you."

Lance doesn't recognize the voice as his. He's thrumming with new energy, like he's grabbed hold of a live wire and can't let go. Darren's surprise is exaggerated by his red cheeks.

"You're crazy."

"What's wrong with you, Lance?" Miriam sobs.

"We'll leave him," Darren says. "We'll just leave his ass here."

Lance turns and walks slowly toward the fire, fighting the pull of Bend's gravity until something snaps like elastic and he's free and rushing toward his new orbit. Breanna sees him coming and her posture loosens, like Lance just added his hands to something too heavy to carry.

"Thanks for coming back," she says.

"I'm fine," Stone says, still sitting. "Not a big deal, people."

"You're not fine." Breanna is crying. "James."

"Sorry if I burned your friend."

"It's okay. He kind of deserved it."

Stone shrugs, staring at the fire. Around him, vacant logs. They've all left. Lance scans the clearing and the trees. Panic flutters in his chest. He will not find her. She's gone.

Dakota is gone, and you are going home.

In the shadows, a shape that isn't Dakota. Coming fast. Charging. Lance turns to the side, bracing for impact.

"Darren," he says, raising his fists.

"Just me," Jonathan says, stepping into the light.

Lance's body goes limp.

"So. Funny thing."

"What?"

"We still don't have shoes. Darren's riding Mason up the hill."

"Wow," Lance says.

"So," Jonathan says, looking at his socks.

"Oh, I see." Lance sighs. "Well, I'm glad this isn't awkward."

"Me too."

Lance turns around. Jonathan's legs lock around his waist, voice in his ear.

"Thanks, man. So, hey. What's the story with Dakota?"

"I can't talk," Lance says. "You're too heavy."

"C'mon."

"Seriously. I can't breathe. You've really let yourself go."

"Is there a thing with her? Yes or no? You can just nod. C'mon. Was that a nod?"

Lance climbs the hill, step by step, and tries to keep his head straight.

27

Their skin is translucent under white parking lights. The Bend crew is alone, and there's a feeling like someone might've hit the reset button on the entire night. Maybe Darren isn't burned. Miriam and him are still okay, and everything can go back to normal. But there are lost hours to account for. Two friends with no shoes. And a strange new silence, like the sheet music has gone blank in the middle of a concert.

Jonathan has always been good at improvisation, and he's good tonight.

"So, Lance. Need a hand with your stuff?"

When they get to his door, it's hard to make the key fit. It takes him three tries. Once he and Jonathan are inside, he has to say it:

"I'm not coming home."

His sinuses burn when the words come out, like he's just been punched.

"Yeah?" Jonathan says. "I thought you might say that."

The cats on the wall are unimpressed. They, like Jonathan, have seen this coming.

"I can't leave my car," he says.

"The car. Right," Jonathan says. "You know, I found a wineglass under the sink."

A hot tingle rushes up from his stomach.

"I didn't mean to find it. I was looking for toilet paper. Then I was thinking, why would you hide one wineglass?" Lance can only stare back.

"It's not a big deal," Jonathan says. "Unless it is."

The air conditioner clicks off, peeling away a layer of sound. A nervy silence. If another unnoticed thing turns off, Lance will scream.

"Are you sure you want to do this?" Jonathan asks.

Lance nods.

Jonathan looks over the room. Sighs. "Okay. Let's break the news."

They pack up the empty beer cans and bags of chips, then each grab a side of the cooler and carry it downstairs. Miriam and Darren are waiting. They watch in silence, then Miriam says:

"Where's your stuff?"

"He's not coming," Jonathan says. "And we gotta go."

A rattle in Darren's throat, like he's going to spit.

"You're not coming?" Miriam's eyes are wide, searching for the joke.

"Not tonight," he says.

"Can we talk?"

"Okay."

The two of them walk to the center of the parking lot. Parked cars, blue and silver. A skin-peeling glow that makes Miriam's veins stand out in dark blue streaks. She looks breakable.

"You don't want to come home with me?" She slurs a little. He's surprised. She's actually a little drunk.

"I didn't ask you to come get me," he says. "My mom sent you."

"But you don't want to come with me."

"I don't know."

Sad, wondering eyes. He could drift back into Miriam's arms now. A current, flowing east. There was no Seattle anyway. An easy float back home, into the churn of summer, Oregon State, Bank of the Cascades, life as he knew it.

And he'd never be here again.

"Come home," she says, stepping closer.

Her open hand. Like seeing it for the first time. He cannot move.

"Is this over, Lance? Are we done?"

An answer sits in his mouth like a stone, but he will not spit it out. He does not want to hurt her. It's still fixable. He could mash his lips against hers until the earth stops and spins backward. They can leave together tonight and just start over. But the thought of starting over with Miriam makes him so tired. So tired he can't raise his hand to her shoulder, or even look her in the eye.

"Can you say something?"

It's all so plain. This should hurt more. He looks straight into her blue eyes, damp and staring. He needs to feel the splinter and snap. To make it sting and bleed the way two years should sting and bleed. And this is too much like nothing. In Bend, a week ago, he'd be curled up in a ball, crying on her carpet. Sobbing and screaming into his pillow. But they are not in Bend. Four short days. Things fall away. And now there is only hard light and concrete and nowhere around them is love.

"Is it over, Lance?"

Her whisper is deep and throaty. He's never heard this voice from her before. A shaky feeling, because there will be so much he never knows about Miriam.

"Yes. It's over."

He can't believe his words, but the impact is there, in her face. She is watching him, looking for something.

"Were you going to write me a letter, like your dad?"

He stops his leg from shaking.

"Miriam."

"I'm glad you missed the party," she says. "Say something. Can you just say something?"

She waits. Keeps waiting, then walks back to the car. He gives her time to get there. Darren has one foot on the cooler. Jonathan is standing by the passenger door. Miriam shakes her head and gets in the car.

"You're really not coming," Darren says. "Have an awesome life, buddy."

Darren looks unsteady. Lance keeps his distance.

"I'll do my best," Lance says.

"C'mon," Jonathan says. "Let's go. Get in."

"Cool. Just one for the road," Darren says. He flips open the cooler lid and screams, jerking backward.

AHH-HAHAHAHA!

Mr. Jangles stares up from a bed of beer cans.

"Stupid," Darren says. He gets in the car and slams the door.

"Nice work," Jonathan says. He picks the figure up by the foot. "It is important to maintain a sense of humor."

"Isn't it?"

"Oh, dang. You know what? I forgot something up in your room." Pats his pockets. "I'll just run up there real quick."

"Not a chance, dude."

"Okay. Just remember. We'll all be waiting."

He and Jonathan hug.

"Stay in touch," Jonathan says.

"I'll be home tomorrow."

"Yeah, sure," Jonathan says. His voice sounds tight. "Just stay in touch, okay?"

In the car, Darren and Miriam are sitting still, like the drive has already started. Jonathan climbs inside and the interior lights dim. They are all facing straight ahead. No one yells goodbye through an open window. No one turns and waves. Three faces in the dashboard's submarine glow, and Jonathan is speaking to them, words Lance can't hear. The car glides to the edge of the parking lot.

The pulse of a blinker. Two red taillights shrinking into darkness. Gone.

The parking lot is quiet.

Then someone is moving toward him from the woods. A face, hovering like a pale coin in the darkness, slowly gaining dimension until it's Breanna.

"Lance," she says, eyes damp. Unfocused. "Will you please go?

Someone needs to go see him." He wants to ask *who* and *where*, but it will only delay what he knows she's asking him to do. He walks down the hill. The trail is dark. Tree roots, thick and slippery, bulking up from the soil, making him slip. The forest smells like the damp-moss musk of a cave and as he picks his way down the slope, Jonathan's face lingers in his mind. Whispers in his ear.

Just stay in touch, okay?

That awful way Jonathan's voice had sounded. Like he knew Lance was never coming back.

28

Stone is standing beside the fire with a certain repose, the way a person only stands when they think no one's watching. Lance walks closer until Stone's features clarify in the flickering light. Vacant eyes. His mouth, without expression.

"James?"

He twists toward Lance. Military training springs out like a blade: straight back, tensed fists. A different person.

"Who is it?" Stone asks.

"Just me. Lance."

"Why are you calling me *James*?"

"That's what you told me to call you. When we met."

"Bullshit." Stone turns away, looking bored. Lance gets closer.

"You were in the car. With blood all over your face. I remember it pretty well."

"Huh," he says. "Maybe you're right." The military part of him retracts, and he's just Stone again. The guy grinning through the service window of The Float. Easy smile. Soft eyes.

"Sorry about my friends," Lance says.

"No big deal," Stone says. "It's universal." He stares at the tracks and shakes his head, losing a silent argument. The flames make a dry flapping noise.

"You're not going back to Bend?" Stone asks.

"Not tonight."

"Bend sounds nice," Stone says. "Mountain town. Breanna says it's awesome."

"It's no Telluride. We should've gone while we had the chance."

"Yes! Yes, we should've," Stone says. He looks over his shoulder, searching the shadows. There is no one there. "You know it was voted the most beautiful main street in America. Have you seen pictures?"

"No."

"It really is, man. If you have the money, you could just sit in a café all day. Your whole life could go by while you're sipping coffee. The mountains are right there. They come right up out of the fucking town. You climb. You ski. Sit in the cafés at night. Maybe work a restaurant gig. Life can start over that way. Find a shit job in a beautiful place and go from there."

"That sounds about perfect," Lance says.

"I can see it." He shuts his eyes. "Just like a picture."

"So what's stopping you?"

"I can't see myself in the picture," Stone says. He opens his eyes. Looks at Lance.

"You don't know unless you try," Lance says. But his words sound flat. Stone, in his cooking pants. Those giant black boots.

"This place," Stone says. "This fucking place."

"So go."

"It's like a horror movie. You can't outrun it," Stone says, his eyes sharp. "Mason's right. That's why I enlisted. To get away. I brought all my favorite books to basic training. Even wore my glasses. A few of the guys started calling me *professor*, you know?" Stone's gaze moves down the long, dark tracks.

"I believe it," Lance says.

"But it always catches up with you," Stone says. "We were in the mess hall for dinner, and I made a joke—I don't even remember what. And this guy McQuarrie flung a spoonful of mashed potatoes at me. They hit me right here, in the chest. He's this rich prick who everyone likes and he says, *Ain't too bright, are you, DeWitt?* And other guys started in with their own stories. And this place found me again. Right there at the table."

"So you left?"

"Nope," he says. That small smile. "I went over the table. I'm not even that strong, but no one could pull me off the guy. I was going to rip the box straight out of his throat. My fingers were all dug in. Someone hit me with a chair, and that was it."

"You left?"

"Discharged. Want a shot?" Bottle on a stump. The whisky goes down like hot water from a rusty teakettle. Lance chokes it back, eyes stinging. Stone pats his shoulder, something opening up between them.

"Nice job. You're getting good at this, Wildman."

"Blower," Lance says, exhaling.

"To hell with that. Fuck Mason. You're still Wildman. You

know what's crazy? The only people who know my real story about basic training are you and this guy who comes into The Float sometimes, John Ganz. Giant beard. Old timber dude."

"What did he say?"

"He got it," Stone says. "Same deal, you know? This guy listens to classical music. Reads like three books a week. But who knows that about Ganz? You'd have to pay attention to know that. So there's the fry cook and the broke-down lumberjack sitting at the bar talking about *The Martian Chronicles* and *The Clan of the Cave Bear.* And I'm telling him things nobody knows about me. I'm telling John Ganz, this total stranger."

"Yeah," Lance says, looking at the fire. The way Stone's voice is, it's hard to look at him.

"He got me," Stone says. "You ever had that feeling? When someone gets it?"

"Yeah," Lance says. And he's looking back toward the woods that lead to a parking lot and a window where she might still be awake. Then he makes himself look at Stone, who says:

"How can a total stranger understand you better than the people you've known your entire life?"

"I don't know."

"But it's fucked up, right?"

"Yeah," Lance says. "It is." Stone nods and walks toward the tracks. His boots crunch on the ballast. He hops up, balancing on the nearest rail.

"So how about you?"

"What about me?" Lance asks.

"What's your Telluride?"

Lance is warm and light-headed from the whisky and before he can say *I don't know,* he says *Dakota.*

"Ha!" Stone lights up. He claps, hops down. "I knew it! No wonder Mason's been such a prick. Man. The way she looks at you. Goosebumps."

"Yeah?" Lance says. "Do they have a thing? Dakota and Mason?"

"Not yet," Stone says. "He's working on it. Has a bet going with Rocco, I think."

"He still owes me a thousand dollars."

"Good luck with that," Stone says. "So hey, what are you still doing here?"

"What do you mean?"

"You're leaving tomorrow, right?" Stone says. "Why aren't you with her?"

"Why aren't you in Telluride?"

"Hey," Stone says, crunching down toward him. "Telluride is a thousand miles away. Dakota's right there in her bedroom."

"It's too late, man. She's—"

A hot flash of pain and Lance staggers sideways. His right cheek burns, tears dribbling from his eye. Stone just slapped him. Lance laughs a long, rolling laugh. It's amazing. Hilarious, being slapped for that.

"Wow, Stone," he says. "That really hurt."

"It hurt when you put those towels behind my head," Stone says.

"What?"

"After the accident. When you saved my life. That hurt too."

Stone grabs him by the shoulders. "I will slap the ever-living shit out of you, Wildman, if that's what it takes to wake you up. Go get her."

Lance wonders if there is enough time. The woods are dark, but it's not far to her door.

Stone laughs.

"What?" Lance says, barely hearing him.

"You're freaking out," Stone says. "It's not too late. Go!" Stone pushes him, and Lance stumbles. He's out of the firelight and walking, almost to the trees when Stone calls out:

"Lance! You told the cops I was driving?"

"Yeah." He stops, turning back. "That's the story, right?"

"That's the story," Stone says. "Promise me you'll get Dakota. No matter what."

"Yes."

"So we're even," Stone says. "You saved my life. I saved yours. Deal?"

"Deal."

Lance walks back to the fire. They shake hands, and Stone claps him on the shoulder.

"Goodbye, Wildman."

Then Stone is alone, orange and flickering by the fire. Same easy posture. Same faraway look. Like Lance had never been there at all.

He is already moving—climbing up the slope through the trees, heart pounding, counting his steps, shedding the weight of Darren and Miriam and Breanna and even Stone. Sweating through his clothes and sucking in night air and breathing it out until there's only Dakota and his footsteps, shrinking the distance between them, dissolving the woods into a parking lot, magnifying her window until he's there, fist raised in front of the glass.

Is this happening?

He knocks. Three stiff raps, but the knocks keep beating, echoes reverberating in walls and windows. He can still run away. There's still time. Then the *zzzwwoooooop* of a cord and clattering blinds. There is only a thin sheet of glass between them. Dakota stares as if taking in a painting. She unlatches the window. Slips it open.

"What are you doing?"

"Ghost hunt," he says. "Want to come?"

A smile breaks through, wild and bright. She vanishes from the window, leaving a dark void of space and the distant blue flicker of a television. The sigh of weather stripping and she's out the door, pulling on shoes.

His teeth are chattering so hard they're bouncing his right leg. Or the other way around.

"Trying to tell me something?" she says.

"What?" he asks.

He looks down. Locks his knees.

"Want to come over?" he says. He can barely talk. Done talking.

"Yes."

That moment of unreality: her hand slipping into his. A new sensation he's coming to know. The drop of shoulders. Opening of lungs. The heart-hammering, gentle drift of Dakota's company. All that's left for them to do is cross the parking lot, so the parking lot becomes treacherous. Every creak and rustle, someone racing to stop them. An impossibly long walk and somehow they're across, upstairs, and standing at the door to his room.

The key won't fit. This key never fits.

He's drilling at the lock when Dakota runs a finger across the back of his neck, right at the hairline. The sensation! A tickling, shivering, stop-and-do-it-again. He's up on his tiptoes. He could melt into the floorboards and live for a week, just on that touch.

The key slips in.

The door closes behind them, and he and Dakota are alone in a dark room. He turns and she's staring at him. Such a small space between them. He tries to close the gap with words, but they go liquid in his head, sloshing into one another, leaking from his mouth. He doesn't understand himself.

"What do you, so, do you—"

She leans in past the place where words snap off. Their lips touch. Heads tilt, mouths opening and he's drinking her in. Her mouth is hungry, moving against his, a pulsing rhythm. A current, carrying them downstream, their bodies together, crashing onto the bed.

The kiss deepens, unbreakable. When he moves his head or brushes back her hair, she always rushes back to rescue him. Like breathing for one another. There is a dark velvet cloth over everything.

Hunger turns feverish. Hands fight their way through buttons and zippers, snaps and clasps, until everything is skin and Dakota's mouth. Every part, surprising. The channel down the center of her back, the shape of her breasts and how they fit in his hands, the glide of her stomach under his palm. How she moves. Her hips, shoving against him until it hurts. No shyness. Only what they both want.

It's too much. Fingernails on flesh. Her tongue against his earlobe, buried in his ear. The taste of arms, calves, and thighs. Sweat. Suffocating under bedsheets. Her mouth around individual fingers. Index, middle, shaking, laughing. So many sensations, all flooding toward one place. He stops her.

"It's my first time." She's breathless, glowing. "What do you want?"

"I want to try."

"Try."

He goes to his suitcase, takes out the blue plastic bag he'd gotten in Seattle, unwraps it. Wrestles through cardboard, trying to find the edge of the packet.

"Let me help," she says. "Come here."

She opens it for him. Helps him put it on. Helps him the whole way. It's not like he expects. No sudden pop and blur. No moment where everything turns to golden light and he stops thinking. He's thinking now. He worries. There are mechanical issues. Is it still on? Is he doing it right? Even the kissing gets tricky, and his head is so full that maybe it's over too soon. Was it? He's shaking again, peeling things off. Tissues. Crossing back and forth to the bathroom. Is this just what people do, every time?

Finally they're back under the sheets. Back to blue light and smiling.

"Are you okay?" she asks.

"Yeah," he says. "Are you?" He laughs.

"What?"

"The way we're talking. It's like we've just been in a car accident."

"A train wreck," Dakota says.

"Was it?"

"What?"

"A train wreck?"

"No!"

"Good," he says. He slips his arm beneath her neck, pulls her close. "So I'm a natural."

"Supernatural," she says.

They're kissing again. That is their magic—an endless kiss. When hands come off clocks and words crumble and the room loses traction and they're slipping off a ledge, flying or falling, too fast to tell the difference.

29

A scratching thing is right outside their window, much larger than whatever lives in the motel walls. It's tapping on glass, chewing wood. Something with claws and teeth big enough to break the skin. Lance wants to investigate, but it's behind the blinds. He's afraid to wake Dakota.

He shifts his position and she bolts up, bundling the sheets around her. She looks toward the window and the scratching noise.

"Mr. Jangles?" she says.

"Stop," Lance says. "Don't even joke."

The noise stops. They look at each other. It's quiet.

Dakota sighs and collapses on the mattress. She stretches out, arches her back, and gives a happy-morning shriek.

"Wow," he says. "Is that how you wake up?"

"Mmmm. Only when I've just had the best night of my life."

"Yeah?"

"Yeah," she says. "That was pretty much my first time, too."

He shivers.

"Are you cold?"

"No," he says. "You make me shiver."

"Yeah? You make me hum."

He smiles, kisses her lips. He wants to tell her she's perfect without making it sound like some stupid movie or some stupid song, but writers have taken all the good lines and ruined them, so he doesn't say anything. He wonders about *pretty much my first time* and stares at the sleep lines on her cheek. Touches one. Smoother than it looks. She smiles. Has a boy ever done that before? Touched a sleep line on Dakota's face?

The thing at the window is back. Loud scratching.

"Wildman!" She clutches his arm. "Save me!"

Lance smiles, but his stomach is fluttering. He pounds his legs into his underwear and lands his right foot squarely in the crotch, tearing fabric. He wrestles them on, then his jeans.

Shtk, Shtk, Shtk on the glass.

Someone's phone buzzes. Lance freezes at the window.

"Damn it, phone!" Dakota says.

Lance pulls the lift cord and blinds snap up. A squirrel, ghastly up close. Dark mouth parted over crooked teeth. Eyes like black glass. It tucks its head and cheeps—a sharp little alarm. Lance steps back and the rodent is a ripple of fur on the banister, winding down to pavement, bolting across the parking lot. Past a police car.

"Squirrel?" Dakota says.

"Chickaree," he says.

A police car. Lights off. No one inside. The first rip in the fabric of a normal day. And everything suddenly feels a little off. No vacuums running. No chatter outside the front office. A fresh-snow stillness in June.

They still have last night's magic locked inside. This room is a submarine, ocean leaning on all sides. If he opens the door, those dark waters will rush in and sweep them away.

Dakota is standing.

The room has already sprung a leak, through her phone. Dakota makes a choking sound.

Lance opens the door.

The warm breath of summer. Police cars at The Float. People shuffling in the parking lot. Small groups. Gray faces and white Styrofoam cups. So many white cups. A crowd with its own gravity, pulling them.

The door is wide open and Lance cannot breathe.

"Stone," Dakota says.

She makes a sound he's never heard before. The wail of something breaking, deep inside her. Lance stands and watches her scream and there is nothing he can do.

They are in the parking lot now. Red-rimmed eyes. Crumpled faces. They, too, are holding white cups. They have cried and shaken and transformed themselves until they belong here with these people. Lance does not remember who gave him the coffee.

Dakota cries out again, making him jump. A yelping sound, like a kicked dog. She's talking to an older man he doesn't know.

She makes the sound again and Lance gags, coffee coming up the back of his throat. Almost loses it. The crowd makes its low, steady churr:

whywhywhywhywhywhywhywhywhy

The strike happened just there. By the fire pit.

Right at 2:26 A.M. Same time every night.

Didn't even see him.

Diverted to Seattle. That's what they do.

Drunk—

Discharged—

Police—

Stone—

Stone—

Stone—

The strike happened just there. By the fire pit.

Right at 2:26 A.M. Same time every night.

Facts, repeated like mantras. Repeated like prayers.

Lance lifts his head, looking for Dakota. He finds Mason, whose face has a damp, surprised look. He keeps glancing backward, as if someone invisible is tapping his shoulder and running away. Then Mason is talking to Dakota. He drapes an arm around her, like a bear.

He pulls her into his wide chest. She leans into him.

Lance's Styrofoam cup bends, turning from a perfect *O* to a long zero, coffee spilling over the rim, hot on his fingers. The cup is about to split. His feet twist away from Dakota and Mason and carry him to the field. Crunching weeds.

One foot in front of the other until he's back at the Trainsong. There is no one outside. Cheri's office is dark for the first time. His phone comes alive in his pocket and he pulls it out, squeezing, trying to choke it quiet. Make it stop. He doesn't recognize the number.

"Hello?"

"Lance? This is Robert."

"Robert?"

A loud sigh, distorting to white noise.

"Uh, ye-ah. Your car. The Buick. The one you love more than life itself. Ring any bells?"

"Oh, Robert. Sorry."

"Well, she's done."

"Done?"

"Fixed. Runs like a beauty."

Lance can't move. A warm breeze shakes the leaves. He scrunches his toes, feeling the rub of cotton.

"Lance?" Robert says. "Lance?"

"Yeah."

"Just get yourself to the bus stop. Bea can pick you up. Okay?"

They hang up and The Lance Hendricks Machine is moving again, carrying him to the road. His phone buzzes and it's Dakota. She's calling and he's walking. That's all he's doing, just walking, and there's nothing wrong with that. She calls again and again, and he's just walking to the bus stop. He cannot answer calls. He is nothing but feet on pavement.

The sun is a small yellow bulb, thinning the grayness.

This could still be a beautiful day.

He's on the shoulder when the pavement trembles. A rumbling in the soles of his shoes, just like the rails. A force is twisting toward him, through the woods. Hissing air brakes. An engine. Closer. Its first long metal edge rounds a corner. A semitruck with a big silver trailer.

What would *struck* be like?

A bone-breaking buckle. A quick twist in the air. Snapping wrists, cracking molars. Compression, then blood finds its way out. Over in a few seconds. The driver of the truck is eating potato chips. Lance can see the yellow foil of the bag, but the driver does not see him.

Lance tastes exhaust, like the day Miriam saved his life.

Jump.

A one-word command. One simple impulse, brain to feet.

Jump.

The truck's grill is a steel wall. He bends his knees and does not know what The Lance Hendricks Machine will do.

Jump.

The truck passes with a punch and drag of air. Skittering leaves.

Lance leaps into the empty road.

Exhales.

His phone buzzes again, and he is feet on pavement. He is just walking to the bus stop.

30

In Robert's office, the fish is waiting for him. Silver lip protruding, it stares him down. Not swimming. Lance wonders how the fish catches the monkeys it eats, then wonders if the aquarium lid is on. He takes a step backward, and the office door bursts open.

"She's ready!" Robert says. He smiles at Lance. Scowls at the fish. "Be nice."

"Is the Buick really fixed?"

He puts his hands on his hips. "Would I bullshit you?"

"Sorry. It's just that so many people have tried to fix it."

"Yeah," Robert says. "But only one mechanic. C'mon."

Back in the garage, a fleet of gleaming hot rods surrounds the Buick like the setup for a joke. But Robert greets Lance's car as respectfully as a gentleman taking a lady's hand. He pops the hood and props it open with a rubber-tipped rod, opens the door with a gentle pull, and gets inside. He points to the engine and turns the key.

It starts.

The boom of the engine fills the space like a song in a cathedral. Robert revs the engine, grinning, raising his wild eyebrows. Lance's jaw locks, eyes stinging, shaking his head. Robert shuts off the engine and gets out. He squares his shoulders with Lance. Looks him up and down. Robert is very tall. Lance steps backward.

"It runs," Robert says. "Now let's get down to business. Analysis, parts, and labor."

"Okay," Lance says, doing his own calculations. He had Goodview Towing's $187 invoice plus whatever he still owed at Macland's, plus four nights at the Trainsong. That, taken with 11 unheard voice messages on his phone and 4 minus 1 people returning to Bend would leave him with exactly $0 of his mother's money to spend.

"Ready?" Robert asks.

"Ready."

"First: analysis!" he says. "This. Well, this was a special case." He paces, circling the Buick like a detective. "Quite a story, too. You've been here how long? Four days?"

"Five."

"Five." Robert whistles. "You know a little about cars, Lance. Is that right?"

He starts to say *no*, then stops himself. "Yeah. A little."

"So you know as a mechanic, you apply logic first. Then equipment. Then skill. In that order. Understand?" Lance nods.

"First!" Robert lifts his index finger like a struck match. "Logic. Your dash was failing. That's electrical. So that's where we start.

Follow the path, my friend. Electricity comes from the battery. It goes where first?"

"I don't know."

"The starter, Lance. The starter. This will be important later. You need two things to start an engine. Spark and fuel. Remember that. So I check your starter, and there's a spark. That means your battery is functional. And your starter is functional. Not a long walk to the dashboard from there, but a couple fuses along the way. And there, we find culprit number one!"

Robert plucks a fuse from his shirt pocket and throws it at Lance's chest. Red plastic with metal buckteeth. It bounces off him, plinks onto concrete.

"Blown fuses?" Lance says. "But I changed—"

"One problem was the fuses," Robert says. "*One.* But like people, it's never just one thing, Lance. Cars are complex. See, when the fuse to your speedometer blew, it spiked your needle right up the center. Like you told me, remember?"

"Yes."

"But there were two blown fuses." Robert throws another one, and Lance catches it this time. "And whereas a speedometer might give you a flashy show before it dies, a fuel gauge will just plain *freeze.*"

"Freeze," Lance repeats. Eyes narrowing to a squint.

"I'm guessing that happened back in Seattle," Robert says, circling closer. He holds up two fingers. "Two things to run an engine, Lance. Spark and fuel. Spark you had. But fuel? Well." He steps so close Lance can feel his breath. "You were just. Plain. Out."

"Out?" Lance says. "I was out of gas?"

"Case closed!" Robert claps his hands.

"Out of gas," Lance repeats.

"Now back to parts and labor. This job took me exactly half an hour. I installed two 20A fuses in your vehicle. And two gallons of premium-grade American gasoline." A plastic gas container appears in Robert's hands. He drums the hollow side with his fingers. "And you, my friend, are as good as new. Or as good as 1993. But that was a good year, son. A damn good year. Now let's get you squared away."

Back in the office, Robert pulls out his calculator. Two fuses at two dollars each. Eight dollars for gas. Sixty-five dollars for diagnostics. Robert charges Lance's card a total of seventy-seven dollars.

"Thank you," Lance says.

"Just doing my job," Robert says. "Bea tells me you're off to graduation."

"Yeah. On Friday."

"So what happens after that?"

Lance had a scripted answer to this question. But his script is gone, and pressure is building behind his eyes. He stares at Robert's desk.

"It's okay. You don't need a plan," Robert says, tossing him the keys. "You got a car."

Lance catches the keys. Heavier than he remembers. Robert rockets up from his chair and by the time Lance is in the Buick, he's already back to work. Cursing and shaking his head. Pacing his concrete palace left to right, right to left.

The Buick's engine fires.

Lance lifts his foot off the brake and is in charge of three thousand pounds of steel. The upholstery, embedded with 156,000 miles of memories. Dried mud from a hundred trails worked into floor mats. The cling of stale cigarette smoke, winning its battle with Febreze. And swinging from the rearview mirror, the brass treble clef his grandmother gave him on his twelfth birthday.

Twenty miles an hour feels fast.

The forest rushes around him. Strange to sit and move so quickly, choosing your direction with a flick of the wrist. Back on Highway 2, the feeling is so surreal he almost forgets to stop for more gas. He sits for five minutes, but no one comes out. He's in Washington. He'll have to pump his own.

The road back to the Trainsong motel feels too steep and fast, like driving down the side of a mountain. He bombs over hills, slips around greased curves. When the road straightens out, the clouds and pavement join into a single silver chute and there is no stopping him. He learned to drive on a country road like this, and can see his father chewing on an apple in the passenger seat, tapping the dashboard to Jethro Tull. Rolling papers, flapping in the wind. *Don't ever do this, okay? Don't ever do this.*

The Trainsong comes into view, and Lance pulls into the parking lot. The breeze through the window dies. The Buick bakes in the sun, and Dakota's front door is closed. He moves fast.

His motel room is still a wreck. His life in folders and suitcases, strewn over the carpet. An unmade bed with dents in the sheets. He imagines the bed cordoned off with yellow tape. A crime scene. The things he's done. When he leaves, this room will be cleaned and used by someone else. They will have no idea what happened here. What could've happened.

But there is no Seattle. There is no other option. Never was.

An animal jolts awake in the cage of his chest.

Run, the animal shrieks. *RUN*.

Things and memories. He will stuff them all into bags and throw them in the trunk. Dark and safe and all locked up.

Plastic folders bend and crack as he shoves them in the duffel. A fat ball of dirty clothes. The suitcase zipper will not swallow the lump. Cram it in. Stomp it down. Too much to fit. These khakis won't fit. These jeans won't fit. Stone's body will not fit. *Goodbye, Dakota* will not fit. And he's breathing hard, he is wiping his face and the room is neat with a suitcase, a trumpet case, an orange duffel bag.

He looks over the walls. The cats stare back, trying to tell him something.

The bathroom!

A massacre of toiletries. Squashed tubes, plastic bottles. Evidence of last night, staring up from a wicker trash can. Obscene. He unspools a glove of toilet paper and piles it on top. He slips a finger under the bathroom mirror and it opens. Empty.

He remembers gaps in a medicine cabinet.

The morning he found the letter there was a missing comb, toothpaste, razor, aftershave. His father's lines of absence were sharp and clear in cupboards and shelves, in the tools missing from the outlined Peg-Board in the garage. Lance closes the medicine cabinet. There is still a wineglass under the sink.

Outlets clear.

Nothing under the bed but a wooden block.

The parts of the room that belong to him all have handles. He hangs everything on his arms and shoulders. He can barely carry it all. Grip, slipping. One trip to the car. He'll reverse out of the parking lot, reverse down the highway, reverse this trip all the way back to Bend, all the way to last Saturday.

NOW! RUN!

Alarms, air-raid sirens. He's out the door and moving too fast. He might spill headfirst down painted steps. He makes it to the car. He shuts the trunk and is in the Buick with locked doors and all is still.

Something jabs his thigh.

A room key anchored to a broken plastic train and a conversation with Cheri and hundreds of dollars he does not have. Cheri is in her office, a horizon of frizzy hair over her monitor. No time for Cheri. Lance starts the car. He pulls forward, rolls down the passenger window, and tosses the key. It lands on the wicker mat with a bounce. *Ha! Perfect!* His engine purrs, carrying him to the edge of the highway. One right turn and he'll be gone.

Blinking, clicking. As soon as this white pickup passes.

C'mon, white pickup!

In the rearview mirror, a parking lot. No one chasing him. He can do this.

You are valedictorian.

You are the first-chair trumpet player.

You jumped a train.

Dakota is in love with you.

He could've said something. Left a note.

Or a letter.

He could've left a letter.

Lance's foot flattens the brake.

"No," he says. "No, no, no."

He jerks open the glove box: starlight mints, registration, receipts, a small flashlight, two rubber rings, crumpled carbon copies—and he heaves them onto the floor. *Please just be here! Can you just be here?*

There is no letter in the car. The highway is clear. Turn signal, clicking.

He could go. Can't go. Lance makes a tight U-turn. He pulls back into his space. He's out of the car, heaving himself up by the handrail, a balcony sprint to his room. A stone doorknob. Locked. He pats his pockets. He curses, turns around.

His room key is on the mat downstairs.

Lance makes it down around the corner and—*no*—Cheri is standing up. Rising from behind her computer. She never stands up. Why is she standing up? Slowly, she moves toward him. He'll be caught. He runs faster but his legs are moving at slow-nightmare speed and he can't go fast enough, can't get there until she's at the door, scowling behind glass.

He smiles, lifting his key.

She opens the door and he's already halfway up the stairs.

"Breakdown!" she yells. "Hey Breakdown! What the heck are you doing?" He slams the door to his room and bounces off the corner of the mattress, hand closing on the nightstand drawer. He jerks it open, contents slamming forward: Bible, phone book, letter. The letter. He pulls out the envelope that says LANCE. He breathes, holds it to his chest.

Across the room, there is a pad of paper on the small desk. A blue pen.

Could he do it? Could he lift that pen? Could he write the name *Dakota*?

Now there are footsteps, coming up the stairs. Cheri is after her money. He walks to the door, hoping to beat her to the knock. If he can open the door and smile and say *Hey there*, she won't be suspicious.

But when he opens the door he is not smiling at Cheri.

It's Dakota. Dakota, climbing out of memory. With a scent and a body and a sour, electric feeling between them. Red-rimmed eyes. Eyes that have cried all day wrap themselves around him and his packed bags and an empty motel room.

"I'm glad I caught you," she says.

"Caught me?"

"Before you left. You were moving pretty fast."

She comes in and sits on the bed. Their bed.

"They want to see you before you go," she says.

"Dakota."

She's staring at the sailboat. "Just say the words. If you have to go, just say the words."

"Which words?"

"'I truly appreciated our time together. And I must ask that you please don't follow me home.'" She looks at him with glassy eyes. He can't look back.

"I'm not leaving," he says.

"Okay."

"Who wants to see me?"

"Everyone," she says. "They need your story."

31

Dakota still steals ground when she walks, moving faster than her small steps should allow. Gliding across the parking lot, down the hillside. She does not look back. Not once.

The fire pit is abandoned. Cordoned off with strips of yellow and orange tape, knotted around sunken rebar. Some of the group's things are still inside where they left them. Empty bottles. Tipped-over cans. A black fleece. It all looks important now.

They continue to walk. They are five hundred miles into the woods, and it will be five hundred miles out. The sky is already losing light, and the place she is taking him is nowhere he wants to be. Halfway down the path they once walked from Sugarville, Dakota turns into the brush and steps into the space they've carved out for themselves.

The fire pit sits in a thicket of blackberries and nettles. Logs have mossy tops, and Meebs and Rocco are standing over a smoldering hole in the ground. They're trying to start a fire without

Dakota. She steps forward and thorned branches swallow the path at her back. Lance couldn't get out if he tried.

"Well, look," Mason says.

Lance is looking at the blond girl by the fire. A girl he does not immediately recognize as Breanna. She has cried away her makeup and hard eyes and any trace of cleverness, as if Stone's death cracked her shell wide open and a real girl came pouring out. She looks about fifteen. Maybe she'd always looked this soft when she was alone with him. Maybe she'd look this way tonight, and never again.

They are all raw.

Tragedy and Meebs are a poor fit. His eyes are too wide, mouth so small. Like a sad cartoon. Mason looks old. Hunched and scowling. Overnight, he's a few years closer to his father. Rocco is the most together.

Put that log here, Meebs. C'mon, man.

Did he care? Was Rocco used to this? How much had he lost in his life?

Lance's eyes are stinging. He can't help it. He wipes his cheeks. They all look different and new. Did he ever really know any of them? Does he know anyone at all?

He sits next to Dakota. Looks down at her hand.

"You brought your horn?" Meebs asks.

Lance nods, pulling the case close.

"Blower," Rocco says.

"We heard you talked to Stone," Mason says.

"Did you go back down like I asked?" Breanna says, her voice thin.

"Yeah, I did."

Her shoulders sag. "Thank you for going. Thank you for talking to him."

"That kind of depends on what you said, Blower," Mason says.

"What did Stone want to talk about?" Breanna asks, only looking at Lance.

The campfire remains a gray, smoking pit. Dakota coughs. Meebs and Rocco shuffle around, jabbing it with twigs.

"He said a lot of things," Lance says. He tries to push his voice out smooth, but it's cracking, ready to snap. "He told me about basic training. He seemed to feel better after we talked. I didn't know he would do it. If he'd said anything, I would've told someone."

"He didn't say anything about Telluride?" Mason asks. Something is creeping up behind his eyes. A wolf in its cave. Lance stares at the wolf, wondering what it wants.

"Did he mention Telluride?" Rocco asks.

They are leaning forward now. They all want something from him.

"Yeah," Lance says. "He did."

"Yep," Mason says, leaning back. They're all nodding, listening to a drumbeat Lance is just beginning to hear.

Their fire has finally started. It's a flimsy thing, no core. It will not hold up unless they keep feeding it, blowing at the smoke until they see stars and taste soot and feel sick from it. But you can keep that kind of fire going a long time.

"I guess he finally went for it," Rocco says.

"He should've known better," Mason says. "Guy couldn't jump trains for shit."

They're looking at him again. Lance's turn.

They need your story.

He just has to say the words. This story will catch and burn. *Stone was trying to jump a train to Telluride.* Breanna is still looking at him. She wants something different than the rest of them. She wants the truth.

"He was so sad, Breanna," Lance says.

She's crying, hard. Staring at the ground.

"Hey," Mason says. "Leave her alone."

Breanna's shaking her head.

"That's not it, Mason," Lance says. "He wasn't that bad at jumping trains."

"You don't know," Rocco says. "He fell twice before."

"Did you drop him?" Lance asks Mason.

"Excuse me?"

The wolf is out now, baring its teeth. *C'mon, Mason. Jump and bite.* Tonight, he is strong enough. He will grab that wolf by the throat and strangle it.

"Did you let go of his hand? Like you let go of mine?"

Breanna stops crying.

"Did you drop him that night?" she asks Mason. "Did you do that on purpose?"

"Are you questioning me?" Mason snaps.

"Yeah. What are you going to do, Mason?" Breanna says. "Fire me?"

"You're seriously talking shit to me, Bre? Who gave him a job when he got discharged?" He's talking to everyone, using his ringmaster voice. "Answer me! Who found him a place to live when he got bounced from his dad's? Who's closing down his whole place tomorrow to host a party for his ass?"

"Yeah," Lance says. "You're such a good friend."

"You got something to say, Blower?"

"Was he too good at guitar?" Lance says. "Is that why you called him Stone?"

"Shut your fucking mouth—"

"Did Dakota like him better?"

"Okay, I'll shut it for you."

Mason is standing.

"Come on over and try," Lance says. He stands, and everyone is standing.

"Calm down," Dakota says.

"Look," Rocco says. "It's no one's fault. No one pushed Stone in front of that train."

Lance is shaking his head, *no, no, no.*

"Stone was riding to Telluride." Meebs uses a clear, monotone voice. Like the comment is designed to play on a loop.

"You're wrong, Meebs," Lance says.

"Blower," Rocco says. "Shut up."

"You want to know what he really said about you all? You want to know what he said about his friends right before he jumped in front—"

Something knocks his head to the side. The world tilts and his eyes water and when he wipes them clean it's Meebs, seething, panicked by what he's done.

"Go away," Meebs says. "Just go away!"

"Andrew!" Dakota says. "What the hell are you doing?"

Andrew? Who's Andrew?

Lance plunges into the brush. Thorns and nettles rip his skin. He's fighting through, hacking at the forest until it loosens his grip and dumps him onto a path. He can't swallow the thickness in his throat, can't move it down far enough to breathe.

And someone is crashing after him.

He turns, but cannot fight. Can't protect himself from what's coming.

Dakota.

It's Dakota, and she's carrying his horn.

A flood is coming, choking off his voice, and Dakota is wrapping her arms around him and there are no words when it all comes crashing down. They hold each other through a long, hard wave, and when the worst is over, they wipe their faces dry and breathe.

Lance expects someone to come for them. Someone must want him to finish his story. But when he and Dakota go, no one follows. There is a new numbness. Novocain in the moonlight. His arm is around her waist as they stumble down the path, cuts scabbing over in the breeze.

He smells the flowers before he sees them.

Honey, lavender, and that singular smell that will always be his first night at the Trainsong. The path spills into a field Lance has only seen from an open train car. White flowers, holding the moon in their petals. The breeze comes fast and cool, and he clutches Dakota with both arms, pulling her to his chest.

"Will you stay for the trainsong?" he asks.

"Yeah."

"You aren't mad?" he asks.

"I don't know what I am."

They find a patch of bare earth. The dirt is still warm. Her hands, still electric. He breathes clean air and holds her left hand. He focuses on her thumb. This thumb is a world that makes sense. A world he can climb inside and build walls around. The ridges on her nail, the softness of a knuckle. The way it can be pinched between his fingers. This tiny piece of Dakota. If he looks and holds on long enough, maybe he can understand just this.

She sees him looking.

"Your thumb is a clue," he says.

She smiles. "Yeah?"

She pinches his thumb back.

"I was thinking maybe they aren't clues," she says. "Maybe they're gifts. They just never felt like gifts, because I couldn't share them. Like I never saw this field."

"Or a hand," Lance says.

"Or a hand."

They hold each other. At the first sound of the train, Lance sits up straight.

The headlamp comes like dawn to the field, swallowing the flowers in a blaze, unclasping their hands, filling his eyes until they burn. He blinks, gobs of color turning solid, becoming a yellow car with black letters.

LARSON'S LUMBER

It coasts down the tracks and shudders through a curve. Next, a silver flash.

They're coming. He feels them before he sees them, and then their car is drifting past in slow time. Mason, feet perched on the car's edge, holding the metal handle. Meebs, right beside him. So close he might've been leaning on Mason's shoulder. Rocco is farther back, in shadow. They're staring out at the field, expressions fixed and flat.

Lance is right there in front of them. Dakota is right there. But the group does not see them. They're looking for something else, watching the horizon. Their car takes the curve and folds into line behind the others, twisting off through a tunnel of trees. The rumble echoes, then is gone.

Lance stands and unsnaps his hard case.

Dakota follows him, wading through the tall grass, climbing the slope to the crunch of ballast. Lance's leg is shaking when he places it on the nearest tie. Or maybe that's the train. Maybe the tracks here always hum a little.

"What are you going to play?" Dakota asks.

"A request."

He puts the brass to his lips and plays Stone's song.

32

According to the sign, the Trainsong office opens "most days between 9 and 10," but today Cheri doesn't show up until eleven. Turns out she still has his mother's card on file from the first night. He can sign all the charges over to *Mrs. Hendricks,* and has no trouble doing so.

"You sure, Breakdown?" she says. "Is this really goodbye? Want to throw your key at me again?"

He throws the key at Cheri. She catches it.

"Good arm," she says.

"Good catch."

"Police still after you? Is that why you came bat-outta-helling down the stairs yesterday?"

"No," he says. "I think I've settled things with the police."

"How about her?"

"Who?"

"The one leaning against your car. Like she's waiting for a ticket."

"Dakota."

"She's nice. You should take her with you."

"Really?"

"Sure. What's the worst thing that happens? She's pretty and she wants to ride with you, even in your broke-down old car. I'd take her."

"You want to, Cheri? I can tell her you're interested."

"Don't start. Hey. What happened to your cheek?"

"I got punched."

"By one of them boys?"

"Yeah."

"Just means they like ya."

"Maybe."

"You are a wild thing. You can stick around. I'll give you a discount."

"Do I still have to clean my own bathroom?"

"Bet your boots!"

Lance walks out the door and a bell rings overhead. The air smells like sunbaked leaves and freshly trimmed grass. The smell of early June, like a clear runway into summer when anything is possible and days don't end and nights don't end and nothing good will ever end.

Dakota is standing beside the Buick.

Their goodbye has chased them on trains and across fields, over long winding roads and through cemeteries and motel rooms and has finally caught them here in this parking lot.

She holds one hand up, shielding her eyes. The sun shines in her hair and he wants to press his face there, breathe in how that hair smells in the sun. He has never done that, and may not have another chance. His hand is moving through the warm air, reaching up to brush her hair, her cheek, but her hand comes up first. She's holding something.

A worn envelope that says LANCE.

"I found this in your room."

"Did you read it?" he asks. A flutter of panic.

"No," she says, handing it over. "But you keep leaving it behind. Are you sure you still want it?"

"I don't know."

"That's why you came back, right? Yesterday?"

He looks at the ground.

"I was wondering if I'd get my own letter."

Her eyes. They won't stop looking.

"I couldn't even write your name," he says.

"Yeah," she says. "I tried to write you a letter in my book, but it didn't belong. Maybe if we can't find the words, we don't say goodbye."

"We'll have to sing it. Write a song."

Her lips curl down, trembling.

"Dakota."

"What?"

"We can't."

"Can't what?"

He sighs. "We don't have any money."

"Okay."

"I didn't get into Seattle."

"So?" she says.

"So?"

"So it's one school. Are you going to stop playing music?"

She is not hiding now. Her face is bright in the sun.

"What do you expect me to do?" he says.

"Yeah? What do I expect? Oh, part of me—" she starts. Takes a breath. "Part of me expects you to go to Oregon State. Give your speech about stars. Catch some shit from your friends. Become a successful businessman who plays his horn on the weekends. Or maybe never."

"So what about you?" he asks. "Work at The Float? Give Mason a try?"

"No. I saw too much," she says. "I have to buy an RV now. Recording equipment."

"Waders."

She closes her eyes. "Fucking waders." She looks over him, toward the road.

"I can come back. I'll call and—"

"Don't," she says. "Please."

He wants to stitch this back together. He leans in past the point of no words, and Dakota does something she has never done before. She turns away.

"I can't kiss you, Wildman," she says. "Our kisses are like a million hellos."

"I don't know what to do."

"That's what awkward hugs are for," she says.

So they hug. He squeezes her so tight he expects her to gasp, tell him to stop, but she doesn't. Her lips are beside his ear. Breathing. She hangs on until it's over and he's climbing into his car. He turns the key and the engine fires. And he will leave now and not look back.

But he looks. Then he waves. Then he rolls down his window. The Lance Hendricks Machine is not following orders. He cannot make it drive away.

The engine hums, his foot on the brake.

"I hate this ending," he says.

"Classic fade-out," she says.

Those eyes. His memories will be worthless because they can't be her, and they can't be now. Dakota is real fire, and he's driving back to Bend with a suitcase full of ashes.

"You got an alternate ending?" he says.

"I do. You ask me if I'll come with you."

"And what do you say?"

She's staring and he is biting his cheek. Eyes, stinging.

"I think I say *Yes*. Then you say: *Grab your bag, Dakota. We're leaving.*"

"And you come running out your door?"

"Like I'm on fire."

"And jump in the Buick."

"Yep."

"And then?"

"Music." Dakota smiles. "Roll credits. That's the end of the movie."

Lance nods. It's like he's back under the willow tree. He can't say what she needs him to say, or touch what she needs him to touch. He must leave. His nose and eyes are stinging and he just needs to feel the wind through his hair and play some music. He'll drag this shitty goodbye over mountains and swing it around turns for six hours until it pulls its claws out. He'll leave this goodbye on the side of the road, and bury it in the wilderness.

He is nodding. She knows this cannot work. She moves her hand away from the window so he can roll it up. And he's just driving.

She is not leaving. Not walking out of the parking lot. His turn signal is clicking. She will never walk out of the parking lot. She will never climb out of his rearview mirror.

The Lance Hendricks Machine keeps moving. He is on rails to Bend. A speech, a summer job. It has always been this way. Nothing has changed. The Buick is running like a dream.

He is barely out of the parking lot when the shaking starts. It begins with his hands. They tremble on the wheel until the tremors move up his arms and shoulders, spreading down to his knees and then his foot stomps the brake.

One quick U-turn removes Dakota from the rearview mirror. He can barely breathe as he presses the pedal until she is real again, right in front of him, and he is shifting into park and leaping out of the car.

"Say it," she says. "I need you to say it. Say it."

"Grab your bag, Dakota. We're leaving."

She pinches him.

"You're supposed to ask."

"Will you come with me?"

She looks at him. He stares back.

"Yes," she says.

Her eyes brighten until they aren't the same eyes, won't ever be the same eyes, and she walks back to her door and disappears. He waits halfway between her and the Buick. Inside, things open and slam. People talking too low to hear. He rubs his hands on his jeans. Remembers to bend his knees. Can't pass out. The door swings open and Dakota has a suitcase. He's never seen her run before, and she's breathing hard when she reaches him.

"You're packed?" he says.

"I've been packed."

They race to the car. Their footsteps are a two-piece arrangement of light percussion, and it sounds like a symphony. Dakota is in his car and she has a suitcase.

It's all terrifying. It's all possible.

"What happened to *We don't have any money*?"

"We do have money," he says, turning the key. "I have a thousand dollars."

33

The Buick's slamming door is the only sound in The Float's parking lot. The echo skips across pavement and crashes into the woods. Dakota sits behind the wheel. She rolls down the window.

"How long until I need to worry?" she asks.

"Five minutes," he says. "This will only take five minutes."

He unzips his orange duffel bag and upends the contents into the trunk. Folders, packets, applications. He shuts the trunk and carries the empty bag across the parking lot. The sign on The Float's front door has been changed.

CLD. PRIVATE PARTY.

Lance's hand wraps around the cool brass knob.

Unlocked. He opens the door.

A wash of cool air chills the sweat on his back. The wooden pirate is solemn, and The Float is empty. Vacant booths stare back at him, stools like polished stumps. A few center rounds have been draped with table coverings that resemble medical-examination paper. There's a frosted rectangular cake on gold-laminated card-board with a string of pink letters: WE WILL MISS YOU. Letters spaced with blue and green hearts.

Lance moves as quickly as he can, but the room stretches out. He's walking through a bog, mud to his knees. He just needs to get to the register, but it's hours before he reaches the bar. There's shuffling in the kitchen. Someone is coming. Lance finds the gap where the bar-top door opens. His fingers curl beneath wood.

"Blower?"

Mason stands in the kitchen entrance.

"How did you get in?"

"Door's unlocked."

"Yeah? Well, we're closed for Stone's party. You're not invited."

He stares back at Mason.

"I'm here for my thousand dollars."

"What?"

Mason walks toward Lance.

"Want to repeat that?" Mason says. He flops his arms on the bar.

"I'm here for my thousand dollars," he says.

"You want a thousand dollars? Take off your shoes and spin the wheel."

"No."

"You know your problem, Blower?" His breath hits Lance's face. Mason's been drinking. "You don't know when to leave." Mason turns away from him. He's holding something in his right hand. A pair of black boots, laces knotted.

"Mason."

"The door, Blower. It's right there. Bye."

Mason's got one boot by its meaty, rubber sole. He's using it to spin the other in wobbly circles. Clockwise, then counterclockwise. He searches the rafters, pacing the length of the bar. Lance has seen those boots before.

"Those are Stone's boots," Lance says.

"Ding, ding, ding! You're a genius."

Mason stops behind the cash register. Lowers his arm once, twice. Lance makes a choked sound. All he can say is:

"Don't!"

Mason lets them go. Heavier than they look, the boots barely make it to the rafters. For a moment, it seems like they might tumble back to the floor, then the laces catch between a jumble of sneakers. One boot chases the other, toe after heel. A slow-motion dance. They spin until they've webbed themselves to the beam, turned outward with the tension.

"I wonder what I'll win?" Mason says.

He walks past Lance and stops at the prize wheel.

"Those aren't your boots. You don't get to spin."

"You're hilarious, Blower."

Mason cranks on the wheel. The sound fills the bar: *clickclickclickclickclickclick*. The pointer stops on FREE BEER. Mason grabs a pint glass from a stack. It makes a sharp ring, like the unsheathing of a blade. He fills the glass with dark beer and puts it on the bar.

"That's not your beer," Lance says.

Mason takes a long, loud slurp. He belches and blows the air in Lance's direction.

"Everything here is mine," Mason says. "Don't you get that? Go home."

"Pay me and I'll go."

"Oh yeah? Anything else?"

"Yeah. You're not going to finish that drink."

Mason takes a giant gulp and gets foam on his lips. He wipes it off, and flicks the liquid at Lance's face. Beer on his own lips, in his eyes. He blinks, wiping it off.

Mason laughs. "You look great, Blower. Just perfect."

Lance turns and walks toward the front door.

"That's right, big man. Go back to Bend. Tell Dakota *hi* for me, okay? I'll take good care of her. Don't worry. Hey. What the hell are you doing? Blower. Hey! Hey—Wildman! Don't touch the pirate! That shit's antique. Step the fuck away! What's wrong with you!"

It takes a few twists to loosen the glue, then the sword's handle comes free. A soft pull and it's his. A real sword, heavy as a fistful of baseball bats, snapping into his hands like it was meant to be there.

He walks toward the bar.

"You owe me a thousand dollars," Lance says.

"You owe me a thousand dollars for wrecking my statue! Put that shit back."

Mason reaches for his beer.

"Don't," Lance says, raising the sword.

Mason's shoulder moves and Lance swings. The beer explodes. A wet confetti of glass sprays across the room. There was a pint of beer, and now there isn't. Lance cocks the sword to the ready position. Using his elbow, he flips open the bar-top door and steps forward, feet squishing onto a rubber mat.

Mason throws back his shoulders. Makes himself big.

"Think you're tough, Blower? I think you're a piece of shit."

Lance steps forward. Mason stands his ground, glances over his shoulder. Lance takes another step. Mason steps back.

"Get in the walk-in," Lance says.

"You don't have the balls. You won't cut me."

"I think I will," Lance says. "Only one of us can be right." He takes a step. A piece of glass slips from the side of the bar, lands with a *plink*.

"You're going to jail," Mason says.

"You're going to the walk-in."

He keeps the sword steady, cocked over his shoulder. One step, then another, and Mason is walking backward. A dance down the length of the bar, through the swinging door of the kitchen. Mason twists his feet for a second, like he might run. He doesn't. He stops in front of the cooler.

Lance steps forward. Mason's back touches the door.

"Stop walking at me!"

"Open the door," Lance says. "All the way in."

Mason opens the door. Condensation curls into the kitchen. The smell of old cabbage.

"I will hunt you down." Mason steps inside, seething. "I will kill you."

"I think you'll stay right here. In this bar."

Lance steps forward and slams the freezer shut. He grabs a broom and slips it in like a dead bolt. Mason's full weight comes smashing against the door. The handle shivers, but holds tight. He expects Mason to pound and shout and break jars, but he is quiet. Fifteen seconds later, it's like he's not even there.

Lance backs out of the kitchen and is alone in The Float. He could be out the door in ten seconds. Instead, he lays the sword beside the cash register and climbs on top of the bar. It's higher than it looks. He slips on the puddle of beer and his right foot shoots out, kicking the cash register with a *DING*. The till pops out. It's empty. Lance plants his feet, and stares up at the distant shoes. He lifts the sword and gets a swimmy touch of vertigo.

Stone's black laces are twisted over a bundle of blue and white threads, not yet part of the rafter's DNA. He nudges the sword's steel tip into the nest of laces, gives a twist. Not enough. He stretches, standing on the tips of his toes. His legs tremble. Another twist splits the laces, and Stone's boots drop with a rubbery clap.

There are noises in the kitchen. Mason, tinkering with the door.

Lance leaps down and grabs his duffel bag. He races over to the American flag and jerks the cord. His breath catches. He hears "The Star-Spangled Banner." "You're a Grand Old Flag." There's so much here.

He finds his own bill first, right where he remembers it.

LANCE

That one is easy.

When he blasts out through The Float's front door, he has the duffel in his left hand, Stone's boots swinging from his right. He's ready but Dakota is giving him the wrong kind of look and somehow the car is not running.

Why is the car not running?

"Dakota! C'mon! Start the car!"

"It won't start, Lance. The car won't start!"

She twists the key. Twists again. The engine is clicking. Clicking hard.

"Stop! Don't turn the key again," he says. "Pop the hood."

He glances at The Float. That door will burst open. Mason will come running out. He lifts Stone's boot and smacks the starter with the thick rubber sole.

"What are you doing?"

"Try it now!"

Click. Click.

He whacks the starter so hard he feels it in his shoulder.

"Again!"

The engine fires. Purring. Ready. He drops the hood with a clap. Dakota slides into the passenger seat. Lance jumps in.

"I thought this car was fixed," Dakota says.

"Cheap starter," he says. "Made in China."

He shifts to drive. They make it all the way to the edge of the parking lot, then Dakota turns on the radio. A deafening F-sharp, blaring from the speakers. Lance pounds the player with his fist. And the tape ejects. He gasps, pulls the cassette from the stereo, and throws it in the back. Dakota turns. She is staring at the orange duffel bag.

"I take it you're not giving your speech tomorrow," she says.

"Not the speech you read," he says, lifting his foot from the brake. "I'm learning how to improvise."

And before anyone can stop them, they're gone.

Hi, everyone.

There's a proven formula for giving a valedictorian's speech. It's been researched and well documented. I'm going to tell you the secret now.

You start with a question. Then a big metaphor, preferably one that involves nature. Mountains, rivers, and shooting stars are great. I went with outer space. You introduce the metaphor in paragraph one, then tell three to five amusing anecdotes about your classmates. It's best if you name-drop popular students and teachers. You should tell stories everyone already knows. The more familiar, the better. You conclude with a few words of wisdom, and a piece of advice for today's graduating seniors.

Most of you know I've always been more of a math person. But it turns out words matter. Stories matter. The stories we tell about each other. The stories you end up telling yourself. Since I can remember, my story has always been about becoming valedictorian. About being the first-chair trumpet player. Getting a full-ride scholarship, and going to business school. I'm not sure where that story came from. Maybe from me, before I knew what it meant. Maybe my mom or my teachers.

Your story might be different. Your story might be about being a burnout. Or a nerd. The smart one, the dumb one. The person in your family who is going to succeed, or the person who is going to fail. Maybe you have a nickname, like me. Maybe you feel trapped. Some of my friends do. My dad did.

That's what happens when you grow up and spend a lot of time in one place. It's hard to avoid a nickname. It's hard to avoid becoming a character. And you don't want to be a character. Even a good one. It can ruin you. Because people are complicated. And people change.

So I'm not going to tell any familiar stories today. I'm going to stick to math.

Most of you are eighteen years old. That's two hundred and sixteen months of living. Six thousand five hundred and seventy days of people telling you what to study and how often to practice and why you should care. When to wake up and go to sleep. Where to live. Who you are, and who you will be.

And if you've survived six thousand five hundred days of that, you've finally earned something. You've earned independence. At eighteen, for the first time, you can legally own things. You can vote and gamble and get tattoos. You can check into motel rooms and buy a car and drive anywhere there's a road. Your parents can't stop you. You can go to any school that will let you in. You can quit your summer job. You can cancel your scholarship. You can love who you want. You can even change your name.

So here's my advice to today's graduating seniors.

You should know what it feels like to be a stranger. Leave this place, and go somewhere new. Because someone you've known for five minutes might know you better than the people you've known your entire life. You can always start over. You've made it this far. And if you're lucky enough to know one person in this world who really sees you, know that's a rare thing. A precious thing. Grab their hand and run.

Of course, with adulthood comes responsibility. Everyone will remind you of that, all the time. Mr. Leeds wants me to remind you that your first big decision is whether or not you will throw your graduation cap in the air at the end of my speech. As a reminder, you're expected to keep your cap on. So think about risk and serious life consequences. Consider aerodynamics, and the volatility of foam. Choose wisely.

Everyone's life is on the line.

Telluride

A thousand miles from Bend, the town of Telluride, Colorado, is said to have the most beautiful main street in America—a panorama of beautiful mountains, and a road framed by beautiful shops and a seemingly endless supply of beautiful people moving among them. There are high cables strung across Colorado Avenue, anchored to buildings and trees, often adorned with banners and bright lights. Everyone takes pictures. With so many people and so many cameras, not much goes unnoticed in Telluride, and nothing out of place lasts long. Which is what makes the pair of black boots hanging from the final cable on Colorado Avenue so strange.

Even at the easternmost end of the street, those boots shouldn't have lasted a day.

But someone within the City of Telluride's Streets and Sanitation Department must have liked the way they looked there, at the edge of where high-end shops snapped off into wilderness, hanging with a backdrop of snow clinging to the mountains. A bold statement, like an exclamation point at the end of a sentence.

So the boots hung for a day. When no one complained, they hung for a week.

People noticed. They photographed the boots. They sent the pictures to friends and posted them on websites, and within just a few months, the hanging boots became a place people sometimes stopped when they came to visit Telluride.

They hung there, durable boots, through summer, fall, winter, and spring. When they'd hung long enough to be photographed in all seasons, the pictures were assembled in a four-photo frame and sold in one, then many of the shops in town. They were seen and admired by visitors and residents until they were just as much a part of Telluride as the people who lived and worked there.

The pictures were stunning. But nothing like seeing those boots in real life.

It was crisp that night. Only one star they could see. The boots were heavy and the lines on Colorado Avenue were so much higher than the rafters at The Float, but it had to work. When Lance let them fly, Stone's boots kicked up and pedaled that impossible distance, climbing their way into the sky and landing on the line with a perfect final step. One boot above the other. Like someone had reached up and placed them there.

"Lance." Dakota grabbed his hand. "I just saw one."

Lance did not know if he'd seen a ghost, but he'd learned from Dakota the most beautiful moments are the ones you don't plan for, and the ones you'll miss if you aren't paying attention.

So when Lance looked in the rearview mirror for his last glimpse at Telluride, he was watching for the boots. He expected what he saw to be moving. He expected to cry. What he did not account for was the way the road sloped up on the way out of town, and how the cables strung across Colorado Avenue would appear to stack themselves into five perfect parallel lines. How with the treble clef dangling from his mirror, those lines would become a clear stave of music, and the boots would shrink to black dots, like a melody's first pair of ascending notes. Like Dakota's hand in his. A riddle, a clue, a gift.

A song, unwritten.

Acknowledgments

This story would not exist without the life-altering break-down of my own '93 Buick and the support of the following people:

First, my love and gratitude to Emily Kemp, who has held my hand and taken the wheel and ridden shotgun on this trip longer than anyone who is not a blood relative. Also, the wonderful blood relatives: Dad, Sarah, and Brett. My mom, who texted *I recognize some of myself in Lance's mother. She seems like a fabulous and loving individual.* And Kelsey, who kept her shoes on and made that drive.

Thanks to Matt Brown—my coolest mentor—for introducing me to both Batman and Tobias Wolff. (How cool is that?!) Thanks to Kendra Bradley for telling me I was ready, and Michael Lucker for telling me LA would wait. It did. Thanks to those whose work helped me build my own lens and kaleidoscope: Capote, Cather, Berlin, Wolff, Kafka, Rand, Dahl, Dali, Bradbury, Steinbeck, Stephen Gammell, and Christopher Pike.

Thanks to The Head and the Heart and Blind Pilot for rocking it on the Buick's tape deck.

Thank you, Tamathy, for knowing when I got it right. Bryan, for slapping some sense into me at the Longbranch. Jacob Boyd, for being my first editor, and the Wordos and No Shame Eugene for making me a better writer.

I want to thank the outstanding, exemplary, spit-and-polish team at Hyperion for believing in me and giving me flowers and defying all reasonable expectations. Thanks to my agent, Sara Crowe, for discovering Wildman, changing my life, and always using her superpowers for the forces of good. And Stephen Barr, for an act of literary altruism that elevated him, his profession, and my view of the world. A shout-from-the-rooftops thanks to Rotem Moscovich, my glorious editor, who saw this book and heard the train whistle and always knew exactly which star to follow.

I want to thank SCBWI for giving me a community and a writing retreat worth driving to.

I want to thank Robert for fixing my car.

I want to thank readers for continuing to think as they travel through the world. And I want to thank the artists who have missed their share of sunlight and parties, and have excused themselves from friends, partners, and children for reasons not commonly understood. The universe depends on you.